THE ELLIOTT FILE

GORDON SILVER

The Elliott File
Copyright © 2023 by Gordon Silver

ISBN
978-1-961250-53-6 (Paperback)
978-1-961250-54-3 (eBook)
978-1-961250-52-9 (Hardcover)

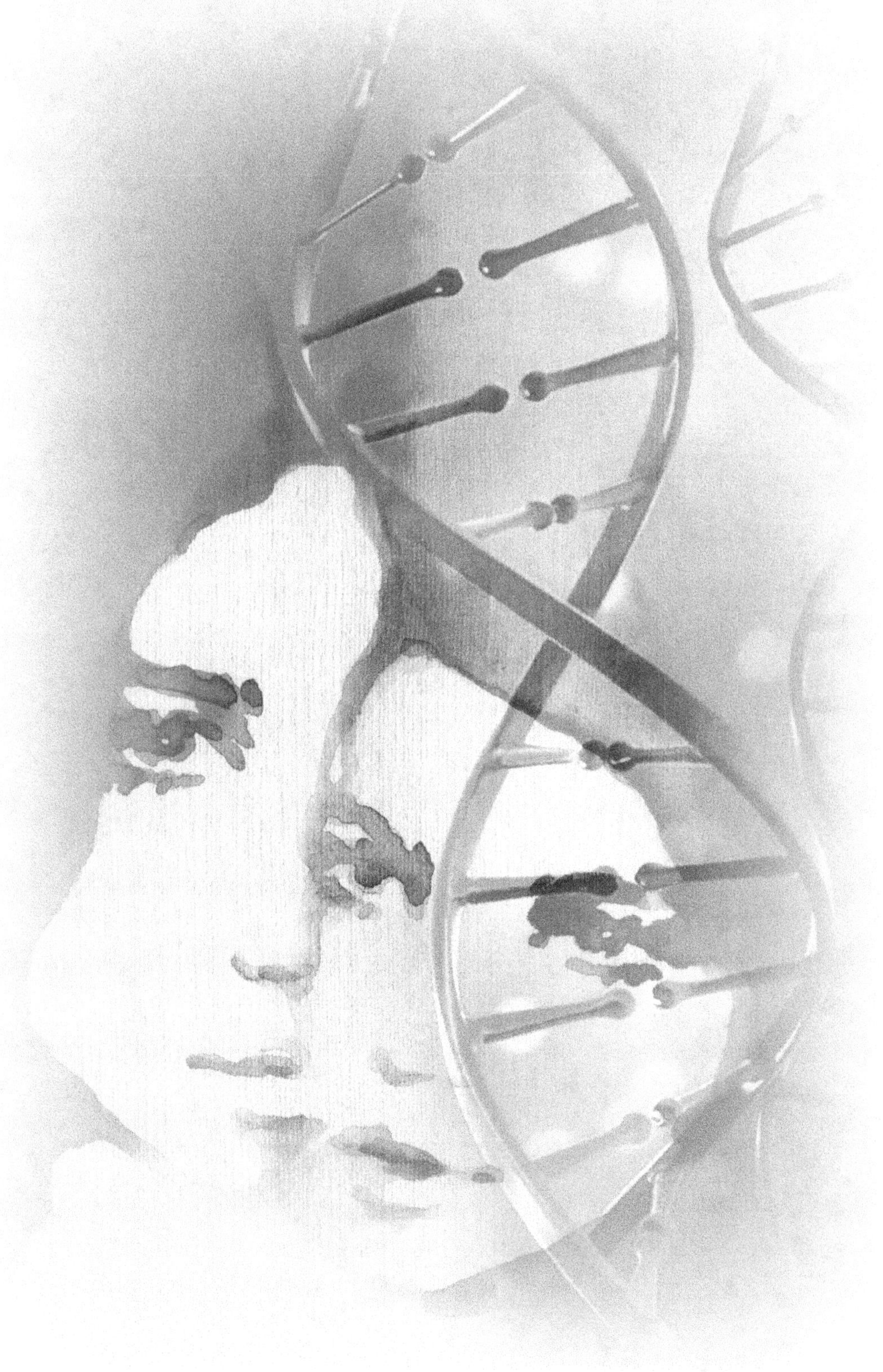

TABLE OF CONTENTS

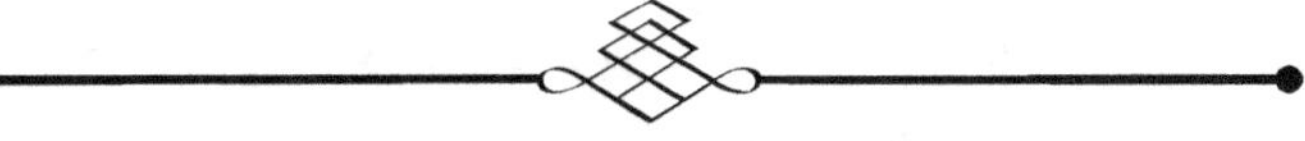

ONE

"BABY KILLER!" "BURN IN hell!" "You murdering bitch!"

The chanting seeped into Dr. Leslie Craswell's brain and brought her to the brink of a panic attack. "These protesters are crazy; I do not perform abortions." A drop of sweat trickled down her forehead triggering a painful stinging in her eye that amplified her anxiety. Afraid she might hit one of the rioters, she slowly and carefully navigated her Range Rover down the narrow ramp that led to the exit of the Baywater Women's Clinic parking garage.

She winced as she emerged into the bright, late afternoon sunlight typical of the Tidewater area in the spring. As she maneuvered onto Decatur Street into the throng of a rather large and disorderly group of demonstrators, her eyes straining to see as she reached for her sunglasses. "This is the third riot this month. These lunatics scare me. They will surely succeed in killing me one day." As protesters rapidly surrounded her vehicle, instinctively she slammed her foot on the brake pedal, while simultaneously trying to shut out the abuses hurled at her.

The group jostled around the Rover. Slowly, she edged forward as some of the demonstrators from the angry crowd beat their fists against her windows and doors. A few of the protesters stepped out of the way to let the Rover pass, but the most aggressive and violent demonstrators wouldn't budge. Craswell could feel her heart racing as several angry men climbed atop the hood of the Rover like a pack of blood-thirsty wolves.

Her sight was obscured by shaking fists and waving placards that shouted *Stop killing babies!* and other insults. The protest was quickly deteriorating into mayhem.

Random thoughts flashed through Craswell's brain. *They have no idea who I am or what my work is. I don't kill babies. I perform research to find a way for women to conceive with another woman. I am trying to create new life potential.*

Dr. Craswell was used to seeing anti-abortion rallies outside the clinic, but she hadn't experienced such a violent crowd before. She tightened her grip on the soft leather steering wheel as she perceived the visceral hatred on the faces of the demonstrators. Internalizing her feelings, she thought, *How horrible! How awful to be screamed at in such a vulgar manner.* The vocal abuses and twisted faces were shocking and made her wonder whether this could possibly be called free speech.

Okay car, do your thing. You better live up to the publicity and protect me, she mumbled under her breath, terrified as she urged the car slowly through the crowd. She hoped her investment in an armored car would be her salvation. *Will I ever get past these hysterical people? It's amazing how effective mass hysteria is, and I am terrified of them!*

A tall man with his head shaved bald stepped in front of Dr. Craswell's car. The man, Mike Wagner, had spent his life listening to antigovernment propaganda and was a pro-life activist. He hated all doctors. He believed that anyone who worked at a women's health clinic performed abortions and deserved to be executed. Dr. Craswell waved her hands frantically when she saw Wagner with a gun in his hand. She looked directly at his face and could see the frantic rage in his eyes wild like a madman as he raised his arm, pointing the weapon directly at her. She felt beads of sweat slide down the back of her neck as she looked down the barrel of a pistol.

Oh my God, this is the end. The shock of the moment registered on Dr. Craswell's face as the scene in front of her seemed to take place in slow motion. Her brown eyes glinted in the sunlight as tears started to well up. Alarmed, she watched her tormentor take aim through the windshield, and she cringed when she saw his finger tense as he slowly squeezed the trigger. She instinctively ducked with her eyes tightly shut, expecting to be hit, but a few seconds later after not hearing glass shattering and feeling no sudden pain, she opened her eyes.

The bullet had ricocheted off the windshield and whizzed through the air, back into the crowd. She was relieved and a little surprised that the bullet had not penetrated the windshield. The Range Rover had lived up to its reputation. A blood-curdling scream shook her back to reality, and she searched the crowd for the source of the shriek. Then she saw a man clutching his face. The bullet, intended for her, had hit one of the other demonstrators. She stared in horror as he staggered and fell to the ground with blood streaming from a gaping head wound.

Sergeant Mila Preston had been watching the Range Rover exit the garage and the crowd swarm around it. The police usually maintained an uneasy vigilance at these demonstrations, but they did not intervene to stop a rally unless violence erupted. When Sergeant Preston saw Wagner draw his gun, she shouted a request for backup into her police radio. As soon as she heard a response, Sergeant Preston sprinted across the road toward the vehicle and the assassin. The assassin was easy to spot among the crowds; he still held the gun in his hand.

Preston was tough and unafraid as she moved in with speed. She pushed the killer to the ground and simultaneously kicked his arm hard so he would drop the weapon before he could do any more harm. She had the advantage of surprise on her side as she wrestled him to the ground. Within seconds, Preston had him handcuffed and immobilized.

With one foot on her suspect's back to keep him subdued, Preston spoke clearly into her walkie-talkie, "Send an ambulance at once. Man down." She was a dedicated police woman who through hard work and resolve had earned the respect of those who knew her. She had received many commendations since joining the Chesapeake police force.

"What is the condition of the man?" the dispatcher asked.

Preston stated plainly, "Severe head injuries."

She replaced her two-way radio on her belt when she heard the dispatcher reply, "10-4." A hangover from the days when the police used codes, it still seemed to be the universal acknowledgement.

Forgetting her own safety, Dr. Craswell leaped out of her car. Her one thought was to try to save the fallen man's life. Kneeling beside him, she felt for his pulse more out of habit than any hope he could still be alive. She saw blood and brains pouring out of his skull. Even if he was not dead, he soon would be.

It was awful to witness such violence inflicted on another human being. Here was another murder by anti-abortion extremists in their ironic right-to-life quest. Dr. Craswell stood upright slowly and carefully feeling unsteady from the shock. She faced her tormentors, who had suddenly become quiet and seemingly immobile. Even they were shocked by the violence. She spoke slowly but in a raised voice, "Is murder what you people want? You kill people, while professing your righteousness and belief in the sanctity of life." Her anger overtook her fear, and she shouted out, "You are a bunch of hypocrites."

The crowd's silence settled in as the demonstrators realized what had happened in the frenzy of the moment. The demonstrators remained quiet even though they didn't want to listen to her. One of their cohorts was dead. They blamed her even though it was not her fault. Why was she meddling with God's creations? The police were swarming all around securing the crime scene so any retribution would have to wait until later.

Preston summoned Max Leland. Leland was a Detective with nearly a decade in the force, and Preston felt she could trust him. "Please restrain my suspect while I repossess the gun," she said. Leland was a large, strong man who immediately relieved Preston of her prisoner. He was always ready to help Preston and hoped that one day they could be friends.

Preston retrieved the weapon and recognized the sinister Sig Sauer, a gun that many assassins use. She opened her police notebook and meticulously recorded the gun's serial number and, following police protocol, allocated an identification number, which would allow her to positively identify any evidence recovered at a crime scene. She then carefully marked the weapon with her initials and her identification number. She placed the murder weapon in an evidence bag and sealed it.

Leland helped Wagner from the ground to a standing position. He held Wagner's right arm with his left as Preston pulled a card from her breast pocket. She then read Wagner his Miranda rights, "You have the right to remain silent. Anything you say can and will be used against you in a court of law. You have the right to an attorney. If you cannot afford an attorney, one will be appointed for you. Do you wish to give up these rights?"

"No," Wagner's black eyes flashed menacingly as he replied emphatically. His fanatical views had been shaped when he was a young man listening to and being mentored by Paul Hill who later became the first person executed in the United States for murdering an abortion doctor. Wagner grieved for Hill and revered him as a hero. He rejoiced when the abortion doctor George Tiller was killed while in church. He would happily follow in the footsteps of these radical murderers. But today, he had missed his mark and had instead killed a cohort. Wagner silently vowed he'd make this right. He'd eventually get his baby killer, whatever her name was.

Preston marched Wagner to the police wagon. The arrest transport vehicle was quickly brought to the scene as a temporary holding cell for use when any demonstration turned violent. She was relieved to have him in custody.

Dr. Craswell climbed back into her armored Range Rover that had protected her from this deadly attack. She felt thankful that she had been spared, but this violence only increased her resolve to succeed in the experimental procedure. She had been working for years on these types of procedures, and now she was working to help a lesbian couple give birth to a baby girl without the use of a man's sperm. She was very excited about her latest experiment.

The historic *Roe v. Wade* Supreme Court decision, which had legalized abortion, turned the subject into one of the most divisive issues in the United States. Ever since the ruling, activists protested, many times with violence, against clinics where abortions were performed. In recent years, these activists expanded their protests to include cloning and stem cell research. Any research that involved conception and birth became fair game for the conservative extremists. As she sat in the car, she fought the urge to throw up. The violence, the blood, the hatred were sickening.

Soon, Dr. Craswell heard the high-pitched scream from an approaching ambulance. The paramedics quickly assessed that Paul Bachmann was beyond any help and that any treatment was futile. The quarter top of his head had been blown off, and both brain and blood were splattered on the road.

Richard Hayward, an arrogant policeman, approached Dr. Craswell. He tapped the window showing his police badge, "Doctor, can you step out for a moment and tell me what you saw?" he inquired, notebook in hand. Craswell steadied herself and tried to remain calm as she opened the door to climb out of the car.

"As I drove out of the parking lot, I was surrounded by this screaming crowd acting like wild animals. I couldn't turn back. I couldn't do anything. I thought I was going to die. Then I saw a gun pointing directly at me. I was terrified," she replied.

Because of an inappropriate sexual encounter as a young girl, Dr. Craswell had an aversion to men. In fact, generally she just didn't like them, especially aggressive men such as those who had surrounded her car. And now this policeman was making her feel uncomfortable even though he was simply portraying his undetached professional demeanor. He brought back the awful memories of her childhood encounter with the priest she had trusted. He had displayed the same undetached professional demeanor as he told her to not tell anyone about what had happened.

Hayward could see that she was obviously shaken, but she also displayed her contempt for these anti-abortion extremists who frightened her and threatened the doctors and women who sought their services.

"You work here?"

"Yes."

"What is your full name and address?" he asked rather officiously.

"I'm Dr. Leslie Glenda Craswell. I live at 5012 Woodbury Avenue in Norfolk," she answered courteously, but with a flat tone.

Dr. Craswell was a tall, imposing woman with shoulder-length brunette hair. Hayward couldn't tell her age. She looked forty, but he recognized her name as a leading researcher at the clinic and he recalled reading an article that placed her in her early fifties. In the last four decades since the first test tube baby was born, there had been many advances to in vitro fertilization, and Dr. Craswell was in the forefront of much of the progress making several important contributions in the reproductive field. She was recognized as one of the world's leading IVF researchers.

"What do you do at the clinic?"

"I specialize in reproductive medicine. But ignorance is bliss to these demonstrators. The fact that I don't perform abortions, but instead create life, escapes these rioters." She was starting to feel angry.

"Answer the questions Ma'am, without adding your innuendos," Hayward's tone was gruff and he sneered at Craswell. "Explain the general conditions as you drove out of the parking garage," Hayward said, growing impatient with Craswell.

Dr. Craswell nervously described the chaotic scene that led up to the shooting. "People, mostly men were like animals pounding on the doors and windows and blocking my exit from the garage. Some of them even jumped onto the hood of my car in their efforts to make me stop the car."

"Then what happened?"

"One of them jumped forward from nowhere and confronted me. He had a crazed look in his eyes and shouted something at me. Then he raised his pistol and pointed it in my face. I was looking down the barrel of a gun. I was scared. When he pulled the trigger, I saw a flash and ducked thinking it was the end. But the bullet must have ricocheted off the windshield. It all happened so fast. But my car's armored windshield protected me. Then there was a blood-curdling scream, and I saw a man clutching his bloody face and head. There was blood flying in the air; he was thrown into the air like a rag doll. I thought that it would be impossible for him to have survived, but I jumped out of the car anyway to try to save him. After all I am a doctor."

"What did you do then?"

"It was obvious he was dead. I mean, I took his pulse, but Christ, half of his head was blown away and the blood was gushing through the gaping wound." She began to sob. She struggled to continue to tell her story. "He was killed instantly, and the man who did it meant the bullet for me!" While Craswell was a doctor, most of her work has been in the labs so she wasn't used to seeing trauma from this kind of violence.

"Dr. Craswell, do you need me to call someone to pick you up?" "No, I'll be okay. But this was totally uncalled for. It is a tragedy.

What happened here today is the logical consequence of the illogical actions of bigots. I only hope you can stop these fanatics before more people are killed."

"Thank you for your statement, Doctor. We will be in touch if we need any more information. Try to take it easy tonight if you can."

A visibly distraught Dr. Craswell climbed back in the car, and then with shaking hands put the car into drive. She was feeling almost physically ill. What a nightmare! How was she going to get this ugly specter out of her mind? *Well,* she thought, *no sleep for me tonight.* She wanted to get home as soon as possible, but she felt that she ought to be careful. She felt both nauseous and shaky. Oh, to be home safe and sound.

She screeched the tires as she sped away from this ghoulish incident. It distressed her that men could be so foolish. It had been a long day, and she was tired, and the added stress of the last twenty minutes had taken its toll.

There were still a few members of the crowd standing around gawking. They didn't seem quite ready to leave although there was nothing they could do. However, the police would be looking for witnesses.

Most of the demonstrators, who had realized the implications of the botched and bloody protest, had vanished. They feared the consequences of an investigation. There were always large numbers of people who sympathized with the pro-life movement, who could be rallied by the rabble rousers to turn out en masse at this kind of event, but they were not there to sanction criminal activity and they certainly did not want to be associated with a killing. These demonstrators believed that they were merely obstructing access to clinics where women got abortions. This kind of violence was not what they wanted to be a part of, although they couldn't really do anything to stop it.

Police were everywhere, cordoning off the crime scene. They tried to list everyone who was involved in the protest and took statements from some of the demonstrators who were still milling about.

Bachmann was the victim of his own quest to protect life. He lay there motionless as the investigators photographed him from all angles. After conferring with the officer in charge, the paramedics covered Bachmann with a sheet and left him lying in the road. Then the inevitable coroner's van arrived to take him on his last journey.

Sergeant Preston left the crime scene as the other investigators remained in full force to gather all of the evidence. Every little detail of the scene was photographed, marked and carefully documented, then placed in evidence bags for forensic examination. It was a hive of activity.

Preston went straight to the courthouse on Albemarle Drive where she waited among the throngs of people all there for various crimes. When her suspect, Mike Wagner, was brought in, she presented the facts to the magistrate and requested a warrant. She then took him to the jail and turned him over to the officers to execute the tedious but necessary processing of her suspect, so that for tonight, at least, he would be behind bars.

Back at the station, Sergeant Preston greeted the officers at the front desk and proceeded to climb the stairs to the deserted detective's office. Most of her colleagues had left for the day, and the detectives on duty were investigating a homicide on the Southside. She always documented everything as soon as possible; she feared forgetting important details that could alter a case.

As she was concentrating on her report, her nemesis, Richard Hayward, arrived and sat at his desk to write his report of the incident. This felt awkward to Preston. She didn't like being alone with him, but Preston told herself that was silly and tried to concentrate on her report.

She knew that Hayward would try to muddy the waters in his report. For one thing, even though he had been the only other officer at the scene before the shooting, she hadn't seen him until after the shooting.

And when she did first see him, she had been tagging Wagner's gun and Hayward hadn't seem to know what had happened.

Oh well, she thought. *I've got to concentrate on my report and forget about Richard. I've got to make this report as detailed and exact as possible, and thinking about that dud will just distract me.*

But instead of shaking off her feelings of discomfort, she could feel the hairs standing up on the back of her neck. She turned around in her chair and let out a startled cry. Hayward was standing four inches behind her chair. He had come up behind her so quietly, that she hadn't heard him.

"Hey, what are you doing?" she asked in a loud, bold voice.

"Laughing at you. I didn't mean to scare you, M-i-l-a," he said, dragging out her name and smirking, obviously pleased at his success in scaring her.

"Do you mind, Richard? Back off! You're in my space," she said, standing up and taking a step forward, forcing him to take a step backward. "For the record, you don't scare me, Richard," she said, with a slight snarl on her face.

This guy had been difficult to deal with ever since she was promoted to sergeant ahead of him and he asked her out. She, of course, turned him down flat. She'd rather become a nun than go out with this jerk.

"I just don't like being able to tell whether you used deodorant this morning. And by the way, Richard, you really should try a different brand," she said, turning her back on him, trying to move slowly and casually as if there were nothing wrong, nothing to be afraid of.

Then she decided to take the offensive. "By the way, where the hell were you this afternoon? You were nowhere to be seen until after I had the suspect collared."

"Oh I was around. But anyway, I'm trying to make up for lost time. But for some reason, you just don't seem to like my company."

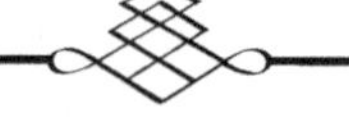

TWO

"IT DISTRESSES ME TO think that poor man would still be alive if you had not persuaded me to buy that armored Range Rover," said Dr. Leslie Craswell, her forehead tensed showing her anguish, "But then it would me who would have been killed in that crazy attack."

"You have every right to feel distressed, Leslie. That riot was really malicious, and you stared death in the face. It will probably haunt you for many years to come," Olivia said, using her most soothing voice to calm her partner. She picked up the bottle of Merlot and refilled Leslie's glass. They still enjoyed sipping on a glass of wine in each other's company after so many years together.

"You know, what happened yesterday still horrifies me." Leslie's gripped her face in both hands and started sobbing.

"Take a sip of wine, and try to think of your ground-breaking research." With a calming demeanor, Olivia stroked Leslie's hair.

When a woman reaches middle age, there is a fork in her life in which she can choose which path to follow. One leads to the wisdom and desire to help others. This is the path Dr. Craswell selected. She could have basked in the glory of a successful career and gone down a path of vanity and self-centeredness, but that was not in her nature.

The path Leslie chose to follow is a life that capitalizes on her experiences she gained over the years, helping the next generation and the community. It is one that consolidates, builds on the loving relationships in her life and allows her to become a role model.

"Why do we need men, anyway? My research will hopefully make them redundant," said Leslie, feeling very annoyed. "Men are just power hungry, potentially violent humans. More brawn than brain." Speaking with a determined voice, she continued, "Men will never truly understand women, and most men are only interested in controlling women anyway!"

"Don't get yourself worked up again. Tonight you just need to enjoy this delightful Virginia Merlot and relax. You deserve it after this very stressful week," Olivia replied, offering her partner some baked brie on crackers with apple slices.

Olivia looked at least ten years younger than her forty-two years. Her long, straight blonde hair framed her tanned and reasonably attractive face with green eyes and a clear complexion. She was still proud of her slim figure with long shapely legs and slender hips that were hard to ignore.

"You do spoil me with your mothering, Olivia. And I love it."

As Leslie began to relax, Olivia watched. Leslie was still attractive, but with some obvious mileage on her. Her auburn hair framed her beautiful face and set off her hazel eyes. Most of the time, Leslie wore her trademark glasses, which matched the color of her hair. They were like a security blanket. She fiddled with them constantly. And when she was deep in thought, she would take her glasses off, hold them in her hand, close her eyes, and chew on the stem of the glasses.

"Have your experiments with nucleus transplantation succeeded yet?"

"Yes, the host does not appear to be rejecting the nucleus in this experiment."

"Have you managed to overcome the problems of genomic imprinting?"

"Yes, the embryos look like they are developing. It is a very promising trial."

Olivia continued to press Leslie for more information, "Did your experiment using only the maternal genomes result in developing embryos?"

"It's too early to be sure, but I am very hopeful."

Olivia had been hired to be Leslie's nurse and assistant. They had been a team in the hospital, and they had started spending most of their time together socially. Inevitably, the two fell in love, and it was not long before Olivia resigned from her job and moved in with her former boss.

"When do you think you will be ready to start working with human cells to fuse a female gamete with another female gamete?" Olivia asked.

"It will be soon. I think I have solutions for the remaining obstacles, and I am confident we might be able to help the Elliott couple conceive a baby. And then watch the anti-gay marriage activists' protest.

It will draw everyone from the conservative movement out in droves. I am dreading that."

Olivia was always sensitive to Leslie's moods. While Leslie was generally even keeled, when she was harassed by right-wing protestors at the clinic or, worse yet, anonymous mail or phone calls, she sensed a prickling feeling throughout her body.

"Leslie, do you need to see Dr. Samuels about what happened at the clinic? After all, it was traumatic and you have a lot of stress with your latest research."

"Olivia, don't worry so much. I am fine. I am sensitive to any signs of depression, and I'll call Dr. Samuels if I need him. But I think I just need some time to get over the attempt on my life and the vision of that poor man with half his head blown off, which could have been me."

"Okay, Leslie. If you promise me," she said, touching her partner's hand and making a vow that she would be vigilant to watch for any signs of depression. It was something Olivia was used to doing, because often Leslie didn't recognize her own signs of depression. *Sometimes,* Olivia theorized, *brilliance exacts a price.*

Olivia always tried to make home as comfortable as possible for Leslie, and even more so when the pressure was on. She did everything she could to help Leslie stave off episodes of depression. She focused on comfort meals, quiet nights, and anything that would put Leslie at ease.

She fussed over Leslie at these times, worried that Leslie would stop eating and lose weight. Although Leslie was the perfect weight for her height, when she was stressed, she would drop a few pounds, making her appear gaunt. Then Olivia would work even harder to get that weight back on, enticing Leslie with gourmet foods, healthy breads, and caloric pastries.

As Olivia and Leslie relaxed on the sofa, they raised their glasses to each other, and with a clinking sound, they took a sip and wished each other good luck. "I will be fine, Olivia. You just fuss too much." Even though Leslie protested, she loved the way Olivia fussed over her.

Olivia mulled over the implications of Leslie's research, "Removing the nucleus from an egg and then using it to fertilize another egg will have an enormous impact on human society."

Developing a procedure to extract the nucleus from an ovum grew into an obsession for Leslie Craswell. If she succeeded, it could become the biggest breakthrough for human reproduction. She believed that she could use the nucleus to fertilize an egg from another woman and that it could be made to behave the same way as a sperm fertilizing the egg. She was convinced that her experimental idea could work. Her theories had already attracted some media with a recent article and photo of her published in the local paper. It had been picked up by the Associated Press and carried on internet blogs. After what she thought would be only local notoriety, she was deluged with requests from lesbian couples wanting to be her first patients. She turned them all down because she felt she wasn't ready to go to the next step.

But then she and Olivia had become friends with Gisele and Azure Elliott. Olivia couldn't wait to tell them about Leslie's research, and she got them excited about the possibility. Leslie recognized that they might be the perfect couple to take her research to the next level. They were in a committed long-term relationship, and they would love to conceive a baby that was their genetic child. They could not believe that one day they might be able to give birth to a baby who would be the genetic offspring of both of them. Most importantly, Leslie could see they were stable, would stick to the harsh drug regimen, and would be good parents if they were lucky enough to conceive.

Leslie's work had revolved around helping couples conceive babies, using female ova and male sperms. When the first test-tube baby had been born in England in the late 1970s, Leslie had been fascinated. When she finished her internship, she chose to specialize as an obstetrician gynecologist. Soon after she qualified, she started practicing reproductive medicine, which brought her to Chesapeake, Virginia, to a new facility that pioneered in vitro fertilization.

It was at this facility that the doctors used a new process to stimulate the development and growth of oocytes within ovarian follicles by administering various medications. The mature oocytes were recovered from the follicles and placed in special solutions. The oocytes were then combined with semen in petri dishes, hence the name *in vitro fertilization*.

The resulting blastocysts were nourished in an incubator until they were mature enough to be transferred into the uterus where normal fetal development could continue. This hospital pioneered the technique in the United States, and as a result, one of the first test-tube babies was born at the hospital in the early 1980s.

Olivia understood her partner and realized how driven she was to find a way to make babies without men. Leslie really didn't like men. Her father had been cold and distant, and while a lot of women shared that history, Leslie had also suffered at the hands of her church priest from the time she made her first communion at the age of seven until she was ten. When she first learned in sex education classes that any child could say no to unwelcomed touching, Leslie realized that what Father Draper had been doing was not only wrong, but also something she could refuse.

Right then, Leslie vowed never to let another man touch her. She kept her secret to herself. But when she first heard about in vitro fertilization, she was mesmerized. She decided she would become a doctor and search for a way to be able to have a baby without using a man's sperm.

She was considered a top scientist and pioneer in the field of assisted reproductive technologies. Dr. Leslie Craswell had written several textbooks and hundreds of papers on her research into infertility. Working on improving various reproduction techniques, Leslie worked to perfect the technique of isolating the nucleus to use it to conceive a baby.

She was extremely proficient with the intracytoplasmic sperm injection, which was used when a man had fertility problems. In this procedure, a single sperm was injected directly into an egg. Using this procedure Leslie, would inject the nucleus extracted from one woman's egg into another woman's egg simulating normal conception.

After the procedure, the resultant pre-embryo would be immersed in a cell culture and placed in an incubator. Leslie would check it each day for signs of fertilization. Then the blastocyst, which was the stage before it became an embryo that had developed for five days after fertilization and had divided into four or eight cells, would be transferred into the mother's uterus. The blastocyst would continue normal development, transforming itself into a growing fetus until nine months later when a baby girl would be born.

"Don't you normally fertilize many eggs when you carry out this procedure?" asked Olivia.

"Sometimes we are lucky and retrieve as many as two dozen eggs, but that is rare."

"If you successfully fertilize many eggs, then you could transfer a blastocyst into both of the women making them both pregnant. Will that increase your chance of success?"

"You're so right. We do not normally have the luxury of picking a parent for the transfer. Only one of the parents usually has a uterus, not like in this case with Gisele and Azure. Both of them have agreed to participate in the trial and try to get pregnant."

"If you do transfer a blastocyst into each woman, will the babies be considered twins?" asked Olivia.

"Not necessarily. But that is an interesting discussion, because although they will have originated from different eggs, they will have the same parents. And even though they will have each developed in a different uterus, they would probably be considered fraternal twins. However there is no guarantee that they will be born on the same day."

Leslie Craswell felt sure she could eliminate the need for a man's sperm to reproduce the human species. The two sex chromosomes determined the sex. Males always inherited their Y chromosome from their fathers because their mothers, being female, had no Y chromosomes to pass on. Therefore, Leslie reasoned, if she could fertilize a woman's egg with the nucleus extracted from another woman's egg, the baby would have two X chromosomes and would always be a female.

"Wow, this could change four hundred million years of the evolution of the male species. Men might become extinct," said Olivia.

"Yes, you're right. Since males have only one X chromosome, they tend to express all mutations they inherit from their mother's X chromosome. Diseases that only affect males, like hemophilia and Klinefelter's syndrome, will be eliminated."

Olivia quickly added, "And women will almost certainly govern the world much more compassionately. We will most likely abolish war, but ironically, men will fight to stop you."

Getting serious, Leslie put her drink down and reflected on the violence perpetrated by the pro-life extremists. "I am already a target for the anti-everything lobby. The assassination attempt yesterday scared me. Do you know what it is like looking down the barrel of a gun?"

"We can thank our lucky stars that you bought the armored Range Rover last year," replied Olivia, reaching for her lover's hand.

"Those protestors will stop at nothing," said Leslie. "Once they started killing abortion doctors on a regular basis, I felt anxious they would try to kill me one day. Now it's happened. Ever since that magazine article, the newspaper article, and the flurry of information on the internet about my experimentation, there has been an increasing presence of these fanatical protestors outside the clinic. Freedom of speech is one thing, but this violence is quite another, and the law does not seem to be able to stop them. I thought that it would be only a matter of time before someone would take a shot at me."

"By the time they realize the full implications of your studies, I'm sure there will be a lot more activists hovering around the clinic. Men will really feel threatened by this, and the Bible thumpers will go crazy, accusing you of playing God," said Olivia as she leaned across to refill Leslie's glass.

"Who can deny that!" laughed Olivia.

Leslie joined in the laughter; at last she was able to relax, leaving behind the stress and horrors of the week. She loved her life with Olivia. If she perfected this technique, maybe she and Olivia would one day have a baby. Olivia was still young enough to carry a baby to term. She could see Olivia barefoot and pregnant.

THREE

The Virginian-Pilot
April 21, 2019

Mike T. Wagner, an antiabortion leader and activist, was arrested and booked on charges of involuntary manslaughter and attempted murder on April 19 in the 700 block of Decatur Street outside the Baywater Women's Clinic.

Police responded to a report of a shooting that occurred during an anti-abortion demonstration and found Paul Bachmann, 32, face down in the middle of Decatur Street with a gunshot wound to his head. He was pronounced dead at the scene.

Police said that a gunman aimed a pistol at a well- known Embryologist and researcher, Dr. Leslie Craswell, as she left work for the day. The bullet ricocheted off the windshield and fatally wounded Bachmann.

Detectives arrested Wagner at the scene.

Wagner has been active in the anti-abortion movement for the last 10 years and more recently has been vocal against research undertaken at Baywater Clinic. Dr. Craswell is believed to be conducting research on samesex egg fertilization.

MAX LELAND NOTICED THE discarded Sunday newspaper next to the coffee machine. He quickly scanned the article. *This is going to be one hot case,* he thought to himself. Leland was not pleased to be assigned to the homicide case that had occurred outside the Baywater women's clinic late Friday afternoon.

Leland spotted Preston on her way back from the evidence room. "Hey, Sergeant Preston, have you got a moment?"

"Sure Max, cut out the formalities. What do you want to talk about?"

"The police chief, Jack Chisholm, seems to be irritated that the demonstration had gotten out of hand."

"I had already called for backup even before Dr. Craswell's car was attacked. But I was told that it was a routine demonstration and that no men could be spared," answered Preston somewhat defensively. "It wasn't until the actual attack occurred that we got the backup we needed. Apparently, someone phoned the emergency call center, just about the time we called for support."

"I know that. I know you did everything by the book. Just be prepared. The chief is on the war path," Leland said. Max Leland had started his career in the force as a police officer after attaining a college degree in police science. He was a tall man of Native American decent with dark hair and a bright smile. He had a rugged look, but Preston thought he was very handsome. He obviously worked out every day to maintain his slender muscular frame. He was transferred to the Criminal Intelligence Division after eight months on the force. Leland built a reputation for being a hard-working detective with integrity, good judgment, honesty, and a sense of responsibility.

"Why? We've got a good case. We've got my eyewitness account and the surveillance tape from the center's parking deck."

"Well don't say I said it, but the chief and Wagner go to the same church. Of course, it's a big church. Lots of people from the area attend. And I'm not saying he and Wagner are friends. But I can't think of any other reason he'd be in such a bad mood." Detective Leland had learned a long time ago that there was no such thing as an open-and-shut case. Anything could happen.

The first thing he had done after being assigned this case was interview Sergeant Mila Preston. He had helped her at the scene of the crime, but she was one of only two officers at the scene who had observed the shooting first-hand. He trusted Sergeant Preston and admired the attractive, young policewoman who exuded enthusiasm for law enforcement. Sergeant Preston had been thorough in collecting evidence at the scene, mainly the weapon.

Preston raised her eyebrows and frowned. "There are many officers in the force who sympathize with anti-abortion groups who obstruct access to hospitals and clinics that provide abortion services. Some officers have even said some vile things to me about Wagner's arrest."

Leland replied, "The Wagner case is politically explosive. Sentiments within the police department will run high as this investigation progresses. Those of us who are ardent pro-choice supporters will have to keep our opinions to ourselves."

"But for them to think that Wagner is not to blame is ridiculous. The evidence is overwhelming," said Preston.

"You know I agree with you, and that is what is so frustrating." Leland mulled over the evidence gathered so far.

Sergeant Preston had turned the gun over to the evidence room as soon as she had returned to the station. It was sent to forensics to match it to the bullet taken from the skull of Paul Bachmann. Forensics had carefully dusted it for fingerprints to match those to Mike Wagner. These were all standard police procedures, and as expected, the results would corroborate Sergeant Preston's report of the events. Wagner's prints were on the gun.

Preston interrupted Leland's thoughts. "You know the CSI retrieved a surveillance tape that captured the whole scene."

Leland replied, "I had heard about the tape, but I have not yet had the time to view it."

"Neither have I," Preston replied.

"Just make sure the surveillance tape stays safe. You don't want that to walk," warned Leland.

"Well, I hope the tape helps to fry him. Even though Paul Bachmann was not the intended target, Mike Wagner fired the gun with the intent to murder Dr. Craswell. Therefore, he should be indicted and stand trial on both counts of involuntary manslaughter in Bachmann's death and attempted murder for firing into the windshield of Dr. Craswell's car." Preston's eyes glowered showing her anger.

The shooting had affected Preston. Leland could see that, and he hoped Preston would be able to get her emotions under control before the case went to trial. But Leland was confident that Preston would pull herself together. She possessed what many on the police force lacked: good communication skills. She had the ability to withstand pressure and make sound, objective decisions in difficult circumstances. She'd be a good witness.

Officer Richard Hayward was altogether another question. Leland had talked with Hayward, who was also at the scene but seemed less certain about the events leading to the death of the demonstrator. He was fuzzy on the details. Apparently, Hayward had been stationed on the other side of the street and did not have as clear a view as Preston. His evidence was unreliable. He was saying something different from Preston. They would have to keep him off the stand. He wouldn't be a good witness. It didn't matter; Preston's testimony would be enough to clinch the case in court.

"Tell me about the research they're doing at the clinic. The paper said something about same-sex egg fertilization. What's that about?" Leland said, changing the subject.

Preston gazed up at the ceiling as she gathered her thoughts. She did not understand the scientific details of the research. But she knew what the objective was.

"Dr. Craswell is attempting to help a lesbian couple have a baby."

"So what! There have been many lesbian couples who have used artificial insemination and other procedures to get pregnant and have babies. What's groundbreaking about that?" exclaimed Leland.

"With same-sex fertilization, both women will be the natural parents of the baby."

"How could that be?" Leland asked.

"I don't really understand it myself, but I think that every baby will be a female," Preston replied. "You know a male baby only comes when a Y chromosome is donated from a sperm."

"Wow, this is huge. No wonder these right wing extremists are trying to stop her. In their world, they believe she is meddling in God's work. She is carrying out research that, if successful, will change human life on Earth," stated Leland.

"Well, we need to protect her and most importantly the integrity of this case without incurring the wrath of our police chief," said Preston.

"I will keep you informed of progress in this case. You will need to testify at the trial anyway. So I am sure that you will receive a subpoena when the trial begins."

"Okay, Max. I have already filed my report, with every detail about what happened. I am fully prepared to recall all the details when I testify," Preston said.

"Thanks for your excellent police work and cooperation. I will call you if I need any more information." Leland walked back to his desk to continue his work.

Preston went to the kitchen to get a cup of coffee. Then she settled down at her desk to read the file on the anti-abortion activists. It was very disturbing to read about their objectives and the methods they used to achieve their goals.

"Hey Mila," called Hayward, "I think I'll have to start calling you eagle eyes. You're saying you saw Wagner pull the trigger? In a lot of people's books, he's a hero."

"Well, I saw what I saw. And I certainly don't think you can classify Wagner as a hero," she retorted. "He is a menace to society. He stirs up his followers about a cause, and then incites them to commit violence. Anyway, too bad you didn't see anything. We could use your testimony in court."

Preston was irritated with Hayward. He should have had a clear view of the doctor's car. She was always aggravated by Hayward. He was the department bully. And he liked to pick on Preston. Even though she was a sergeant and outranked him, she didn't outrank him by much. He thought she was easy to rankle, but he had always managed to sidestep any reprimand from annoying her. He had never really made her mad, but he could tell he was infuriating her.

"Well, whoever aimed at the doctor was trying to do the world a favor. I hear that bull dyke, excuse me, Dr. Craswell, is trying to raise little queer babies in a jar," Hayward spoke with venom in his voice.

"Well first of all, she's a very attractive woman, and whatever her research, that is not the issue or our business," Preston snapped back at him. "It is our job to uphold the law regardless of what you think of the law. These radical demonstrators are vigilantes; they are violating the law to exact what they believe to be justice. They are taking the law into their own hands to pursue their misguided social principals. They accuse researchers and doctors of playing God, and they play God. They say they are pro-life and yet they take life."

Trying to aggravate her even more, Hayward continued, "Oh, Mila, I didn't know you swing both ways. You sweet on her yourself?" he sneered speaking loudly enough to attract an audience.

And people were watching. They had seen these standoffs between Preston and Hayward before. Preston usually tried to remain cool, but every once in a while he managed to push her over the edge and she'd lose her temper.

This time, however, Preston had decided she wasn't going to lose her cool. She'd been practicing this for some time, and decided to try it today. She was tired of his pushing her buttons. And she couldn't pull rank on him, which would be a win for him and a loss for her. This time, she decided she would humiliate him in front of their colleagues.

Preston casually stood and leaned against her desk. She nonchalantly began mentally undressing Hayward. Slowly with each piece of clothing that her eyes removed, she imagined a man at his worst. His chest, as she saw it, was as hairy as an ape's, his belly button full of lint. *This is kind of fun,* she thought, and the hint of a smile began to spread on her face, and then she got to the good part. As she stared right between his legs, her gaze fixed on his crotch. She lifted her cup to her lips and had a sip, then placed it back down on her desk and smirked. "Richard, now I understand why everyone says you have a very, very small, really remarkably small," and she hesitated to allow the insinuation to sting. She continued squinting at his fly trying to see something that just wasn't there. Everyone could tell Hayward was beginning to feel the heat of her scorn. He shifted his stance, and his face burned bright red. It was obvious he was becoming self-conscious.

And then she said slowly and distinctly, "Mind; a very, very small mind," and she held up her hand with about three inches between her index finger and thumb. The other men in the squad room let out an audible sigh of relief, and then they burst out in a raucous laughter.

Hayward did have a reputation for having a small member. Years ago, he had failed to back up his partner at a crucial moment. His partner survived the incident, but Hayward's reputation had suffered. His fellow officers thought that he did not have any balls. They lost all respect for him. Besides, he was extremely thin and he also had small feet, so behind his back, they had nicknamed him "Pencil dick". When Preston had paused, every man held his breath, afraid that the derogatory nickname would be revealed to Hayward's face.

Max Leland was the first to regain his composure and speak. "Hey Richard, lay off Mila. She's doing her job, and she's right. We are not the judge and jury. And we're not getting paid to enforce our personal opinions."

Leland liked Preston and thought she was good looking as well as a good cop. And mostly, he thought Pencil dick was a real redneck, to the point of being an ineffective cop.

Hayward left the squad room, grousing. Leland walked up to Preston and said, "Great job putting him in his place. By the way, do you know his nickname around here?"

"No, I don't," she said, "I suppose you don't include us women in your chatter." But that was gossip she craved to hear.

"Well, I tell you what," Leland said, "If you can find some time to have a hamburger with me, I'll tell you the whole story."

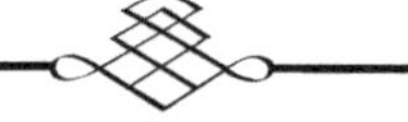

FOUR

COMMONWEALTH'S ATTORNEY ANTHONY COLEMAN glowered at the throng of media reporters who were assembled for the gory details of the breaking story. Coleman did not approve of the publicity generated by the news media and eagerly devoured by the masses. A case should be heard in a Court of Law, not in the court of public opinion.

"It is my understanding that Mike Wagner intended to shoot Dr. Craswell, but he missed and hit the victim, Paul Bachmann. How did Dr. Craswell avoid getting shot?" asked Libby Chen, an up-and-coming reporter from the *Virginian-Pilot*.

Coleman believed that the media hype could damage a criminal case, where a jury could be easily swayed. The case of *People v. Wagner* was particularly sensitive in that it included the explosive issue of abortion.

"Mike Wagner is one of our suspects," Coleman said answering Chen's question politely, he was hoping to sway public opinion to help Wagner. "Dr. Craswell was driving a custom built armored Range Rover and the bullet fired at her ricocheted off the bulletproof windshield and hit the victim in the head. He died instantly." Coleman relaxed a little.

"Has Wagner been questioned about his attack on Dr. Craswell? What evidence do you have that he tried to kill her?" asked Amy Parker, a young reporter at the back of the pack.

"We have an eyewitness account from one of our police officers at the scene. While Mr. Wagner denies that he fired the shot, we believe we have a pretty good case proving that he did fire the gun." Coleman was trying to play ball with reporters, even though he didn't want to.

Chen was persistent in her questioning and asked, "Do you have you any idea about his motive?"

"During questioning, Wagner told us that he believes that the Doctor performs abortions at the clinic," replied Coleman.

"Does she?" an unidentified voice from the left called out.

"Ironically, no she doesn't. She conducts research involving in vitro fertilization advances. Specifically, I don't know what those developments are," said Coleman.

Then Todd Jameson of the *New York Times*, knowing his opposition to same sex marriage and parenting, dropped a bombshell, "Are you concerned about her research project helping a lesbian couple conceive a baby without the use of male sperm?"

"No! My own personal opinion on her experiments does not affect this case," replied Coleman dodging the accusation. Trying to remain calm, he tugged his ear nervously. A body language expert would argue that this habit suggested he was being untruthful.

Jameson continued, "You have been known to speak out against Dr. Craswell's research. I have heard you say that God would not approve."

"I repeat my own personal opinion on the services or research carried out at the Women's Clinic is not relevant to this case," Coleman said emphatically still tugging at his ear nervously. He remembered his interview with the local reporter, who was sympathetic to his views and felt annoyed at himself for making that off-the-cuff remark.

He turned around as though to speak to one of his assistants and muttered under his breath; *don't let these fools in the press get to you. Think carefully before you answer their fool hardy questions.* Then he took a deep breath and turned to face the microphone again.

"It would seem that you support the pro-life lobby, Mr. Coleman. Will that keep you from prosecuting this case?" Jameson asked, pressing forward on his questioning.

"Certainly not. And my moral beliefs are not on trial here," Coleman retorted indignantly. His ear tugging was becoming frantic. Coleman hated reporters and especially Jew reporters. He was quite certain that Jameson must be a Jew. After all, he worked for the *New York Times*. Weren't they all Jews? Or queers?

Peter Herman of the *Tidewater Times* fired off another awkward question, "Why has Mike Wagner not been indicted yet?"

"We are still investigating the circumstances of the demonstrator's death and the attack on Dr. Craswell. We are still reviewing the evidence," replied Coleman. He was again tugging on his ear and feeling uneasy about the direction of the questioning. "I will convene a Grand Jury and present all the evidence and leave it up to them to indict."

Jennifer Granger of NBC asked, "Is it true that Wagner and you belong to the same church? Are you trying to protect him? I mean, is this a conflict of interest?"

"No, that is not true. I mean, yes, we do go to the same church, but it's a large congregation. My church membership will in no way interfere with this case. And I resent the implication!" Coleman started sweating and his hands began shaking. Granger noticed his strange habit of tugging on his ear and wondered whether he was telling the truth.

One thing he knew, there wasn't a red-blooded American in the bunch. None of them loved their country. None of them held the values that he cherished. And he was certain, none of them was a church going family man, or God forbid, woman. The worst reporters were the women. They were just like little bull dogs. When they got onto something, they just couldn't let it go, like a dog with a bone. And that bitch Granger always went for the cheap shot, the below the belt question. Obviously, she needs something below the belt to put her in her place.

As Jameson and the other reporters continued to fire questions at him, all he could see was their mouths like the barrel of a shotgun, aiming down on him, or like sharks coming in for the kill. Especially that Jameson. He thought he detected some spittle in Jameson's mustache. What a worm he was! Coleman didn't give a damn about his Pulitzers; he was the lowest form of life. Coleman hated the 'lame-stream media' and he wanted to retaliate, but that would have to wait for another day, another venue.

Coleman wanted to end this news conference before it got out of control. "That is all for today ladies and gentlemen. I do not want to compromise this case." He picked up his papers and tried to leave the lectern as quickly as he could.

But the throng of reporters blocked his exit and he was forced to shout, "As I have already told you, we will be moving swiftly to gather and evaluate all the evidence in this case and present it to a grand jury to see if we should move forward with a trial. Now gentlemen and ladies, I really must end this conference and continue with my work."

At last, Coleman's public relations flack had made his way to the lectern and took over. At last Coleman was able to push past the reporters and make his exit. He just wished that Mike Wagner had aimed his gun at these assholes.

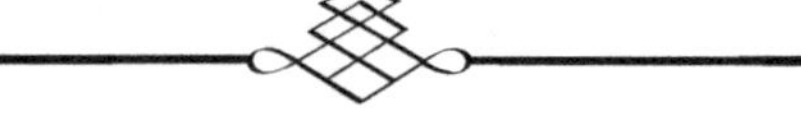

FIVE

AT FIVE SHARP, CHISHOLM arrived at the northwest corner of Main Street, parked and entered the historic *Virginia Club*. When the door opened, he noticed the plush red carpet, the heavy frosted glass doors, the granite clad walls, the masculine looking leather chairs and captains' tables, and the shinny polished mahogany bar. Chisholm loved the look and feel of the place. He'd love for this to be his club one day.

As Chisholm looked around the club, he saw Coleman at a table in the far corner. It wasn't as if there was a crowd, other than the two elderly gentlemen sitting at the bar. But Chisholm also liked the fact that the club wasn't crowded. If they were going to discuss the Wagner case, he wouldn't want any nosey witness within earshot.

Chisholm strode across the club floor, feeling confident as he extended his hand toward Coleman's. Coleman rose and shook hands, as if sealing the devil's pact even before it was discussed.

Coleman was magnanimous, as he invited Chisholm to order a cocktail, "Be sure to order what you like. And damn well order a call brand so the bastards don't give you some rot gut stuff," Coleman said, as he whacked Chisholm on his shoulder and sat back down first emphasizing his superiority.

Coleman didn't like meeting after hours with the police chief. He thought of it as somewhat beneath him to socialize with the police chief or even appear to be socializing with the police chief. But, sometimes you had to do unsavory things when you held an elected position such as commonwealth's attorney. Coleman wanted to get a feel for where

Chisholm stood on the Wagner case. He thought Chisholm was a stand up kind of guy. He would agree with him that those cops of his needed to be reined in and that the courts should go easy on Mike Wagner.

"Thank you, Mr. Coleman," Chisholm said humbly. The enthusiasm in his voice was obvious. A good working relationship with the commonwealth's attorney was important to his career. And so far, Chisholm felt like he hadn't made a good impression on Coleman.

"Call me Tony, all my friends do," Coleman offered bigheartedly.

Jack Chisholm, even though socially and politically not Coleman's equal, still had a slight advantage. He was handsome and at ease with his body. He was essentially a man's man. Coleman on the other hand was out of shape, obviously a book worm, an egg head turned lawyer, and then eventually elevated to Commonwealth's Attorney.

Coleman calmed his feelings of inadequacy by pointing out to Chisholm the obvious. "Jack, this place is great. The only thing it's missing is dames. But if you had women here, well there would be problems. Dames always cause problems," he laughed.

"You are right Tony. Times have changed and women are now infiltrating every business and service. They're all over my squad room now," Chisholm uttered in a low voice. Tonight he really needed a drink after dealing with those difficult cops of his all day. That Mila Preston was determined to get Mike Wagner. Officer

Richard Hayward, on the other hand, wasn't so dogmatic. At any rate, a gin and tonic would help sort things out.

"Speaking of which, what about those girl cops in your house? They are coming down on Mike Wagner hard. One of them says she saw Wagner actually shoot at that clinic doctor. I'm sure that she really didn't see that. Aren't you, Jack?" asked Coleman.

Chisholm liked the fact that Coleman wanted to be on a first name basis with him. And he'd want to play ball with Coleman. But there was a slight problem. Not only did Preston see Wagner point the gun at Dr. Craswell, but the security cameras even recorded the action. There weren't but so many ways to slice this cake.

"Well Tony, Preston saw it go down, and it was caught on camera. From what I hear, it pretty much substantiates everything she said."

"Was the whole action captured on the tape?" Coleman displayed his disgust for the modern technology that made his job harder. He swirled the deep amber gold single malt Scotch whisky in his glass. Then he drained the glass of the last drop of his peat smoky Lagavulin, and raised his hand to attract the bar tender's attention for another.

"Yes, the clinic set up additional security cameras because of the frequent demonstrations, and the incident happened within visual range as Craswell was leaving for the day. So yeah, it's all on camera."

Coleman got a sour look on his face. He was deep in thought, and apparently didn't like the narrowing list of options. But then, Coleman put his poker face back on. He was all smiles. "You know, I sort of feel sorry for Mike. I'm sure he didn't mean for the gun to go off," Coleman said.

Chisholm knew that Coleman and Wagner went to the same church as himself. He hated getting between church buddies. That's why he kept questioning Preston, and why he was really pissed off when he learned of the surveillance video. The tape just didn't leave any wiggle room. It put him in a tough place with the commonwealth's attorney.

"Well, I guess it's an open and shut case, as long as the surveillance tape doesn't go missing. If you know what I mean, hey Jack?" As Coleman said this, he looked long and hard right into Chisholm's eyes.

Then he added: "You know, I've been watching your work. You're good. Someday, when you're ready, you might run for political office. I could help you get your nomination and initial funding." At that, he held his glass up as if in a toast. "Now you take good care of that video tape, you hear?"

Chisholm liked the idea of a political future to make him even more important and able to enjoy the good things in life. He wanted to belong to the Virginia Club. He wanted eventually to be more than chief cop. So he held his glass up and touched Coleman's glass. "I'll take good care of it. I'll make sure it's in good hands."

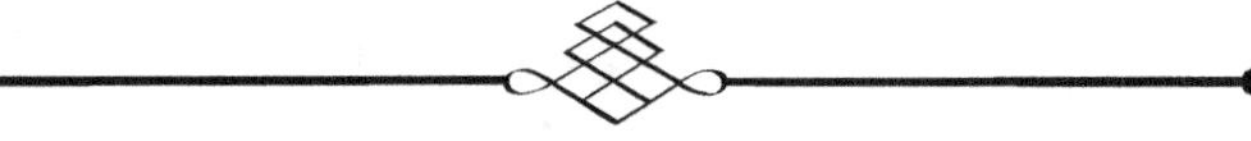

SIX

GISELE AND AZURE ELLIOTT loved each other and wished that they could have a baby that was genetically theirs just like any heterosexual couple. They wanted a baby who would inherit their personalities, Gisele's golden blond hair or Azure's coal black hair, Gisele's beautiful soprano voice or Azure's artistic talents. They wanted a baby that might inherit Azure's mole right at the end of her eyebrow or Gisele's Mona Lisa smile, not a baby that would come from the sperm of a stranger. And so, when they heard about Dr. Craswell's research into egg-to-egg fertilization, the couple begged to be included in the experiment.

On the day of their fairy tale wedding in the rose garden amidst the elegance of the Hermitage Gardens with its beautiful waterfront views, the sky matched Azure's sky blue eyes and the perfectly manicured lawns were the color of Gisele's bright green eyes.

The words "Do you take this woman to be your lawful wedded wife?" brought Gisele back to reality as she gazed lovingly at the angelic Azure in her dress of shimmering satin silk with ethereal flowing silk georgette sleeves. The "I do," slipped out of her mouth in a whisper.

And then it was Azure's turn to confirm her vows to Gisele, who wore a slinky silk-Carmeuse gown with a deep cowl neckline, which had delicate tiered beading down her back creating an alluring waterfall effect. Her "I do," was louder and confirmed her commitment to her partner. As soon as they were pronounced wife and wife, they fell into each other's arms. Their family and friends applauding their union, made possible only a few years earlier by the passing of same-sex marriage laws.

When she first met this loving couple, Dr. Craswell was hesitant. She didn't know if she was ready to make the leap from research to reality. Dr. Craswell had spent almost two years experimenting with various techniques to extract the nucleus from an ovum. She believed she could successfully extract the nucleus from an ovum recovered from one of the women and then inject it into an oocyte retrieved from the other woman. From that, according to Dr. Craswell's theory and research, a pre-embryo should start to develop normally.

While she was hesitant to take her experimentation out of the lab setting, she had to admit that Azure and Gisele were good candidates. They were in a committed relationship and they were healthy young women.

At their first appointment Dr. Craswell explained the risks associated with the procedure and the high probability of failure. "Since a procedure of this type has never been attempted before, a baby conceived this way might be born with sever genetic deformities," she stated matter-of-factly.

Azure looked at Gisele and glimpsed a drop of moisture as tears glistened in the corner of her eyes. Turning back to the Doctor she gathered her thoughts and asked, "Is it possible to determine any of these deformities in the early stages of pregnancy?"

"About ten weeks after you conceive, we will perform chorionic villus sampling, a test that can identify chromosome abnormalities and other inherited disorders."

Azure, still sniffing, asked, "What will happen if the results suggest that our babies are not normal?"

Speaking in her most professional voice, Dr. Craswell suppressed her own emotions, "Then we will need to make a decision about carrying the child to term. We may have to infuriate those murderers outside the clinic and abort your baby."

After an hour of consultation, Dr. Craswell referred her candidates for psychological evaluation. Dr. Craswell was nervous when she received the report. But as she started to read the opinion of the analyst, she broke out in a smile. The assessment was that Azure and Gisele Elliott would be loving mothers and they would provide a stable home for the babies.

"Thank you for coming to see me again," Dr. Craswell held out her hand and greeted both women warmly. "Did I scare you at our last meeting?"

Both women answered in unison, "No! We would love to try, no matter what the risks."

Even with their positive attitude, Dr. Craswell hesitated before telling the couple, "Yes, there seems to be no reason why you two wouldn't make good candidates. If we can use the nucleus from your egg to fertilize the other we will make a major breakthrough in human reproduction. It would be a huge step to fertilize an egg without the need of a sperm."

Gisele squealed with delight and jumped up to hug Azure. "Thank you Doctor. We both want to start our own family."

Dr. Craswell became serious and warned, "The drug regimen is tough. If we proceed, we will have to put you both on the hormone treatments that stimulate your ovaries, because we need to recover eggs from each of you. The hormones will cause your uteruses to prepare for pregnancy, allowing both of you to bear children together. This strategy will double our chances for a successful live birth of a baby girl. The drugs will initially throw you into a menopausal state, and that can be hard. You can also experience weight gain and other side effects that we women detest. Are you still game?"

Gisele and Azure looked at each other and then without hesitation, they said, "We want to be your guinea pigs. When can we start?"

In the conventional fertility procedure with a husband and wife, the woman has to suffer the superovulation therapy to stimulate her ovaries so that the number of eggs she produces is increased. In this case, both women would undergo the superovulation therapy. Dr. Craswell would fertilize as many oocytes as she could harvest. Once they reached viability, she would transfer half of them into each of the women's uteruses in the same manner as in any conventional in vitro fertilization.

For a month they were both given the drug called "gonadotropin releasing hormone analogue" to temporarily suppress each woman's natural hormones. This would allow greater control over the treatment cycle and put the woman into a menopausal state. It was difficult enough for a husband when his wife was put on this regimen, but when both of them started showing symptoms such as hot flashes, headaches, mood changes and night sweats, the usually peaceful and pleasant Elliott household got a little nutty.

In this same-sex household where both partners were experiencing similar symptoms, Gisele and Azure showed consideration for each other's reaction to the hormone regime. One morning Gisele woke up to find the windows open and the air conditioning cranked up. She was freezing and called out to Azure only to find her completely naked and fanning herself.

"What are you doing?"

"Aren't you hot? It is so hot in here, I can't stand it."

Both women looked at each other and began laughing, in spite of themselves. Every woman who had gone through menopause could sympathize with Azure as she sweated with a hot flash. They understood what was happening, and that this would be a small price to pay to produce a baby or babies that would be their own, proof of their love for each other.

But both women were willing to go through the rigors of the procedure because they wanted to have a baby of their own, not a baby produced by a male donor sperm. They wanted this baby to be theirs and theirs alone. They were ready and very excited about the possibility of having a baby, in spite of the inconvenience and discomfort of the procedure. In fact, maybe both of them would be able to have a baby, depending on how the fertilization procedure worked out.

Dr. Craswell monitored their progress with regular ultrasound scans to ensure that the women's ovaries were inactive and that the linings of their wombs were thin. She carried out blood tests to estimate their hormone levels in order to ensure the elimination of natural hormones. She needed to determine when they were ready for the gonadotropin injections to stimulate their ovaries.

Without stimulating medications, the ovaries only release one mature egg per menstrual cycle. Reproduction Doctors have several ovarian stimulation medication protocols that are used to "pump up" the ovaries to make enough follicles and eggs. Dr. Craswell had well defined protocols that she used to prepare the women for egg retrieval. These protocols were well understood and had been used and refined over many years.

At their last appointment, Dr. Craswell explained the calendar, "You will take Lupron for seven days. Then I will administer the human chorionic gonadotropin (HCG) shot to induce final egg maturation. Your egg retrieval will be within 36 hours."

On the day the women were scheduled for the retrieval of their eggs, Dr. Craswell sat anxiously at home sipping a cup of coffee. She tried to calm her nerves and wondered if she would run into another protest outside the clinic. The antagonists were not going to give up on their pro-life obstruction of all reproductive clinics. After all, they had no idea this Doctor was performing a conception, and not an abortion.

They were prepped and then wheeled into the operating theatre. The procedure was a tried and tested one, and Dr. Craswell was an expert at collecting eggs from the mature follicles. She operated on Gisele first.

"You will only feel a little pressure. It should not be painful. Tell me if you feel any pain. Are you ready Gisele?" asked Dr. Craswell in her most soothing voice.

Gisele relaxed as she parted her knees to allow the Doctor access to her most private parts, "Go for it Doc. I hope I have what you need."

An ultrasound allowed her to guide the needle through Gisele's vagina into her ovary where she aspirated the mature follicles. She immediately examined these follicles under a microscope to ensure the presence of a viable egg and then placed them in an incubator. She was thrilled that she managed to retrieve thirteen eggs. Gisele's procedure had gone so well, she smiled to herself as she realized that her dream of a major breakthrough was close.

Then Azure took her place on the operating table and as Dr. Craswell viewed the ultra sound, she was alarmed that there were far fewer follicles stimulated.

Gisele noticed the look of alarm in the Dr. Craswell's face and asked with a concerned voice, "What's wrong Doc?"

"Azure's ovaries have not responded to the stimulation as well as I hoped. Let's see what we can find."

She was passionate about her work and guided the aspiration needle into position and started removing the follicles carefully. She took each one over to the microscope to see if it contained an egg. It was painstakingly slow, but Dr. Craswell was obsessed with her task. Several follicles were empty, but she managed to retrieve five eggs. Dr. Craswell was disappointed with this result, because she needed double the normal number. However, she thought that she could still achieve a conception for both women in spite of the small number of mature eggs.

The women were taken back to the recovery room where the nurses monitored their awakening. Because they had both gone through the procedure and there was no one else at home to care for them, they were advised to remain in the hospital overnight.

Dr. Craswell entered the modern pristine IVF Laboratory. She was very familiar with every piece of equipment in there. She was a qualified embryologist. She eased herself onto her stool in front of the inverted microscope and micromanipulation equipment used in the intracytoplasmic sperm injection procedure otherwise known as ICSI. This technique to inject sperm into the middle of the egg was developed in the 90's. The futuristic equipment was a world apart from the chaos outside the clinic where abortion opponents chanted their favorite phase, "Pro-choice, that's a lie, babies never choose to die!"

She was about to start on the next phase of the procedure. She was extremely nervous as she carefully extracted the nucleus from some of Gisele's eggs. Then with the precision of years of experience, she sucked the first nucleus in to the pipette and proceeded to inject it into one of Azure's eggs. She used the technique that had been perfected a couple of decades earlier where they inject the sperm directly into the egg, using the tiny specially designed hollow needle. She carefully advanced it through the outer shell of the egg and egg membrane and the nucleus was then injected into the inner part of the egg where she hoped it would combine with the other nucleus.

She couldn't suppress the feeling she was acting as both God and father. It was almost a sexual feeling, that she was introducing the triumphant sperm, except this time it was woman to woman. No man was involved in any way.

The process completed she carefully placed the embryos each in its own petri dish in the fluid that mimics the lining of the uterus. She then placed the petri dishes into the incubator where they would divide for the next six days. The incubators would maintain a very constant and clean environment for the embryos. Everything looked promising as Dr. Craswell finally retreated from the inner reaches of her cavern.

Dr. Craswell was apprehensive as she entered the reproduction laboratory the next morning to check the embryos for fertilization. After examination under the microscope, she placed the petri dishes back in the incubator and almost ran to see Azure and Gisele.

"Good news girls! Most of the eggs show evidence of fertilization."

"That's exciting," squealed Azure as she burst into tears of joy.

Gisele added, "It's going to work, I just know it. Call it feminine intuition, but I am very excited right now Doc."

Dr. Craswell started to feel the giddy excitement that she remembered feeling as a little girl when her mother and father were about to take her on a long anticipated vacation. "We need to calm down and just be patient. You two can go back home now and relax. I will sign your discharge papers, so you can leave the hospital, but I will need you back here in 5 days. So don't flee the country," she laughed as she added that last bit.

The next day she retreated back into her laboratory to grade the embryos. Usually she would assess the quality of embryos by determining the number of cells, regularity of the size of the cells, and degree of fragmentation. She hoped some of the embryos would consist of at least eight cells. It was very important to assess embryos with higher cell numbers and regular appearing cells with little or no fragmentation. It was these embryos that would have a higher overall chance of implanting.

Each day, Dr. Craswell entered her sterile domain to check the embryos and would nervously count the number of cells. Ultimately, the only true test of the quality of the embryos was whether they implant and develop normally and eventually go home from the hospital with their moms.

Five days after she had retrieved the eggs, Dr. Craswell decided that the embryos were ready. She arranged for Gisele and Azure to check into the hospital for the transfer, a procedure in which Dr. Craswell had a lot of practice; she would not be able to count the number of times she had performed this procedure. But this time she was more excited than she had ever been. If her theory proved correct, she would be making medical history and more importantly, she would be changing the way life starts in the womb. Millions of years of evolution would change in an instant.

As she entered the operating room, she was all smiles, "Good morning ladies."

"Good morning, Doctor," the two women sang in chorus.

"Are you both ready to become moms?"

"Yes ... yes ... yes," was the high pitched excited reply.

As Dr. Craswell's assistant wheeled the incubator into the operating theatre, she said, "Here are your future babies, swimming in these petri dishes."

Then the assistant helped position Gisele on the table, draped her in a sheet, placed her feet in the stirrups. It was like any pelvic exam, cold and awkward.

Dr. Craswell added, "This will not hurt, but you may feel a bit uncomfortable. Are you ready? Shall we begin?"

Gisele looked at up at Dr. Craswell smiled and nodded her head.

Dr. Craswell had graded each fetus earlier that morning and had selected the best ones for transfer. She had selected four, two for each patient. She would have preferred more, but this was not to be.

The Doctor positioned herself in front of her patient and using the speculum she spread the opening of Gisele's vagina so that she could gain access to her uterus. She carefully placed the first fetus onto the lining. She had already graded each fetus and she selected the best ones for transfer. She had selected six, three for each patient.

"Gisele, I am finished with you. Azure it's your turn now."

The assistant helped Gisele to get down from the table. She then lent Azure a hand and carefully positioned her on the table, placing her feet in the stirrups. The Doctor repeated the procedure and stood up smiling.

"Now we have to leave nature to take its course and hope your babies attach to your uterus. I will need to take your blood in ten days to confirm you are both pregnant."

Gisele and Azure sidled over to Dr. Craswell and nearly crushed her with a bear hug. "We will be here whenever you want us," Gisele said excitedly.

Dr. Craswell could hardly wait to know for sure if her dream for a major medical advance would come true.

"I think this will work and you two will soon have babies to cuddle. Your girls will bring a lot of fun to your lives and you will enjoy them all the more as a loving married couple."

"Do you think they will also be gay?"

"No, not necessarily. A person's sexual orientation maybe genetic or it may be the result of a hormonal imbalance during your pregnancy. But one thing is for sure, no one just decides at some point that they want to be gay."

The Doctor handed all the instruments to her nursing assistant who took them out for sterilization.

"Do you girls have someone to give drive you home?"

"No, we drove here by ourselves."

Dr. Craswell went into lecture mode, "Be very careful and watch out for those pro-life demonstrators as you leave the clinic. Remember to relax as much as

possible and take many naps. Do not do anything strenuous."

"Yes mom," Azure laughed.

"Ok then, goodbye. See you soon."

"Good bye, Doc," they both echoed.

The smiles on Gisele and Azure's faces could not be dampened, not even by the rowdy demonstration outside the clinic as they drove out the parking garage.

SEVEN

AFTER ALL THE SHUFFLING quieted down, the bailiff called for Mike Wagner to be brought into the court room. Coleman and Gallagher were seated at the attorneys' tables at the front of the court. As Mike Wagner was brought into the court, they both rose. Joining his court appointed attorney, Robert Gallagher, Wagner looked like he had had a bad night. He had deep circles under his eyes. But they had cleaned him up. He was close shaven, and had a new haircut. He had on a blue blazer and khaki trousers. In fact, he looked more like a banker, than a would-be assassin. His attorney had given him a look of respectability, not entirely convincing, but pretty close.

Judge Burnett asked, "What is the charge?" Coleman replied, "Involuntary Manslaughter and attempted murder, your Honor."

Gallagher interjected, "My client requests the court to release him on his own recognizance. The defendant has strong family ties to the community. His parents have lived in Chesapeake their whole lives and my client owns a home here. In addition, his children also live here with his ex-wife. Mr. Wagner has no record and he is a church going man."

Judge Burnett hesitated as she considered the statement and read the papers on her desk.

Burnett was young for a Circuit Court Judge when the Governor appointed her, but she was accepted by her colleges as she had appeared before them many times and they all had respect for her integrity.

She was very attractive with shoulder length brunette hair that curled naturally, but even so, she remained single. She had a few close friends, all women, who frequently got together for drinks or dinner. This created fuel for speculation about her sexual orientation, but she managed to keep her private life a secret and was never seen on a date with any man or woman that might be considered a potential partner. Her career on the judiciary was her life and her only true love.

One of Judge Burnett's first trials would be a tough one. She had read about it only briefly, and stopped following the case in the media as soon as she presided over the bail hearing and realized the case would become one of hers. It was a hot case with lots of publicity and the public taking sides. A demonstrator had been killed in a protest against the Baywater clinic whose specialization is in vitro fertilization and reproductive research. And now, a man the media was labeling a firebrand was on trial. She hated that her first major case would be a media magnet, sure to get close scrutiny from all sides, especially the ultra conservative right.

She asked Coleman, "Does the state have any objection to the request of the defense attorney?"

"Yes, your Honor. We have police eyewitnesses or at least a police eyewitness and there is a surveillance tape that shows Mr. Wagner with the gun."

"So Mr. Coleman, are you telling me that you have clear proof from your police witness and you have a surveillance tape. I assume you want me to deny bail?" Judge Burnett asked, somewhat crossly. She didn't like having to prompt the Commonwealth's Attorney.

"Well, we are trying to analyze the tape at the moment," Coleman replied, tugging on his ear, showing some slight hesitance.

Detective Max Leland and Sergeant Mila Preston were sitting in the back of the court room listening to every word. "What does he mean, analyzing the tape?" Preston asked leaning over to Leland. "With my testimony and Hayward's being in contradiction, the tape is our ace in the hole. Without it, our case is weak."

"I don't know what's going on," whispered Leland, "But what I do know is that surveillance tape is the only thing we have to ensure that Wagner won't get off. Otherwise, it's your eyewitness account against Hayward's. Wagner could walk out a free man. We can't let that happen." The two women looked at each other, clearly concerned about that possibility.

"And I thought there were two policemen at the scene," the Judge pressed.

"Well, it appears that only one clearly saw Mr. Wagner there."

Gallagher saw his opening. "Your honor, my client picked up the gun after it was dropped by someone else. It's not even registered to him."

"It apparently is not registered to anyone, Mr. Gallagher. Nice try." The judge was clearly trying to move things along, and didn't want to get into the particulars of the case.

"Well, do you think you all can speed up the analysis of the tape, Mr. Coleman," she said emphasizing the words speed up and analysis. "I mean how hard can that be?" she asked rhetorically, obviously somewhat irritated with the way the Commonwealth's Attorney seemed to be hedging his bets. Why was Coleman dragging his feet, she wondered? He usually was a pit bull, always ready to chew up a defendant and spit him out, just in time to make headlines for the next election cycle.

"These are serious charges. I'm not willing to let Mr. Wagner out on the street at this point in time. Bail is denied, while the state analyzes the tape," she said, again making a point of looking at Mr. Coleman. Judge Burnett obviously did not like the way the state was presenting its case and she was letting Coleman know that by her stern looks. She sure didn't want the Commonwealth's Attorney playing politics with this case, and it was beginning to seem like that could be a possibility.

"Mr. Gallagher and Mr. Coleman this case is attracting media attention from all sides of the political spectrum. So just be careful about what you say to the media. I don't want to see any grandstanding to get media attention or any efforts to mobilize the right to life crowd. I don't want to see either of you turn into media stars. We are going to try this in court, not on the streets. Agreed?"

Both attorneys nodded in agreement although Coleman vowed to himself that if he had anything to do with it, he'd raise as much public sentiment as possible against what was going on in the clinic. He was already steadily leaking information to a few sympathetic conservative reporters. This would help set the stage for a plea agreement that would keep this case out of court altogether.

As the bailiff picked up the papers for the next case and started calling for the next defendant to come before the Honorable Judge Burnett,

Gallagher turned to Coleman, expecting the usual posturing that goes along with any case. But what followed next surprised him.

"Call my secretary and set up an appointment to meet me in my office later in the week. Maybe we will be able to work out a plea deal in exchange for a more lenient sentence," Coleman said, looking sour. Even though this was the outcome he wanted, he never liked being backed into a corner. He gathered up his papers, tried to look preoccupied and snapped his brief case shut. He avoided the customary handshake.

Gallagher tried to cover his surprise at Coleman's invitation. "I'll be there." As Gallagher watched Coleman walk out of the courtroom, he felt someone tap him on his shoulder. He spun around to face Mila Preston and Detective Max Leland. Seeing Mila after so long was a surprise.

"Why hello, Mila, it's been a long time since we last saw each other," he said.

"Yes Bobby, you seemed to disappear after we graduated," she replied.

"That's not true, Mila. I just got tired of the repeated rejections," he attempted a smile and tried to sound indifferent, but did not exactly pull it off. The two had dated while he was a law student and she an undergraduate in criminal justice.

Leland interjected, "You two know each other?"

"We went to school together," Mila said as she and Gallagher exchanged brief glances, which told Leland everything he needed to know.

Gallagher tried to focus, "Well, I am sure you came to talk to me about something else, not reminisce about our school days. What's on your mind?"

"I know you are just doing your job, but I was the officer at the scene, or at least, the officer who had the best view of the shooting. I don't want to see your client back in front of the Baywater clinic harassing women who need specialized care from one of the most advanced and respected reproductive institutions in the world?"

Gallagher got a funny look on his face. He didn't relish the idea of cross examining Mila Preston, his old flame, when the case went to trial. This was certainly something they never covered in law school, how to question an old girlfriend.

Then Leland added, "We don't want to see him succeed the next time he tries to take Dr. Craswell's life or some other doctor's life, or an expectant mother."

Preston interjected, "He's dangerous, Bobby."

"Why are you telling me this?" Gallagher glanced at them with a quizzical look on his face, "It is my job to get him off on all the charges. And frankly, Mila, I'm not even sure it's proper for us to be having this discussion." He ignored Leland altogether.

Preston looked him up and down and then spoke slowly, "I know you are not a right wing radical. You are a fine attorney Bobby and Wagner is lucky to have you as his lawyer. But this guy is a fanatic."

Gallagher's face went white as he realized the officers were right, but he composed himself and acted as the perfect defense attorney. "Look officers, I understand your concern, but my job is to represent my client."

Reading the concern on his face, Preston pressed forward with her argument, "I watched him fire the gun at Dr. Craswell. He was intentionally trying to kill her at point blank range. Do you want to see another death at the hands of this man?"

"First of all, my client is innocent until proved guilty and there is very little proof that he committed this shooting. And secondly, of course I don't want anything to happen to Dr. Craswell or anyone else. But really, Mila, this conversation is just not appropriate. The court will decide and I am going to perform my fiduciary duty and do everything I can to represent my client to the best of my ability. I can't discuss this with you any further."

Preston took a deep breath and looked at Gallagher with resignation. She was obviously disappointed, but she also realized that he was right. He had a job to do and it would put them in head to head combat in court. That prospect did not excite her, any more than it excited Gallagher. "I understand Bobby. I just wanted to make sure you understand what's at stake here." Disappointed in the exchange, both officers retreated to their cruisers as Gallagher tried to look cool and professional by calling his office to check messages.

But Gallagher had a sinking feeling in his stomach that Preston was probably right. He knew that Wagner was a radical and that most likely he would strike again, maybe hitting his intended target the next time. He realized that Wagner was a danger to all women seeking abortions and to doctors performing them. He knew Wagner was also violently opposed to all doctors involved in any type of reproductive research.

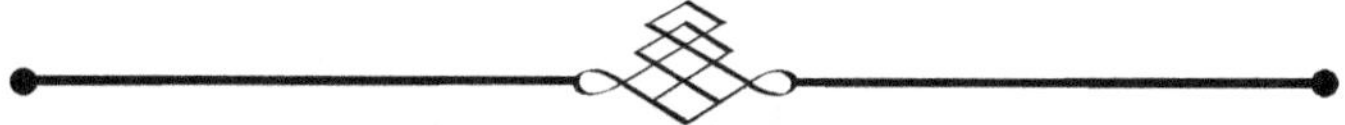

EIGHT

SERGEANT MILA PRESTON REALIZED how relieved she felt that the Judge had denied bail for Wagner. That militant activist needed to be off the streets. Leaving the courtroom and heading back to the station house, she remembered that she had an open invitation to a date with Max Leland and she thought she might enjoy his company this evening. After all, they had something to celebrate. She found Max attractive and a nice guy. She didn't love the idea of 'dating' in the station house. But she'd keep things cool. Besides, Mila was intrigued to find out Richard Hayward's nickname. She knew that it was derogatory by the snickers around the station house whenever the guys talked about him.

Max had mentioned the idea of going out together for a hamburger and gossiping about Hayward ever since the station house incident. Max was surprised when Mila finally approached him and asked, "How about tonight?" "Tonight?" he said, smiling.

"For a hamburger," she said reproachfully, but with a smile. "We have something to celebrate. That worm of a human being, Mike Wagner, was indicted today."

Max returned the smile. "Great, I've got just the place." He was ready, willing and able to celebrate with Mila. He too knew it would be tricky to date a fellow officer. And she did outrank him. But it was only one grade and besides, rules were made to be broken.

It was turning out to be something of an old fashioned date. He was actually picking her up at her apartment. He even went up to her door and laughed at himself when he rang the doorbell. He felt like a high school kid with sweaty palms. He'd definitely have to get a grip or she'd think he was a real loser.

She came to the door in a pink raspberry cashmere sweater with pearls, no less. And what he hadn't fully realized, what her uniform concealed, Mila was stacked. In fact, she was positively smashing. He liked the way she looked in uniform, but this was something altogether different. While she had on very little makeup, her cheeks were pink and her eyes were shinning. Maybe it was the glow from the raspberry sweater.

Most amazingly, she had on a skirt. Max had never seen her legs before. They were surprisingly shapely. There was no doubt she would definitely pass her next physical for the police force. And she would give any wise guy a run for his money. Oh, and he laughed to himself, they had one thing in common with their outfits for the evening. Like him, she had one extra bulge that maybe only another cop would recognize. She was packing her firearm and so was he. He guessed that both of them had a trust issue, even when going to a hamburger joint. You just couldn't be too careful these days. He carried his service revolver and his badge everywhere he went. He just didn't want to be caught flatfooted, and he realized Mila felt the same way.

Max took all this in, with one quick glance. Of course, he couldn't be caught checking her out. This was, after all, still a casual hamburger date, maybe not even a date, maybe an outing would be a more appropriate way to describe it. At any rate, the way Mila looked put to rest any rumors that she might be gay. She had kept to herself so much over the past couple of years she had been on the force, that some of the guys wondered if she was 'playing on the other team'. Well, Max decided that not only was she a player, she was an all star. Then the thought occurred to him that maybe it was the guys on the force who had shut her out, shut her out of the after-work poker games, the jokes, the inside scoop, precisely for the reason that she didn't look like a dyke.

While Max was giving her the quick once over, Mila was doing the same thing to him. She liked the way he looked in jeans, casual, yet still crisp. Unlike his uniform, the jeans showed off his buns. They were spectacular. Not that it mattered; she wasn't going to get involved; she just wanted to be friends. But she did realize that once she really looked at him, he was a handsome guy. And hot too.

She too noticed he was packing his handgun, and she liked a man with a pistol. It made her feel secure. Not that she needed protection, but she wanted a cop to always be able to take control in any situation. You just never knew when a situation would arise.

Max had selected this neat out-of-the-way diner, a real museum piece, left over from the fifties, for their hamburger 'outing'. Amazingly, even though it had been modernized, it still had the original diner trailer and original booths. He loved going there and only took special dates there. He really didn't want too many people to know about it. The diner was a jewel that he didn't want to see ruined by becoming fashionable. But most importantly, the hamburgers were the best in the City.

As they pulled up to the diner, Max jumped out to get the car door. But Mila beat him too it. And as he reached for the door, he grabbed Mila's hand instead. They both laughed, and they both felt instantly shy. Their laughter seemed to cut the tension as they made their way to the front door. As usual there was a short wait to get a table, but they started talking non-stop. Finally the waitress called them and seated them near the back at a semi private table. Once seated they ordered beer, hamburgers, and onion rings and continued from where they left off. They were both army brats, and that meant their paths had probably crossed somewhere in time.

Once the hamburgers came, there was a moment of silence, as they both bit into the juicy burgers that more than lived up to the joint's reputation for good greasy food.

He hated to even get into the whole explanation about why Richard came to be called Pencildick, but, she pressed him to tell her all about Richard's nickname, "You promised to tell me if I went out with you. You are not going to go back on your word are you?"

Max shyly told her, "Everyone loved how you dressed Richard down the other day when he tried to put you down."

Mila jokingly repeated her demand, "Don't try to get out of it, come on let's hear about his nickname."

"Well," he explained, "the guys don't exactly trust Richard. He let his partner down a while back. He froze during a standoff with armed robbers at a convenience mart. And yeah, I know anybody can freeze once in his career, but he tried to make it seem like he was the hero.

But unfortunately for him, it was all caught on the store's security tape, and basically, he hit the floor when the firing started and didn't even try to help his partner. His partner got shot and came this close to dying. Ever since then, everybody's been kind of cool to Richard. Because he has small feet and small hands, the joke is that he has a small u'know too."

"A small u'know; what is a u'know?" she asked, looking at him like he was crazy.

"You know, his privates. We think he has a small dick," he said quietly, blushing. In for a penny, out for a pound, so he continued, "Behind his back, we call him Pencildick."

Bad timing, Mila had just taken a sip of beer, and when Max gave the explanation, she gave a hearty laugh. Her beer went everywhere. They both started laughing and couldn't stop for at least a minute. Well, that really cut the ice, and Max realized he and Mila were really going to hit it off.

Getting serious, Mila asked who his partner was. Max had left out that one detail. "I was," he said.

Mila put her hand on his. "Goddamn that bastard! He is a Pencildick." And they both laughed again. "You seem to have recovered completely."

"It was tough as first, but extensive rehabilitation with sexy therapists helps to regain one's mobility quickly," he mused.

"Well, Pencildick is probably upset that Mike Wagner was indicted to stand trial for the murder of Paul Bachmann and the attempted murder of Dr. Leslie Craswell," Mila stated.

"He's not only a Pencildick, but a right wing extremist Pencildick, at that."

Mila added soberly, "He most likely secretly belongs to the same gang as Mike Wagner, who I think is a danger to society. He is certainly a danger to Dr. Craswell. He hates her for some reason."

"I'll try to drive by her house once a day in my patrol car, just to check it out and make a police presence known. They have a security guard for the neighborhood, but anybody could get past that. I am worried for her too," Max said.

Mila liked Max even more now that he showed he cared about the controversial doctor. Most men condemned her research. They judged her as a weirdo because of her new experimental in vitro fertilization techniques. Mila had read a very vague article about how women might reproduce without men. It was odd, Mila thought. But on the other hand, with male sperm counts dropping, who knows, it could be the saving grace for the human race, one day. One thing that was for sure, Mila thought Max's sperm would be strong swimmers. Not that she ought to care, she reminded herself.

But as the evening progressed, Max and Mila clearly had chemistry going for them. At one point, when Mila reached over to brush off a burger bit from Max's mouth, he playfully bit her finger. They both nervously laughed. Oh yeah, things were going to get hot tonight, he though, he hoped, he prayed. However, his prayers were not to be answered.

Just at that moment, two guys in sweatshirts with hoods walked into the diner. Max noticed them immediately, and Mila noticed how his attention was diverted. It was obvious to the two cops that something was up. As the guys in hoods approached the busy cash register pulling their guns, Max and Mila reached for their firearms at the same time.

Max and Mila both hit the floor and rolled under the table concealing themselves from the robbers and giving themselves a clear view of the cash register, guns drawn and ready for action.

"You stay here. I am going to crawl over to the front to catch them by surprise. We don't want to start a shootout or someone will get hurt badly. I want to take them out quickly, keep me covered," Max whispered.

He slithered out from the under the table and then crawled over to the next table, between two pairs of lovely legs. The hoods waved their guns wildly around and ordered everyone to place their hands on their heads. They picked an elderly couple first and grabbed the woman's purse. Then they demanded that her husband hand over his wallet.

Quickly checking to make sure he was not spotted, Max sprang out from under that table and quietly ducked under the next. The patrons were terrified and he had to shush them as he made his way systematically to the front of the restaurant.

As the hoods moved toward their next victim, Max jumped up and grabbed one of them around the throat. The hood fired his gun in the air and his comrade spun around to face them and pointed his gun right at Max.

Just when it looked like he had a straight shot at Max, Mila sprung into action and fired a round into the second hood's leg. He let out a blood curdling scream as her bullet hit the target and lodged itself against the long bone in his leg. He spun around and started firing at Mila, but he missed and hit a young man in the arm. Blood was spurting everywhere as he took another shot at Mila. Her reaction was swift; she overturned a table and ducked down behind it. She fired off a few rounds and hit the robber in the chest. His legs slowly crumpled beneath him and his firearm fell to the floor with a loud thump. He fell on top of it and rolled over dead.

Meanwhile Max and the first hood were wrestling on floor. The first hood caught Max by surprise with a skillfully executed judo throw. Both weapons went flying as they crashed to the floor. Max quickly recovered from his surprise and threw himself on top of the crook.

Just when Mila thought she could go to Max's aid, another thug burst through the front door and started firing into the crowd. The women were screaming and many men were crying. Two more patrons were hit.

Mila turned her attention to the new threat and kept firing at the thug. This time, Max was relieved that his partner had backed him up, unlike three years ago, when Pencildick turned into a pansy. Yeah, he'd take Mila as his partner any day. In fact, he thought, maybe she'd be a good partner for life.

One carefully aimed shot at the thug's head and he dropped to the floor, also dead. She then came out from behind the table and aimed her gun at the first hood's head. She had to be careful as Max and the hood were still wrestling. As soon as she had a clear line of sight, she fired at point blank range. His blood and some brain tissue splattered out from the wound that opened in his head and splashed all over Max's shirt. The last hood collapsed and died sprawled on top of Max.

Mila placed her gun back in the holster and extended her hand to help Max free himself from the hoodlum and stand up. Neither of them had time to think about what had just happened. Instead, they realized that there were several wounded diners and they rushed over to help others who were administering emergency first aid. People tore the table cloths into bandages and wrapped them around the profusely bleeding wounds.

It was a tossup who got to the diner first, whether it was a flood of police officers, Internal Affairs or the screeching ambulances. It all seemed to happen at once. Emergency crews swarmed into the restaurant and loaded the wounded onto gurneys. Five police cars with sirens blaring and blue lights flashing gave the diner an eerie look. The screech of the tires as the ambulances pulled off together with the screaming sirens, destroyed the peaceful night.

Three members of Internal Affairs asked Leland and Preston for their weapons, routine for a police related shooting, and then took the officers' statements. Their statements were corroborated by a diner full of grateful witnesses. When Internal Affairs had gotten the officers' statements, the diner owner, Ozzie Williams approached Leland. "Man, you've been coming here a long time. I never knew you was a cop. But from now on the hamburgers are on me. And bring the lady too. You two saved our lives tonight."

There still remained a massive amount of police work to carry out. The forensics unit was brought in to recover all evidence as smoothly as possible. The deceased were photographed and every bullet was located and marked on a layout of the restaurant for later analysis.

Once outside and away from the other cops and the civilians, Leland and Preston let down their guard. They stopped the tough act. Max sucked in as much fresh air as he could as he tried to fight back the waves of nausea he felt. Mila knew she had to sit down right away; she could feel her legs turning to rubber. She made it to the car door and was holding herself up by the door handle, as her legs buckled under her. Max saw what was happening, realized the door was locked, and pulled himself together so he could lend a hand to Mila. He rushed to unlock the car door and helped Mila inside, just as she collapsed.

He cradled her in his arms. "You were amazing, tonight, Mila. You saved my butt."

Mila had started crying silently and she was trying to hide her face. She didn't want another cop to see her cry. "Yeah, but I've turned into a wimp now," she said, turning her head, refusing to let Max see her vulnerable side.

"No, Mila, this isn't a made for TV series. This is real life. Our bodies are reacting the way they're supposed to. You're no wimp. You were so brave in there tonight. I'll never forget it," he said, putting his hand under her chin, raising her head so his lips could find hers. They kissed on the lips, only on the lips, but it was the most stirring kiss either of them had ever experienced. For a brief moment, their eyes locked in recognition of what they had just experienced in the diner and now at the car.

To lighten things up and cover her own embarrassment, Mila asked through her tears, "You always kiss your partners? You didn't kiss Pencildick, did you?"

"No, I've never kissed a partner before. You, Mila, are something special."

At that moment, TV crews began to roll into the diner. The spell was broken, at least for that night. They both groaned as they saw WAVY News pull up. They both knew their quiet hamburger get away would be the talk not only of the station house, but the whole town. Oh, God, the jabbing that would invoke!

"So much for a quiet relaxing night out," Mila said, knitting her brow as she envisioned the talk and whispered rumors she'd have to ignore from the other cops, not to mention her noisy elderly neighbor, Mrs. Lovelace.

"Yeah," Max replied, as he shook his head and put his arm protectively around Mila. "But we'll get through this together too. Come on, the sooner we face the media gauntlet, the sooner we can get out of here."

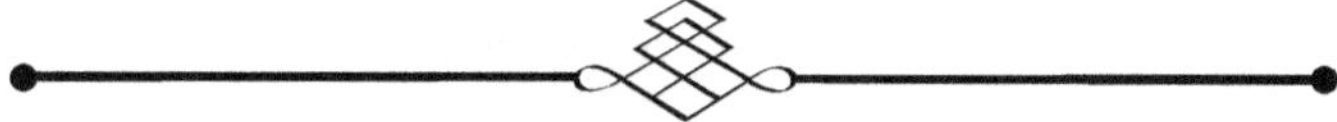

NINE

JUDGE CLAIRE BURNETT SAT quietly in her chambers waiting for the bailiff to announce that the court was ready for her to enter. "All rise, court is now in session. The Honorable Judge Claire Burnett now presiding over the Chesapeake Circuit Court...." The bailiff cried out in his pompous baritone voice. He waited until the Judge came in, robe streaming behind her as she walked swiftly to the center of the bench and sat in her chair. "You may be seated."

The next order of business in this case would be to convene the members of the grand jury. Even with the veil of secrecy surrounding the grand jury process, she knew there would be leaks. As Judge Burnett looked over the prospective jurors, she tried to imagine which ones would leak to the media. Someone always did. While the grand jury system is not perfect, Judge Burnett realized it was part of our system of checks and balances that gives a suspect a fighting chance. True, the grand jury was a prosecutorial tool, but still, you had to convince a jury of ordinary citizens that there is reasonable suspicion or probable cause that a crime has been committed, and that the suspect could be the likely culprit.

After the court was called to order, Judge Burnett explained the importance of the grand jury and its procedures, and she attempted to explain the differences between trial jurors and the grand jury. In reality, she realized that the grand jury had none of the formality of a trial jury, and that often an indictment was little more than a rubber stamp for the prosecution. But in this case, she wanted that to be different. This case was really important and could go all the way to the Supreme Court.

The judge was required to ask a series of questions to ensure that prospective grand jury members would be impartial so that they could determine if there was probable cause. In this case, that was not an easy task.

Would a prospective juror be inclined to be biased because of religious convictions against abortion and against reproductive research and new reproductive techniques? Would a prospective juror be so in favor of a woman's right to choose and so supportive of new scientific techniques that he or she would jump to indict, regardless of the facts presented? She had to screen for bias on either side. The question was not about abortion. It was not about in vitro fertilization and new scientific research. The question was whether the defendant could have committed the crimes of involuntary manslaughter and attempted murder. To Judge Burnett, it was a plain and simple question of whether Mike Wagner likely aimed a gun at Dr. Leslie Craswell at point blank range in an attempt to kill her, and whether in doing so, the bullet had inadvertently ricocheted and killed a fellow protestor.

After the formalities were over, the clerk drew names from the box and placed them on the bench before Her Honor, who began calling the prospective members of the grand jury. The jurors rose one by one, some of them obviously unhappy, and walked over to the front bench, where they sat in sequence.

Once they were seated, Judge Burnett faced the men and women selected for the grand jury. "Please stand and take the oath," she instructed, "and please raise your right hands. Do you solemnly swear or affirm that you will faithfully discharge your duties as grand jurors; that you will faithfully hear and decide all issues and matters brought before you, so help you God?"

A chorus of assorted "I do's" followed, and the grand jury was seated.

"Ladies and gentlemen," Judge Burnett addressed the group, "you have been selected and sworn in as grand jurors for the City of Chesapeake. You have the responsibility to hear cases from the Commonwealth's Attorney and to decide on whether to indict the accused. Mr. Anthony Coleman please stand. Mr. Coleman is the Commonwealth's Attorney representing the Commonwealth of Virginia and will present the cases to the grand jury. Please go with Mr. Coleman to the grand jury room."

Coleman marched the grand jury members down the hall to a small conference room where they seated themselves and were instructed to elect a foreman for this jury. After looking at each other with blank faces, Emily Bowen, a rather matronly looking woman stood up and volunteered to lead the group. The others quickly agreed and Emily took her place as the foreman.

Coleman cleared his throat, "Ladies and gentlemen of the grand jury, I would like to present the case of State of Virginia vs. Mike Wagner to you." This would be a little tricky for Coleman. He'd want to lay out a weak case because he didn't want the grand jury to indict. At the same time, he needed to seem like he was enthusiastically pursuing prosecution of Wagner. So Coleman laid out the evidence but reluctantly included the defense's assertion that the shooting might have been accidental.

"Mr. Wagner was present at the shooting that occurred outside the woman's clinic on Olney Road," he said in his most solicitous voice and tugged on his ear, which if the jurors knew him well, they would have taken that as a sign that he was lying or angry. "Now we have an officer at the scene who says she saw Mr. Wagner shoot point blank at a doctor from the clinic. Now a lot was going on at that demonstration, I'll give the defense that. There were hundreds of people there, and there was a lot of excitement. I'll give them that too."

Usually Coleman didn't give the defense anything. But today, he was trying to present a weak case, while not appearing to do so, and he was "giving" a lot to the defense. "Someone brought a gun to the demonstration. And we think that was Mike Wagner. Now the defense is going to say it wasn't Mike."

Coleman knew how to start generating empathy for a defendant, and using his first name started that process. Also describing the chaos at the demonstration was important to begin planting confusion in the minds of the grand jury. No one would have noticed Coleman's sleight of hand. No one that is, except for Miss Emily Bowen.

Bowen was a rather mousey looking woman, but surprise of surprises, she had real chutzpah. A librarian, she had read for years how one juror can make a difference, and she always longed to be that juror. So Bowen surprised everyone when she spoke up and asked, "Can the grand jury compel witnesses to testify before us?" She already knew the answer; she had done her homework.

It appeared to Bowen that the other jurors weren't paying attention, and that they might let this guy, Mike Wagner, off without even a grand jury indictment. And she was convinced that this case needed to go to a jury trial. All of a sudden, questioning Coleman had the intended effect; her fellow jurors' sat up and listened intently.

Emily's favorite movie was the 1950s classic, Twelve Angry Men, in which a lone juror managed to convince others. She wanted to be that lone juror who was not bowled over by a fast talking attorney.

Coleman couldn't hide his surprise at the questions from this librarian, for God's sake. "Of course you can and unlike the trial itself, the grand jury's proceedings are secret. The defendant and his or her counsel are generally not present for other witnesses' testimonies."

Bowen had one more card to play. She wasn't going to let her fifteen minutes of fame go by one second too quickly. She asked again, "While we discuss this case, can we ask you to leave?" Some of the jurors gasped at how bold she was, how audacious.

Coleman's face turned bright red as he tugged on his ear and you could see his demeanor change to anger. "That is your right," he snapped.

"Then I would like to request that you leave this courtroom during our deliberation," Bowen took pleasure in making him noticeably angry. Now, her fellow jurors were wide awake. She could tell they had taken a new interest in the case, and in fact, those who had been irritated at being called to be part of the Grand Jury, had lost their irritation. Now they were engaged.

Coleman rose and gathered up his files, placing the papers back in his expensive leather briefcase. He then walked slowly to the door, hoping that someone would ask him to stay. No one did. Emily Bowen was their leader now. As Coleman opened the door to leave the courtroom, he turned and looked appealing at the jurors, who were watching him intently. No one said anything.

As soon as the door closed, Bowen immediately asked, "Let's see where we stand in this matter. From what I heard from the Commonwealth's Attorney about this case, Mr. Wagner is charged with involuntary manslaughter and attempted murder. One of the officers at the scene said she saw him aim point blank at the clinic doctor, right at her face, and pulled the trigger. There is a dent in the windshield where the bullet ricocheted. If that had not happened, Dr. Leslie Craswell would be the deceased. As far as I can tell, that shows intent, and the rest is history. An innocent bystander was killed at a notso-peaceful protest. Anybody have anything else to add?" She asked looking around the room.

No takers there. So Bowen proceeded. "Please vote. Those who think we have enough evidence to indict Mr. Wagner, raise your hands." Everyone's hands went up. "And those against." The room was silent as they realized their job was done for today. They all felt empowered.

Bowen called the bailiff, "Please inform the judge that we have reached a decision."

As they returned to the courtroom, Coleman searched their faces to see if he could tell whether they were going to dismiss or indict. The Grand Jury's decision had been swift. Sometimes that meant they had voted to dismiss the case. But you just couldn't tell.

Judge Burnett asked them who they had voted a foreman. Bowman stood, "Your honor, I was voted foreman of the jury."

The Judge continued, "What is your decision?"

Bowen spoke loudly and clearly, "We, the jury, believe there is sufficient evidence to indict the defendant on all charges."

"Thank you ladies and gentlemen. You duties have been discharged for today. You are dismissed."

Dammit, thought Coleman, now we'll have to get down and dirty to acquit Wagner. Even as the Judge concluded her speech, Coleman was already formulating his next step.

Emily Bowen left the courtroom euphoric. True, she wasn't a media star. She wouldn't get to have her name in the paper. But she had mobilized the jurors. She had done her part to at least see that someone would be tried for attempted murder and involuntary manslaughter. She loved the system and she relished her role in making sure that Mike Wagner would go to trial. But Emily was rejoicing prematurely. Neither she nor the other members of the Grand Jury or any other court officers, save one, knew that a very important ingredient in the state's case would soon be missing.

Police Chief Jack Chisholm called Hayward into his office the day after the indictment. He did it in a way that everyone would see and hear.

Chisholm had found that if you wanted to hide something, the best way to do it was in plain sight.

"Richard, come on into my office. I want to discuss what you saw at the clinic. I just don't like it when my cops see two entirely different things. Mila, after that, I'll want to talk with you." It was obvious that the police captain was fuming.

Oh dear, Mila thought, here it goes, this is what Sunita warned me about. He's going to make my life hell.

In a second, Hayward was on his way into Chisholm's office with police pad in hand, ready to suck up to the Chief in any way he could. And as he was soon to find out, there was a way. The minute Hayward entered his office; Chisholm yanked the cord, shutting the blinds with a snap.

"So, it looks like either you or Mila need glasses. I'd like to think it was Mila," the Captain said. "You know, not that it has any relevance to the case, but Mike and the Commonwealth's Attorney go to the same church and I understand Mike's a good guy."

"I just don't like what those baby makers are doing over at the Baywater Clinic," said Richard.

Always the one to miss the point, Hayward didn't pick up on Chisholm's comment about the Commonwealth's Attorney. Oh brother, I'm going to have to spell this out for him, thought Chisholm. No wonder the guys call him Pencildick. He is a dick. Patience, he reminded himself.

"Richard, forget about what they do in the clinic. I'm sure that didn't affect what you saw. Let's talk about what happened outside the clinic," and the Captain smiled to encourage Richard to focus. "You know, I'd tend to take a seasoned cop's eyewitness account over a girl's. They get so excited and think they see all kinds of things."

Now, Chisholm could see that made Richard feel a little more comfortable. Maybe he'd relax enough to play ball.

"Yeah, that's not what I saw. I clearly saw Wagner pick up the gun from the ground."

Yeah, Chisholm thought, what you saw was some pretty little thing's skirt and the fantasy of a little pussy totally distracted you from your job. But, with restraint, Chisholm harnessed those negative thoughts and continued, trying to sound as macho as he could.

"I would think that would be the likely scenario too, Richard. The only problem is Mila says the whole thing was caught on a surveillance camera tape. And she says the tape shows Wagner firing point blank at the doctor's windshield. Now that gives us a problem. Surveillance camera tapes tend to be believed by jurors."

Chisholm spoke slowly and was playing with a pencil on his desk. He stopped, folded his hands, looked into Hayward's eyes and said, "Now, I myself haven't seen the tape. So before I can decide which of my cops is correct, I'll have to look at the tape, unless of course, something happened to the tape. I mean things do go missing from the evidence room. Now, I myself don't go into the evidence room that often. So how's the security in there? Is it likely the tape will be in safe keeping?"

Ever the dimwit, Hayward still didn't get it and reverted back to his talk about the clinic. "Well, I don't know, it's all a mess. But these baby doctors are..."

Chisholm interrupted him. His patience, which wasn't abundant in the best of situations, was running thin.

"Listen, Richard! If you start talking about what they're doing in the clinic ever again in my presence, I'm going to feed you your balls for your last supper. Shut up about what they're doing in the clinic, and concentrate." At last, Chisholm could see he had Hayward's attention.

"The Commonwealth's Attorney is upset about having to prosecute this case. He wants to plea bargain it out. But he can't as long as there is physical evidence. And the surveillance tape is physical evidence. As long as that tape is around, it substantiates Mila's story. Now when you go into the evidence room today," he continued, "check to see how secure that tape is. Will you do that for me? See if that tape's got legs and how fast it can run," he said cryptically.

"I need to go into the evidence room this morning to check on the Harper case," as the light went on in his head.

"Aren't you the lead investigator in the Harper case?" Chisholm knew Hayward was the lead investigator in that case since it was dragging on forever. "I want you to wrap that case up. To do that, you'll need to list all the physical evidence. I imagine you will want to review what you have before writing your report. Right? And while you're in there, check on the video, like I said. If it were to be missing, well, I guess you'd have to break the news to Mila."

The light shone in Pencildick's eyes. He couldn't wait to bust Mila's chops. Yeah, that tape would go missing. He'd see to it. And he'd nail Mila in front of everybody.. .that would get her back for the other day, when she embarrassed him so.

"Right, Captain," Pencildick said smiling.

"And one more thing, Richard."

"Yes sir?"

"Wipe that grin off your face. If you mess this up, you'll have to become a hair dresser. If you know what I mean?"

The insult had the intended effect. Hayward left the Captain's office really pissed that Chisholm had insulted his manhood. It didn't take much to insult Hayward's manhood, because true to the nickname the guys had surreptitiously given him, he didn't have much of it to begin with.

The Captain took a bottle of Tums out of his desk drawer, went to his office door, unscrewed the cap, popped a couple of Tums to try to douse the fire in his esophagus, and bellowed over to Preston, "Mila, I'll see you this afternoon. One of these interviews with cops who see two different things is all I can take this morning." And he closed his office door shut with a little bang.

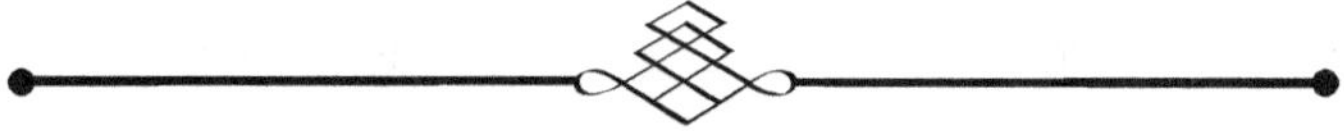

TEN

HEIDI SUSMAN GREW UP in a single parent household. She grew up with a mother that tried hard to make everything possible in her life. Her mother started encouraging her as a child, telling her that she would go to college. And that unlike her, Heidi would use her brain to earn her money, not sweat. Heidi's mother made sure her daughter looked smart when she left the house to go to school, even if it mean she had to stay up until all hours of the night washing and ironing Heidi's clothes.

Heidi took ballet classes with the extra money her mother made editing the theses of doctoral students at a nearby university. When Mrs. Susman had the opportunity to switch jobs and start working as an administrative assistant at the university, she gladly did it. She had better hours and working conditions, and most importantly, Heidi would be able to further her education at the university tuition free. Moreover, the university administration would make an exception and permit Heidi to live at home instead of on campus. In other words, Heidi would receive a very prestigious under graduate education free of charge.

At her mother's urging, Heidi took prelaw, graduated at the top of her class, and was accepted into the Harvard Law School, again a free ride because Heidi came from a low income single parent household and because Heidi was an exceptional student. Heidi headed to the Harvard Law School, heaping more prestige on her resume, and more doors opened to her. By the time she received her law degree, Heidi had every major corporation sniffing out her resume and making fabulous offers to her once they met the five foot ten, shapely blond whose body was as fabulous as her academic record.

Heidi took the highest paying job offer, urged on by her doting mom, who thought it was the chance of a lifetime, their dream come true. But just weeks into the job, Heidi realized that she just wasn't willing to make the sacrifices that the boss demanded; she wasn't willing to help corporations cheat clients, lie as a matter of course, or spend her life and brains on something she thought meaningless. This was the beginning of her hate affair with corporate America. She wanted to quit her lucrative job and dreaded breaking the news to her mom.

As she suspected, her mom did not approve, "Heidi, this is what we've both worked for all of our lives."

"Mom, it's my life."

"Well, Heidi, yes, it's your life. But don't forget the sacrifices we've both made to get you to this point. You can be a rich woman."

"Mom, no one knows better than I how you have sacrificed to offer me every advantage. And I can't tell you how grateful I am for all you have done. Your sacrifices have provided me with great opportunities. But I want to do something more with my life than just get rich. What if I could get rich, become powerful, and make the world a better place?"

"That's not realistic," her mother countered. They had discussed this 20 times in the past week, since Heidi told her mother she was quitting.

"It is possible, Mom. I want to move into politics.

I want to make sure other single moms like you have opportunities that weren't available to you. I want to be a community organizer at one of the city projects."

"Oh brother, and what are you going to organize? Trash pick-up?" her mother asked sarcastically. Heidi hated her mother's sarcasm, especially when it could possibly be true. But she wasn't going to back down from this.

"No, Mom. Not the trash. I am going to organize women so they can become self sufficient. We're going to do this by offering General Education Development classes at night, and help place the women in jobs during the day. Once they get a paycheck, we're going to involve them in a women's investment club. We're going to rely on the career women in these clubs to act as mentors. We're going to lift these women out of their poverty."

Heidi's mother was quiet for a minute, "You know, you've always followed your hunches, and you've always done well. Okay, let's see where this goes. I have to admit I have my reservations, but as you say, it's your life and you never cease to amaze me."

Heidi was so grateful for her mother's support. Heidi had always been able to count on her mom's support. And she didn't want this to be any different. Heidi wanted to reassure her mom that this would work out.

"Mom, I know this is going to work out. But if it doesn't, I'll be the first to admit it and make a mid course correction. Okay, Mom?" The two women hugged and began a partnership that would become legend.

Heidi tendered her resignation to the astonishment of her boss, who thought he and the job he had given Heidi were God's gifts to the world. She became involved in the community organization she told her mom about and she partnered with a women's investment club headed by Tanya Jackson, a career woman she really admired. As her friendship with Tanya grew, as her admiration of self made women grew and as her hatred of corporate America deepened, Heidi saw politics as her way to the top and as a way to help women and the underemployed.

Heidi wanted to make a difference, and she wanted to be in a position that would bring about change to corporate America so that the power of corporations wouldn't replace the power of the people. Her mother still didn't entirely approve of all of this, but alas, her daughter was strong headed, and didn't seem to be following her direction any more. She was proud of Heidi, and just had a hunch, that this girl would shatter the glass ceiling.

So Heidi's mother began throwing all of her energies into Heidi's community self help project. She became Heidi's right hand woman, her best friend and her best advocate. Meanwhile, Heidi's organizational work was really paying off. There had been several news features about Heidi's work and the women she was helping lift out of poverty. It was all over the internet and she was even featured on The Today show and started hitting the talk show circuit. This became the launching pad Heidi needed to test the political waters.

She eyed the seat held by a very conservative, low brow reactionary representing the Seventh Congressional District in her hometown of Richmond, Virginia. His seat was coming up for re-election, and for the life of her, Heidi couldn't understand how this guy ever got elected in the first place.

"You know, Mom, the man has never had an original idea and he's fought against everything that would help working class people. He is nothing but a lap dog for the gun lobby and other special interest groups. He is an effete snob and God only knows why he could be a snob about anything. There's nothing attractive about him."

"Well Heidi, maybe the voters just need a better choice. And you know, I think you just might be that better choice." Her mom just knew the right things to say to support and motivate her daughter. That was all Heidi needed to hear. But instead of trying to work her way through the bureaucracy of the two traditional parties, Heidi thought she'd try a different route to the White House.

Rather than try to get a foot in the door of the existing political parties that had become very lazy at best, or downright corrupt at worst, Heidi decided to try a more complicated approach. She would resurrect Teddy Roosevelt's political party, the Progressive Party. That way, she wouldn't have any political debts to pay off. She'd start with a clean slate. It was risky, but the rewards would be high.

Theodore Roosevelt, America's twenty sixth president who served for two terms at the beginning of the twentieth century, was her hero for several reasons, most of them unknown to the majority of the American public. Everyone knew that Teddy Bears were named after him following a botched hunting trip to Mississippi and that he was one of the four presidents' depicted on Mount Rushmore.

But what most people didn't know is that when Roosevelt ran for president for a third term in 1912, he formed the Progressive Party to run against William Taft, who had succeeded him in 1909. He pulled so many progressives out of the Republican Party that he split the vote and both he and Taft lost that election to Woodrow Wilson. While Roosevelt was a spoiler, he also showed that the right candidate could muster support in a third party run.

Most Americans also didn't know that he distrusted wealthy businessmen and dissolved forty monopolistic corporations as a "trust buster". He was the first United States president to call for universal health care and national health insurance.

Heidi liked to quote Teddy Roosevelt's platform of 1912, "To destroy this invisible Government, to dissolve the unholy alliance between corrupt business and corrupt politics is the first task of the statesmanship of the day." This was music to Heidi's ears. She was disenchanted with the politics of the new millennium, with multiple wars and deregulated businesses that wrecked the economies of the world.

So Heidi decided she'd take the same approach as Roosevelt; she'd bypass the Republican and Democratic parties, and revive Roosevelt's Progressive Party. Her political instinct sensed that the public, especially women, were disenchanted with the status quo and they were ready for something new, different and exciting.

Heidi's mother again thought her daughter was unwise to take such an unusual approach, but then again, she thought, look how successful her daughter had already been. So this time, she didn't try to discourage her daughter. Instead, Mrs. Susman helped her daughter by scheduling speaking engagements, and doing the massive amount of organizational work that was needed. In the process, Mrs. Susman began to see that Heidi was starting to draw larger and larger crowds at her rallies. Her message was becoming polished and people really believed in her daughter's promise of a better future for them and their children.

By the end of the campaign, her mother had a feeling her daughter's good judgment, organizational skills and hard work were going to win her the seat from the Seventh Congressional District. And they did. Heidi was elected to serve as the Representative from the seventh district from the state of Virginia, defeating the powerful Republican congressman that had held the seat for five terms. The conservative Richmond political machine was stunned. And for once, the hapless congressman was speechless, which definitely was an improvement over twenty years of his non-stop prattle and stonewalling in Congress.

As a Representative, she was successful in forming alliances with the most powerful congressmen and women. They respected what she had accomplished, liked her fresh ideas, and were somewhat fearful of her growing feminist base. So she managed to rally support for her progressive ideas for more socially responsible government. And the party originally founded by Roosevelt, the Progressive Party, became a political force in its own right at last.

During her first term as a representative, Heidi managed to sponsor a Corporate Responsibility and Workers' Reform bill. Basically, it ensured that workers would earn fair wages, based on the success of their corporation and that they'd have the same benefits that management had including paid holidays, supplemental health benefits, and a retirement fund partially funded by their company.

It was so impressive to watch Heidi work the House of Representatives that friend and foe alike stood in awe of her ability to form unusual alliances. Fellow Congressmen and women stopped treating her as the junior representative from Virginia. Instead, they began deferring to her, realizing that one day, she could be calling all the shots. In fact, several Senators approached her about running for the Senate. She did run on the Progressive Party ticket and she won again. With one year under her belt in the Senate, she began looking at a Presidential bid.

ELEVEN

RICHARD HAYWARD RELISHED THE idea of taking the surveillance tape from the evidence room and then calling Mila out, contradicting her testimony, and having the Captain side with him. That'd fix the bitch, he thought, sticking his chin out, and adjusting his collar which was just a little too tight around his neck. And Hayward figured it would be easy to fool the evidence officer, Danny Randall. They occasionally were drinking buddies. Danny would be sloppy about watching him. He could easily slip something past Danny.

"Hey Danny," Hayward said, approaching the baby faced evidence room officer. "What have you been doing lately?"

"Anyone I can," and they both laughed at Randall's impotent humor. "How have you been?"

"Not so good. The captain has got a burr up his butt about the Harper case. He wants me to close out my report today. So I need to go over my evidence box. Can you get if for me? I'm going to be working late as it is."

"Sure, wait here and I'll get it," said the ever affable Randall. Hayward sat at the secured booth and waited for the small box of evidence on the Harper case. There wasn't much to go on for that homicide. One piece of crucial evidence was a blood stained wash cloth. That would be the corner stone of any case the Commonwealth might have. In less than five minutes, Randall brought the cardboard box back to the review booth.

Then he went back to get his cup of coffee and would join Hayward. Of course, that was a breach in protocol, since the intake officer was never supposed to leave a cop's side while he looked at the evidence. But, Danny and Richard were friends. Danny never even gave it a second thought. Hayward took the opportunity to slip the wash cloth down his pants. He had plenty of room to stuff the wash cloth in his tightie-whities.

"Damn, Danny. That blood stained wash cloth isn't in the box. Man, do you think you left it out by mistake when you sealed the box?"

A look of panic spread across Randall's face. He had been careless in the past with evidence, and he had been warned that if any evidence disappeared again, it would mean his job. He ran back into the evidence room with his buddy, Hayward, right behind him.

"I will help you look Danny and don't worry, I won't tell anyone." As they started looking, Hayward spotted what he was looking for, the evidence box marked Wagner/Craswell.

"Holy mackerel, Danny! We left the Harper evidence box unattended. Quick before some brown noser walks by and reports you, go get the box and bring it back in here."

Without a second thought, Randall ran out the door. From timing Randall when he got the box, Hayward knew he would have a few minutes before Randall could repack the box and get back into the evidence room.

Hayward headed straight for the box marked Wagner/Craswell. He pulled it down, opened it and saw the surveillance tape. He was relieved that it was a small cassette and snatched it from the box. He quickly removed the washcloth from his briefs and replaced it with the tape. Then he positioned himself in front of the empty space where the Harper box had been, just as Randall was rounding the corner with the box and its contents in his hands.

"Oops, that was close." Danny still looked worried.

"Yeah, and look what I found, Danny. The washcloth. It was on the shelf pushed all the way back," Hayward said, pointing to the shelf and holding out the blood stained washcloth in the plastic bag. "Danny, you got to be more careful, bro. Don't worry, I'm not going to breathe a word. But without this wash cloth, that crazy nigger who killed that white girl is gonna go free."

"Thanks Richard, you saved my butt."

"We're fiends, so don't worry about me telling the Sergeant or anything. But man, that scared me. The Captain would have had my butt, and you'd have lost your job."

By that point, Danny Randall was nearly reduced to tears. He never even considered that Hayward used the opportunity to tamper with other evidence. He was so grateful to Hayward that he put his arm around him.

"Hey, don't go getting girlie on me. What are friends for?" As Hayward turned to go, Randall said, "Hey, don't you want to see the evidence box, now?"

Hayward covered himself nicely."Yes, I thought you'd be bringing it out to the booth where we are supposed to look at this stuff."

"Of course," Randall said, recovering a semblance of professionalism, as he clutched the box and brought it out to the booth once again.

Hayward, sat down, and began jotting notes, pretending to sift through the evidence box. He spent about 10 minutes looking like he was concentrating, all the while, dying to get out of there, and dying to get the tape out of his briefs. Richard Hayward, after all, wasn't use to having much in his briefs, and he felt it uncomfortable. He left, but didn't fail to remind Randall of his screw-up.

"Danny, this will be our little secret," he said, holding his right thumb up. Danny returned the thumbs up, and grabbed the evidence box, taking a quick inventory ensuring that everything that was supposed to be in the box, including the blood stained washcloth was safely inside.

As he was busy doing that, Hayward, left, stopped by the men's room, took a crap, and then flushed the small cassette down the toilet. "Well, Miss Mila, let's see what you have to say for yourself now," Hayward said as he watched the tape disappear with his morning dump.

He called the Chief on his cell phone. "Mission accomplished!" was all he said.

"Where is it," the Captain responded. "Right about now, it's on its way to the Chesapeake Bay, I'd figure.

You see, what I did was..."

Chisholm interrupted him. "No don't; I don't want to hear the gory details. Now, don't say or do anything until Mila learns about this. I'll be sure to make that abundantly clear."

And he hung up without even a good bye.

He decided to talk to Mila at her desk. He didn't want to afford her the courtesy of a private audience. He'd need to shake her confidence, and he'd start by a public display.

Chisholm acted like he was headed out of the building, when he walked by Mila's desk, and then turned back, "Mila," he barked. "I want you to get me a list of your evidence. I just don't like the fact that I have two different cops at the same crime scene, seeing two entirely different things. I want to see that tape, in my office in 15 minutes when I get back. Have it ready for me to see. At least I can trust my own eyes."

"Yes, sir," she said to the Captain's back, as he headed toward the door. This disrespect was not lost on the other cops. They were used to the Captain's bad moods. But still they wondered what Mila had done to incur his special wrath.

Mila headed immediately for the evidence room. Ah, today was Tuesday. She'd have to deal with that imbecile Danny Randall. That guy couldn't find his fly in the dark," she thought. "Hi Danny," she said, wondering if she had startled him. He looked shaken. "I need to see the Wagner evidence box."

"Sure. I've got to finish this paper work, so have a seat," he said somewhat tersely. He wasn't going to hurry for her. Let her cool her heels a little bit. Mila was used to this type of discourtesy from Danny. He always made her wait. She knew in about five minutes, after he stalled as long as he could, Danny would finally go in and bring out her evidence.

Then he'd watch her like she was a common criminal, making sure she'd sign every form and that he would studiously count everything she'd touched. He'd watch her like a hawk. He just didn't like Mila. She was pretty and all, but she was almost as tall as he was. And she was uppity. She thought she was hot stuff. Besides, she'd turned him down for a date. Who did she think she was?

Finally, Danny looked up from his computer keypad, got his keys out, and walked into the evidence room. He slowly brought out the Wagner box and set it in the booth for Mila's inspection. She opened the box, saw the bagged gun, a few other pieces of evidence from the scene, but to her horror, no tape. "Danny!" she shrieked, "Where is the surveillance video?"

"I don't know what you're talking about. If it's not in the box, it's not here. After all, you packed the box."

"It was here. Let me come into the evidence room and check it out."

"You can't come in here. That's against protocol. We'll have to call in the Chief," Danny said, reaching for the phone. "No, let me help you look. I'm sure it's just fallen out of the box."

"Are you asking me to break protocol?" And he finished dialing the chief's number.

"Chief, we've got a problem here," he loved squealing on Mila. She thought she was so high and mighty. "Yeah, what's that," the Captain barked into his cell phone. "Something's missing from the Wagner evidence box. Officer Preston doesn't have any explanation for it and I know it's not in the evidence room; I went over everything this morning," he said, recalling the housekeeping he'd done after his buddy Hayward left.

At that moment, a thought flickered through his mind, as he recalled leaving his buddy Richard in the evidence room by himself. No that couldn't be, could it? He dismissed the thought willing himself not to think about it further. But there was a persistent doubt that maybe Hayward had tricked him. He kept going over his movements in his mind, and then he thought about Hayward's movements. He had the time to remove the tape, but why?

"I'm on my way over. When I get there, I'll want you and Preston to search that evidence room from top to bottom," Chisholm said, flapping his cell phone shut and smiling.

Three hours later, Mila Preston was fighting back tears as she left the evidence room and headed for her desk. It was just at four o'clock, and a lot of the other cops would be in the station house, winding up their day. She didn't want them to see her looking so discouraged and unprofessional. But somehow, she just couldn't put her professional face on. When she entered the squad room, Max Leland saw immediately that something was up.

"What's going on, Mila?" he asked.

"I can't talk about it right now. I'm sorry," she said, visibly shaken. Leland and all the rest of the cops didn't have to wait long to know exactly what the problem was, as the Captain stormed out of his office.

"Where the God is dammed tape, Mila? I've got two officers disagreeing about what they saw at the scene of a homicide, and without the tape we don't have any case."

"I know it was in the box and entered into evidence properly, I have my receipt." she said.

Detective Sunita Singh had just walked into the squad room. "Mila put it in the box," she said, standing up for her friend.

"Well, the only thing I know is that it's not there now. And testimony from anybody who's seen the tape won't be admissible because without the tape, it's hearsay. God damn it, can't you do anything right? Nancy, get me an appointment with the Commonwealth's Attorney. I've got to head this thing off at the pass," he barked. "And make it first thing in the morning. The sooner the better." And he slammed the door to his office behind him.

Preston just sat down at her desk, trying to look busy, trying to keep from bursting into tears. Not only was she personally embarrassed, but Wager was going to get off scot free.

"Well Mila, a bit of sloppy police work, wouldn't you say," Hayward sneered, having the audacity to lean, no he was partially sitting on her desk. She hated him to be anywhere near her, much less having even a half of a body part on her desk.

"Look, Richard, I entered that tape into evidence. And I have the receipt to prove it. It's just not there now. Someone must have tampered with the evidence."

"Wow, that's quite a charge, Mila. Got anything to back that up, or is that evidence the same place the missing tape is," Hayward quizzed her. She just stared at him.

"Yeah, you got to watch the details, little missy," he nagged.

She hated him so much. As he sauntered away, she muttered, "You are a Pencil Dick." Maybe she said it a little louder than she had expected.

"What did you say?" he reeled around. For a long time, Hayward had a suspicion that the guys had been talking about him behind his back. Sometimes when he came into the room, they almost seemed to have smiles on their faces, as if they'd been laughing at something about him. Now Mila was calling him a name he couldn't quite make out.

Every pair of eyes was watching the two officers squabble. Everyone was holding their breath and everyone was rooting for Mila.

"I said, do you have a pencil, Dick?" she covered, grabbing her interview note pad.

"Don't call me that! My name is Richard, not Dick!"

"I'm sorry. I thought you were a Dick. I mean with the name Richard and all. It just seemed like it would fit. I mean, the shorter name fits you. I mean you look like a Dick. You know the nickname."

How she said all that without cracking a smile, with such faux innocence, with the exaggerated movements of one who is flustered, no one in the station house could figure out. But they all agreed that she should get the Academy Award for best actress. And they all began laughing. It was a release of tension after years of the secret nickname, Pencil Dick. And now this.

The laughter died down only when Max Leland strolled over past Mila's desk. He slapped Richard on the back, maybe a little too hard to be a touch of camaraderie. "You know, Richard is a little too formal for the squad room. And Dick fits you better," and he resumed laughing, shaking his head. As the men resumed laughing, some were reduced to tears. Richard left, but not before he cast a look of hatred at Mila.

From then on, he was always called Dick by every officer in the squad room and even by the Captain, who while he hadn't come out of his office, had heard the whole exchange behind closed doors. He really didn't like Hayward even though he'd done his bidding. Even the Captain could be heard laughing behind closed doors.

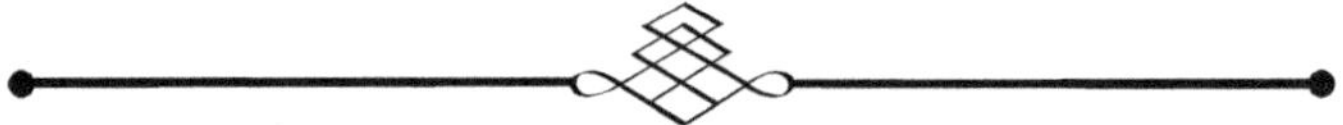

TWELVE

AZURE AND GISELE ELLIOTT once again waited for Dr. Craswell to come and get them from the waiting room. It was unusual for a doctor to be personally involved with the pregnancy test. But this case was special and she intended to continue to monitor the women's progress herself.

For Gisele, this was an especially difficult day. She had undergone artificial insemination two years earlier. They had used the sperm of a donor from a cryobank. A procedure that was relatively simple and less expensive than the treatment the couple were now attempting. The artificial insemination was successful and Gisele was soon glowing with pride when she was told she was pregnant and going to be a mommy.

But four months after the procedure, just as Gisele was beginning to show and just as she and Azure were getting excited about being parents, Gisele began with cramping, then spotting. As Azure was calling the doctor to ask what they should do, Gisele began hemorrhaging, and miscarried their baby. Azure did not truly understand how Gisele felt and their friends tried to comfort her by telling her that she had 'just had a miscarriage'. She was young, they said. She could get pregnant again. But to Gisele, she had lost her baby and all the optimism that goes with expecting your own child. Gisele was grief struck and at times she was near absolute despair and wished that she could join her baby. She had even named her lost baby.

So Gisele was understandably apprehensive. Would the expensive procedure be successful? And if it were successful, would she be able to carry the baby to term. For Gisele the excitement that she felt the first time she become pregnant would never have the same innocence again.

Dr. Craswell came into the room, carrying a bouquet of white chrysanthemums and handed them to Gisele and Azure, as she greeted the ladies warmly, "Good morning. It's good to see you both so cheerful. Come with me to see if you are expecting."

She could see that Gisele looked stressed, and she recalled Gisele's history, and thought she might be having thoughts about what had happened two years ago. As she stood to one side to let them pass through the door first, she put her arm around Gisele's shoulders, smiled at her, and said, "Gisele, what happened to you two years ago was a fluke. It could happen to any woman. It was just bad luck. You must not worry that it will happen again. Once we confirm that you are pregnant, the only thing you will worry about is names, nursery and nanny. Okay?" And she squeezed her. This motherly touch was just what Gisele needed. She felt assured by this doctor who she really trusted. Sensing the change in mood, Dr. Craswell decided it was time to see who would be the mommy.

"Who should we suck blood from first?" She didn't want Gisele to lose her confidence, so she selected Gisele before Gisele had a chance to volunteer. "Okay, Gisele you'll be the first guinea pig. Come on over and have a seat," she said, pointing to the lime green cushioned chair with the folding arm rest. "Are you

comfortable?" she asked as she put a rubber tourniquet on Gisele's arm, preparing to draw her blood.

"Okay, but still a little apprehensive about this test," replied Gisele.

"Don't forget what I told you Gisele," Dr. Craswell said. "This time is going to be a different experience for you, I promise."

"Okay, but I can't relax until I find out we are pregnant and our baby is born," Gisele said, barely noticing that Dr. Craswell had already gotten two vials of blood, all she needed for the pregnancy test.

"Now you, Azure?" Dr. Craswell asked, as she helped Gisele out of the chair, and ushered Azure into the chair.

"Thrilled at the possibility and I told Gisele the same thing. Gisele told me that we can never understand how she really felt then, but I think that everything is going to be okay this time, because we have you for our doctor." These young women had total confidence in Dr. Craswell, something they'd really need to get them through the next few months.

Dr. Craswell was excited as well. In fact, she had been up all night, not just because of the test this morning, but she had the distinct feeling that someone was watching her every move; that someone was even listening in on her phone conversations. She had shared her concerns with her partner, Olivia. They discussed whether this was some kind of post traumatic stress anxiety as a result of the shooting outside the clinic. But Olivia took her partner seriously. They had strengthened the security system around their house, and Olivia decided to call a security company later that day to determine if they needed to hire someone to patrol.

On top of that, Dr. Craswell couldn't sleep because of the upcoming test today. This test could make or break her efforts to produce a baby from two female eggs. A lot of couples get cold feet at this point even in the routine in vitro process and quit if the test is negative, either because of the additional money they would have to spend or because they cannot bear the repeated disappointment.

So in many ways, Dr. Craswell was as invested in the outcome of these tests as were Azure and Gisele. When she saw the young women, she tried to remind herself that this was about her patients; not about her and her ambitions as one of the world's top reproductive specialists. That worked to some extent to calm her down, so she could focus on the couple.

Once she had finished taking the blood samples from Gisele and Azure, Dr. Craswell disappeared with the vials into her laboratory to test whether the HCG hormone was present in the blood samples. The pregnancy test measures a hormone called human chorionic gonadotropin. HCG is a hormone produced during pregnancy. It appears in the blood and urine of pregnant women as early as ten days after conception.

Just being in the lab had a calming effect on Dr. Craswell. She could focus on what years of training and experience required of her. All thoughts of a possible peeping Tom, a suspected eve's dropper and her career ambitions vanished as she followed protocol and hoped for the best for this young couple.

When the test was positive for Azure, Dr. Craswell was ecstatic. She subsequently prepared the test on Gisele's blood sample. As she read the results, she was speechless at first and then let out a shriek of happiness. The HCG was abnormally high. This might indicate that Gisele could have multiples.

She rushed back to the room where she had left the two women to tell them the good news. At first, she tried to keep a straight face, but gave up on that effort as she was overcome with her own joy.

"Azure, I am happy to tell you that you are pregnant." Azure and Gisele were beside themselves, hugging and crying. Dr. Craswell beamed broadly as she said, "There's more, maybe a lot more. Gisele you might be carrying twins." After a moment of stunned silence, all three jumped up and hugged each other.

Now, of course, the next hurdle was to see if these women could get past the next three months without miscarrying. This is one of the most dangerous times in any pregnancy, and Gisele and Azure's pregnancies could be facing unknown complications and dangers. Dr.

Craswell counseled them on what could go wrong in the next three months, but soft pedaled it, realizing that they both knew exactly what could go wrong as they had lived through it once. Unlike she did for other couples who needed to be cautioned and cautioned again, Dr. Craswell told the two women to enjoy this time. She did everything she could to put them at ease, as she considered this the best medicine in this couple's case.

"Enjoy the next few months, Azure and Gisele, because come July you are going to be knee deep in dirty diapers. After that it will be roller skates, sleepovers, frilly dresses, dancing lessons, dogs and cats, then dating. So get a good night's sleep for the next nine months, eat the best meals you can, enjoy the quiet and time to be together alone, because pretty soon, that will be a thing of the past."

This was just what the two women needed to hear. Gisele was feeling much more confident that everything was going to work out this time and she would soon hold a baby that her partner Azure had parented with her.

This was exciting but begged the question, "It makes me wonder why the two sexes evolved in the first place. I mean some organisms can procreate by simply producing an identical copy of them self. Organisms that do this are able to multiply relatively quickly and easily, so what was the evolutionary advantage to sexual reproduction?"

"That is an interesting question, since sexual reproduction is much more complicated," replied Craswell. "Not only must an organism produce sperm or eggs, it must also find a member of the opposite sex, satisfy the potential partner's selection criteria, and then mate with it successfully.

After all that, the organism only transmits half of its genetic makeup to the new offspring. But in evolutionary terms, sex is more important than life itself. Sex fuels evolutionary change by adding variation to the gene pool."

"Fascinating," exclaimed Gisele, "Go on."

Craswell continued, "The drive for sex is one of the most ancient of instincts, dating back at least 680 million years. Most modern mobile life-forms are driven by this same instinct. It is also one of the strongest of all instincts in all of the life-forms that contain it, at times even surpassing in strength the drive for survival. Sexual reproduction is an ancient evolutionary tool. Its significance in the development of the human, genetically and socially, is profound. It is hard to find a cultural rule which does not refer in some way to sex."

Gisele and Azure were captivated by Craswell's explanation and hung onto her every word. They felt so proud to be chosen by this genius doctor for an earth shattering experiment. Azure looked puzzled as she asked, "But why the male and female?"

"Sex is not always determined by DNA. In many reptiles, the temperature at which the eggs are incubated determines the sex of the offspring," said Leslie, "but when warm-blooded mammals with internal reproduction arose, sex determination by temperature became problematic. Shortly after mammals branched off from reptiles, approximately 300 million years ago, a regular pair of autosomes began evolving into what would become the modern X and Y chromosomes."

"Couldn't we all be woman and procreate just like we are doing now? Could evolution still have been successful if the whole world was simply all one gender?" asked Gisele.

After taking in a deep breath, Craswell replied, "There are many theories about the creation of sexes, but my hypothesis revolves around the need for evolution to mask deleterious mutations. But the ensuing problem was probably linked to the violent nature of the Earth itself at that time. The Earth had frequent cataclysmic events, such as earthquakes, volcanoes, electric storms and solar radiation that were probably more formidable than similar events that we observe at this time."

"How did that cause a change from selfreproduction to sexual reproduction?" enquired Azure.

"Any life form that existed then that managed to survive to maturity had a high probability of some kind of unsuccessful genetic mutation that might be passed on to the next generation of the species through procreation by division. But if two individuals from a species come together to reproduce the next generation of the species, then these harmful mutations would be eliminated from the gene pool by natural selection."

Azure looked confused as she absorbed every word of her doctor, "But that still does not explain why males came into being."

"Well," Craswell sighed as she gathered her thoughts and then said, "The sexual revolution, which is still having repercussions in the battle of the sexes today, began between 240 million and 320 million years ago. A study of the key events leading to the evolution of the two sex chromosomes in mammals has revealed they started with the birth of a gene that decides the sexual fate of an embryo. Scientists have found that all the differences between X chromosomes, found in both men and women, and the Y chromosome found only in men, stem from the sudden arrival of a gene that turns female embryos into males. The X and Y chromosomes determine the physical and emotional characteristics of the sexes. Once the gene, known as the SRY gene, came into existence it meant that the sex of an embryo would henceforth be determined by the chromosomes and not, as previously occurred, by other factors such as the temperature of the environment."

"That is a very interesting, but why did the gene appear?" asked Gisele.

Craswell continued her explanation, "All of nature needs to live in balance. Therefore, when two members of an animal species join together for procreation and the primary purpose is to eliminate mutations, there needs to be a selection process for the fittest and healthiest specimens to mate. If you consider the process of natural selection, all animals instinctively want to choose a mate that gives them the best chance to produce an offspring to continue their genes into the next generation."

Azure was enjoying this downtime discussion with the doctor they had come to admire and love. "Your knowledge amazes us. Your explanation is intriguing and thought provoking. How does all this explain the need for the male, who does not have anything further to do with procreation after supplying the necessary sperm?"

"Well every member of an animal species needs to select a mate to produce offspring and the question is if tiny blemishes that might be considered mutations would make that animal undesirable as a mate. In that case there is a danger that if the instinctive nature of the creature is too demanding, then unions will not take place and the species is at risk of extinction. But if the selection instinct of the creature is too lenient then some mutations may be ignored, defeating the purpose of attachment for reproduction purposes." As she finished her explanation, Craswell leaned back in her chair feeling very relaxed.

"That is some very deep thinking."

"So to summarize females are more selective and the male is promiscuous. So you could say that the female is responsible for ensuring the quality of the species, while the male guarantees the continuing quantity of the animal." Craswell smiled and added, "In other words, a man is programmed to have sex with as many women as he can while the woman applies a rigorous standard to select one man she thinks will give her the strongest and healthiest babies."

They started giggling and didn't stop until they hit the first baby furniture store. The women stopped at

Babyland and bought three cribs and three darling mobiles. Then they went out for a steak dinner and had to scuttle their plans for maternity clothes shopping. They were exhausted and so excited because they knew they were well on the way to starting their own family, children from their own loins, their own flesh and blood. And they were thrilled.

Their excitement was so high; they never even noticed that their car was being followed by a red Hummer with the license plates, FAITH98.

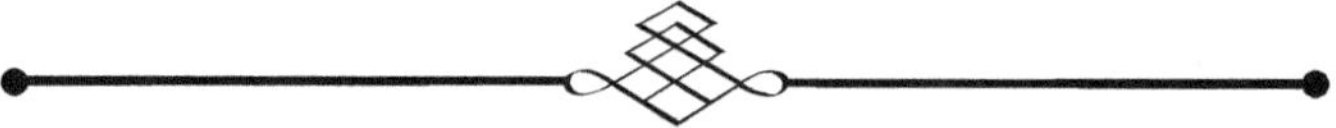

THIRTEEN

ROBERT GALLAGHER ARRIVED AT city hall which housed the Commonwealth's Attorney's office five minutes early for his meeting with Anthony Coleman. As he approached the receptionist he noticed 'Fiona Nolan' on her name plate. She looked like a teenage girl with her green eyes that sparkled and rich amber hair that glistened under the lights. When she smiled her cute dimples framed her mouth.

"Who are you here to see?" Gallagher thought that her Irish accent was lilting and sexy.

"Mr. Coleman. By the way, may I say that you have a lovely smile, Miss. Nolan? May I call you Fiona?"

"Sure you may," she said sounding more Irish than ever.

"And do I detect a bit of an Irish accent?"

"Indeed you do. My mother is Irish married to an American. I've spent most of my life in Dublin, and now Virginia." And she smiled again.

"Well, I guess you can tell from my name, Gallagher, that I'm Irish on my dad's side, and O' Donohue on my mom's. As far as I know, that's a combination of potato famine and tech revolution. Maybe we could trade Irish stories some time." Gallagher was glad he had arrived a few minutes early. He'd like to get to know Fiona a little bit better.

"May I call you sometime, Fiona?"

She nodded, smiled again and picked up the phone.

Nolan dialed Coleman's office to confirm his appointment, "Mr. Coleman, your eleven o'clock appointment is here."

She hung up the phone, "Please follow me." She walked Gallagher down a corridor and showed him into Coleman's office.

When she returned to her desk, she surreptitiously placed a call, hoping that this charming fellow would never find out who spilt the beans.

Gallagher entered the Commonwealth Attorney's office and fixed his eyes on Coleman and his clean shaven face with the steely blue eyes, trying to determine the best approach for this pre-trial conference.

The two men shook hands, and as Coleman sat in his expensive leather swivel chair, he motioned for Gallagher to sit across the desk on the very comfortable visitor's chair, also upholstered in matching leather. Gallagher knew the comfort of the office and chair were somewhat deceptive because Coleman had built a 'hard as nails' reputation for ruthless prosecution of the criminals that fell under his jurisdiction.

"Thank you for meeting with me so soon after the grand jury indictment, Tony," Gallagher decided to take the plunge and address Coleman by his first name. It was always tough for a junior attorney, but Gallagher decided that he needed to elevate himself to an equal footing with the Commonwealth's Attorney. Apparently, it didn't bother Coleman. So Gallagher continued, "You must know that this incident was most unfortunate, an accidental shooting. And..." Coleman interrupted him right there, before Gallagher could implicate his own client.

"Yes, of course, uh, it's Robert, isn't it?" Coleman said. "There has been an unfortunate slip-up in this case. I guess you've already heard about it," he said, knowing full well that Gallagher hadn't heard a word about the missing tape. After all, he had just met with the Police Chief and learned the surveillance tape had gone missing.

Coleman was a bit surprised that Chisholm had managed to have the tape spirited away so soon after their initial meeting. In fact, it was more than he had dared to hope for. This would make things easier in the negotiations with the defense attorney. He did not like the complication of a surveillance tape with its vivid portrayal of the incident. Coleman liked having that damning evidence off the table so early in the negotiations, avoiding any back tracking.

"A slip-up? What are you telling me; what's the error?" inquired Gallagher, ever alert for any advantage that would come his client's way.

"Well, to be honest, the surveillance tape has gone missing," said Coleman, looking very grave and exasperated. "I don't know how the damn thing disappeared. But apparently, they've turned the evidence room upside down. The truth is that without the tape, this suit is not an open and shut case."

Coleman was monitoring himself carefully, making sure he sounded appropriately disappointed and irritated. "But, of course, we do have a cop who thinks she saw your client aim the gun at Dr. Craswell's car." Coleman paused tugging on his ear anxiously, waiting for what he knew Gallagher's response would be.

"Yes, but you also have another officer who says he only saw my client pick up the gun after it had been fired."

Coleman folded his hands, pursed his lips together and nodded his head.

"True," he said, admitting to the obvious flaw in the Commonwealth's case. "And it is always preferable for us to come to a suitable arrangement so that we can save the time and expense of a lengthy trial. Also, if we can reach a plea agreement, we will both be spared the uncertainty of going to trial with the ambiguous nature of a jury."

Sensing that Coleman was feeling vulnerable, Gallagher pounced, "My client is innocent of the charges you are bringing against him. He will plead not guilty. And if some of the evidence was mismanaged, that's too bad. But I'm afraid it will be to our advantage. I will have to question the validity of all your evidence, including Mila's, uh, Sergeant Preston's testimony."

Coleman was secretly pleased that this meeting was going the way he wanted it to, but he reverted to his insistence once again that they can win the case. "We still have a very strong witness in Officer Preston's first hand view of the shooting. You know she will be very convincing on the witness stand and she'll be steadfast in reporting what she saw. Officer Hayward is only able to report what he saw after the shooting. I'll be frank; I think the jury is more likely to believe Officer Preston. And there's a good chance the jury might go for the death penalty. This is Virginia, after all."

Gallagher had learned a long time ago, when someone insisted on being "frank", it usually meant he was lying, or at least, was hedging his bets. So Gallagher decided to go for broke. Besides, even though Coleman was talking tough, Gallagher hoped that he would personally be sympathetic to his client. He knew they both attended the same church, and that it was a very conservative congregation.

"Yes, but there's also a chance my client will walk. A good chance! But my client is prepared to plead guilty to a lesser charge of involuntary manslaughter with," he hesitated for a minute, "no more than ten years suspended. And besides, your police officer's story is not corroborated."

Now Coleman was in just the uncompromising position he wanted to be in. But it still felt like a tight shoe. Even though this was his desired outcome, he felt uncomfortable being squeezed, especially by this little neophyte lawyer. He tugged on his ear, subconsciously indicating his displeasure. This sign of apparent irritation was not lost on Gallagher. He waited like a hunter hearing his approaching quarry. Of course, Gallagher had no way of knowing that, in this case, the hunter was the hunted, that Coleman wanted Wagner to get off.

"Well you're right. Her testimony won't be corroborated. But still, some jurors will be swayed. Others may not," he took a deep breath as he said this. "You know, sometimes in the heat of the moment, demonstrators will bring guns into something like this, never intending to use them, but only to show they mean business. And then the gun goes off. It's really an accident, but once a bullet is fired, intentional or not, it can change things in an instant. I'm sure when Mike saw his friend lying dead on the ground, he was devastated."

That was the opening Gallagher was looking for. He decided to press the issue and sway the discussion to his point of view by adding, "You know I will present the truth about those doctors in their women's clinics in such exhaustive detail. I think once the public knows what kinky things they're doing in these Frankenstein labs and how out of line they are with American values, they will be sympathetic to Mike. Not that anyone would condone a deliberate shooting, but an accident like this, whoever did it, however it happened, well it was just unfortunate. But I think I can present a case that will not only vindicate Mike, but will encourage the public to be more vigilant against these weirdo doctors," Gallagher concluded. He was somewhat frightened at how quickly he could spit out such vitriolic rhetoric. But that's how you play the game when you are a defense attorney and when you are trying to get your client the best deal possible.

"Ten years suspended, huh? I don't like it," Coleman lied. "But I guess a suspended sentence on involuntary manslaughter is better than no sentence. I suppose in this case, the state's caught with too little sure fire evidence. And you know, Robert, the judge isn't going to like this," Coleman continued. "But under the circumstances, what can we do? So you've got yourself a deal."

It didn't feel right to Gallagher. He'd won, but it didn't feel like a win. However, Gallagher wasn't going to look a gift horse in the mouth. He rose quickly and shook hands with the prosecutor and left the office, feeling like he'd just shaken hands with the devil.

But as he left the Commonwealth's Attorney's office, he said a hearty goodbye to Fiona. He was sure she'd brought him good luck. He'd definitely be giving that young lass a call in the near future. His good mood, however, was short lived.

As Gallagher exited the building, a young woman approached him. She looked somewhat familiar and he couldn't place her at first. But the minute she began talking, he recognized her voice. It was Libby Chen, a reporter, and an outstanding one at that. He had talked with her several times on the phone, and she was good. He liked her penetrating questions when they helped him tell an innocent client's story. But he was sorry as hell that she had tracked him down this time.

She was a pretty woman with Asian ancestry. Her long black hair framed her thin face with high cheek bones. She had large dark eyes and a slender figure, 5'3" or so, he guessed. But damn, he was dreading her penetrating questions.

"Mr. Gallagher, I'm Libby Chen. We've talked on the phone before."

Gallagher extended his hand, forcing Chen to fumble with her pad and pencil, as she struggled to free her right hand for the pleasantry. "Call me Robert, please. And it's finally good to meet you, Libby." He was hoping she wouldn't mind him taking the liberty of using her first name, and he was also hoping she'd soften to his charm, as he flashed her the smile that had won several women's hearts.

She did smile, but not much, and she shook his hand, but then like a dog hot on the trail of a fox, went straight back to work. "Are you defending the man who tried to murder Dr. Craswell?"

"Whoa, Libby. There is no proof that my client did the shooting. When his friend was killed by the ricocheted bullet, it was heart breaking for him. The poor man is bereft," said Gallagher, trying to look as sincere as he could. How did you know I was here anyway?"

She ignored that question, of course not telling him that she had made friends with every secretary in the building, and that they were more than eager to follow this case. They were furious as the religious right zealots who blocked women going into abortion clinics, tried to stop couples from getting in vitro fertilization services, and now were even trying to stop any experimentation that advanced women's reproductive rights.

Libby spent lots of time cultivating the little people, the invisible people on her beat. So that meant that not only did she dog the movers and shakers, she also intimately knew the secretaries, the office assistants, parking lot attendants and even the janitors and handymen in key buildings. She always remembered them at Christmas with bars of chocolate candy, and she always spoke to them all by name. It always paid off for her, just like it had today. She was going to get a scoop. She could just feel it. Of course the next time anything happened in this trial, she would not be the only reporter to corner Gallagher. But today, he was all hers.

"So have you and the Commonwealth's Attorney discussed a reduced sentence?"

"Of course, I can't talk to you about that," Gallagher said, looking sheepish and annoyed. Libby pounced upon that right away. "Did you reach a plea bargain?" she fished.

Gallagher was used to relying on his charm with women, not his wits. And so he went for the confidential approach. "Well Libby, I certainly wouldn't want this out yet, and I'll let you know when we're ready to talk, but this was just an accident, a tragic accident. And so we're hoping to get a suspended sentence."

Libby didn't blink, but she was thinking what a travesty of justice this was. She made sure she didn't take notes. She could remember his words and write them in her pad the minute he was gone. But for now, she had to appear conversational and in agreement with Gallagher, whom she had respected in the past. But not today. "Well, accidents do happen," she cooed, hoping he'd add more. And he did.

"Like I said, there's no proof he did the shooting. Apparently the surveillance tape has gone missing."

That was the plum Libby Chen had been looking for. That was a scoop. Gallagher had more or less confirmed that a plea deal was afoot. She wondered what role the Commonwealth's Attorney was playing in this. She knew he had strong leanings against the work going on in the women's clinic and that his sentiments were with the right to life crowd. But was he letting his religious convictions tarnish his good judgment and take the place of the rule of law?

She also knew she'd have to give the prosecutor's secretary more than a box of candy, next Christmas. She was so lucky that Fiona Nolan hated her chauvinistic boss, unbeknownst to him, and tipped her off to every unusual case that came along.

FOURTEEN

THE FIRST FEW WEEKS of their pregnancies were miserable. Azure and Gisele Elliott fought over the bathroom in the morning as they hurled uncontrollably into the toilet. Their morning sickness was wretched. The only saving grace was that Azure and Gisele could really sympathize with each other, since they were both experiencing the same suffering, though it was actually worse for Azure because her morning sickness seemed to linger on into the early evening.

As fall gave way to winter the morning sickness passed. As the nights became shorter they started to actually take pleasure in their pregnancy. In fact as they entered the second trimester, Gisele and Azure positively glowed with the joy of an expectant mother. A snowstorm early in January brought out their childlike spirits and they both behaved like young girls prancing around in the snow. As snowflakes landed in Azure's black hair they added a sparkle in the fading winter sunlight to her already dazzling good looks.

As their bellies grew and they began to really believe there was life inside them, they started looking up girls' names, keeping a list of three names they liked the best. That list changed daily. They also started considering how they would fix the nursery. Both women loved decorating, anyway, and it was doubly pleasing to them to decorate for their little girls' nursery.

Both women continued to work, although it was getting harder for Gisele who, after all, was carrying two babies, not one. One evening after work, as they were sitting in their den after dinner, Gisele got the strangest look on her face. It actually frightened Azure. "What's wrong?" Gisele wouldn't speak at first. Then tears rolled down her cheeks.

"What is it," yelled Azure, now really worried about her partner.

It took Gisele a moment more to answer. "I just felt one of the girls move."

In a ritual as old as humankind, Gisele took Azure's hand and placed it on her belly. After a few minutes, she finally felt the same movement and tears welled up in her eyes as well. They really wanted these babies. And to actually feel one of them move for the first time was a moment they'd never forget. Two days later, Azure felt her baby move and she couldn't wait to share that with Gisele.

Both women started showing that maternal glow, characteristic of the second trimester, after the morning sickness has passed, and before the onset of the other curses of pregnancy such as Braxton Hicks contractions, swollen ankles, back pain and other ailments too numerous to mention. Both women felt like they had limitless energy. Both were so excited about becoming mothers. Nothing could ruin this for them, they thought.

Then one evening, a middle aged man knocked on the door of their condominium. He identified himself as Matt Schuster, a reporter for the Virginian Pilot and he wanted to talk to them about Dr. Craswell and her experimental reproductive methods. Gisele answered the door, and even though she was only in her fifth month, her pregnancy was really obvious; after all she was carrying twins. Gisele's intuition told her that Dr. Craswell would have notified them if an article had been planned. She was uneasy seeing this man knocking at their door.

Besides, he didn't look like a reporter to her. He didn't have on the coat and tie she was used to seeing on the evening news. His hair was slicked back in a style from years ago, not anything current or zippy like most of the reporters she saw on TV. He was a little overweight, and he was, well, in a word, unattractive. He didn't smile or seem polite or show any charm. He just didn't seem like what she thought a reporter should be. Most alarming, Gisele trusted her instincts and she could feel the hairs on the back of her neck stand up. She was afraid of this man; whether he was a reporter or not, she just didn't trust him. She called Azure, who having seen the exchange at the door, slipped into the kitchen and picked up her most wicked looking butcher knife before confronting the reporter at the front door.

"We are not, interested in participating." She told him, as she tried to close the door. But the 'reporter' became aggressive and stuck his foot in the doorway stopping her from shutting him out.

Azure straightened her five foot nine frame and looked him in the eye. "Remove your foot from the doorway, or I will remove it permanently from your body." The knife that she had retrieved from the kitchen glinted in her hand as she threatened to use it on the man. Taken by surprise, he stepped back for a second, allowing Azure to quickly close and lock the door.

As soon as the disgruntled 'reporter' left, the couple called Dr. Craswell, who said she knew nothing of a reporter doing a story. Dr. Craswell sounded a little alarmed. She did not tell them that she was worried because just a few days before, she had found a file drawer ajar, the file that contained personal information on the two women, the Elliott File, had been rifled through. Azure and Gisele next called the newspaper to check out the credentials of the reporter, who had told them his name was Matt Schuster. The Metro Desk Editor said they had no Matt Schuster and apologized for any inconvenience they might have experienced. He also cautioned, "Just to be safe, keep your doors locked. There are all kinds of nuts out there."

This really upset both women. In fact, after a few days and sleepless nights, Azure began spotting. Dr. Craswell admitted her to the hospital because not only did she not want to protect her prize experimental subjects, she also liked the young women and cared very much about their babies. Gisele stayed by Azure's side until she absolutely was told to go home and get some rest herself. Gisele worried all the way home about the man impersonating a reporter, and about why he was visiting them. Was he just a curiosity seeker or did he have some weirdo cause? It was easy to get paranoid in this environment. Lesbian couples were still looked on with suspicion. And a lot of Bible thumpers didn't believe in any reproductive rights, much less reproductive rights for lesbian and gay couples.

It was just dusk as she pulled up to her condo. Lucky for her, there was a parking space right out front.

Gisele noticed that the bushes in front of the house needed trimming, especially the worrisome thorny pyracantha bush with its pretty red berries, which had really become overgrown. As she got her key out and headed for her front door, she failed to notice a shadowy figure on the other side of her porch. As she reached for the lock, the man surprised her. He roughly seized her and grabbed her around her neck. Her scream turned to a gurgle as he throttled her. Then he bludgeoned her with a baseball bat which he left at the scene.

"You are the devil reincarnated and you are giving birth to the devil's progeny," he shouted at her, as he turned away then swiftly kicked her in the stomach. He was told that a blow to the abdomen can cause placental abruption which would deprive the fetus of oxygen and nutrients. A severe case could also cause bleeding in the mother that can endanger both her and the baby.

As she fell, she strained to watch the man running towards an old red hummer. The man leapt into the passenger seat and the vehicle quickly sped away. She noted the vanity plates "FAITH98" and grasped her cell phone to dial 911.

"What is your emergency," came the welcome reply.

"Help me, I was attacked, send help to 3711 Bay Oaks Place," relieved she fainted.

"Ma'am, are you there?" No reply. The dispatcher called all police cruisers in the area to the scene and immediately dispatched an ambulance, instinctively knowing that the woman on the other end of the line needed medical assistance urgently.

Sergeant Mila Preston was the first to arrive. She took in the scene and immediately realized the severity of the attack. She knelt beside Gisele and took her pulse. Her heart was still beating. Good. Gisele's eyes fluttered open.

"Did you see your attacker?" Preston asked very concerned.

A slight nod of her head in the affirmative. "Good. Can you tell me anything?"

"The same man who came to the door a few days ago, pretending to be a reporter. Hummer... Red...

Faith98," she whispered before falling into unconsciousness.

"Put out an APB for a red Hummer; license plate FAITH98," Preston spoke clearly into her police radio.

The emergency medical team arrived and knelt beside Gisele, taking all her vital signs. She was eased onto the gurney and wheeled to the ambulance. Preston walked beside her, assuring her that she would get to the emergency room and they would take good care of her. Gisele beckoned her to come close and whispered in her ear, "Please try to locate Dr. Craswell, you must get a message to her. Tell her I want to see her."

"OK, I will try to contact her. Do you have any idea why you were attacked?"

"He called me the devil. He hates my baby. He wants the baby to die," she sobbed.

"Why does he hate your baby?"

"I am the first woman to become pregnant by being fertilized with another woman's egg."

"Oh, you are Dr. Craswell's experiment." "You could say that."

The ambulance door closed and Preston watched it pull away from the curbside. She took her cell phone out of her pocket and called Max Leland.

"Hey Max, get a load of this. A pregnant Gisele Elliott was attacked outside her apartment tonight. She is a victim of some loony opposed to Dr. Craswell's procreation experiment. Please call her service and find out if she is on duty. Gisele asked for her by name," she was speaking as fast as she could.

Meanwhile a few blocks away a police cruiser approaching the scene of the crime spotted the red Hummer and attempted to stop it. It sped off accelerating to dangerous speeds.

"Suspect spotted corner St. Paul's Boulevard and Brambleton Avenue. Heading South. Giving chase. Send backup."

The police radio crackled into life as police cruisers rushed to aid in the chase. Several cruisers joined in the chase as the Hummer careened down St Paul's Boulevard screeching tires as they turned right onto Waterside Drive. Several pedestrians jumped out of the way as the Hummer careened past them with three police cruisers in hot pursuit.

It took off at high speeds down Waterside. But police chase experts were ahead at the sharp right hand bend next to Town Point Park. They cleared as much of the traffic away as they could and laid down spikes across the road just as the procession of cars came into view. But the muggers in the Hummer spotted the spikes and screeched almost to a halt and then with screaming tires maneuvered into a U-turn to return back down Waterside the other direction towards the interstate. The police were taken a bit by surprise and tried to head off the vehicle as it swerved to get around them and continue the mad dash to get away.

By this time the police helicopter was airborne and following the chase from the air. The pilot was determined to keep these fanatical charlatans from making their escape. But they seemed determined to take a few innocent bystanders with them to the grave. The helicopter pilot radioed control which called for backup from all available police cruisers.

As they entered I-264, they crisscrossed around trucks and onto the shoulder nearly hitting the barriers on the side of the road. The police cruisers managed to stay a respectable distance behind as more reinforcements were brought into position on the highway. They closed the interstate at the Military Highway exit forcing all traffic to exit the highway. They then placed several spike strips across the highway and waited for the Hummer to approach. They had picked a location where the strips could not be seen until it was too late.

As the Hummer came into view the police cruisers behind the spikes formed a barrier driving slowly to block all escape. This time the Hummer hit the spikes and all the tires burst causing sparks to erupt from the rims as they ground into the road surface. The driver lost control of the vehicle and it skidded sideways hitting the barrier. But he managed to straighten the front wheels and tried to continue, only much slower since he found his path blocked by the police cruisers.

The main suspect in the passenger seat leapt out of the moving vehicle and he ran to the side of the highway.

He climbed up onto the concrete wall which served as a guard rail for the raised roadway. The police officers jumped out of their cruisers, realizing that this man was acting irrationally.

Well trained in the dealing with all types of emergencies, the officers got quiet. "Hey buddy, come on down from that wall and let's talk about it. Everything is going to be alright."

"No, you're wrong; it's not going to be alright.

The wicked are taking over the world. We have to stop the Devil from winning. This is the end. You must all be saved. We must..." and then the man stepped back, perhaps not realizing that forty feet separated him from the ground. He released a blood curdling cry as he sailed through the air backwards, looking like he was doing a backwards dive into a pool. When he hit the ground, each of the silent officers heard it. His head hitting the pavement below sounded like a ripe watermelon splattering on the ground. And then that was followed by the sound of a truck slamming on brakes, unsuccessfully trying to stop before running over the man.

The officers came up to the barrier and looked down at what was left of the man. It was a sight they'd never forget, just as they'd never forget the sickening sounds of his fall and the brakes of the truck. His head was split open. The truck had severed his right leg and arm. What was left of his body, strangely looking like it had no injuries, was his headless torso and his left arm and left leg. Adding to the macabre scene, the momentum of the truck whisked the severed right arm along the side of the road, so that it rolled over twice on its own, with its flopping hand seeming to be motioning traffic onward.

As the officers looked over the guard railing, several began vomiting. This would be something they'd not talk about or joke about at the station house, something they'd not describe to their wives or husbands, and something they'd try to gloss over when questioned by the cop shrink. This is when they all hated being cops. As they walked back to their cruisers, the cops avoided looking each other in the eye. They just needed to go home, but they'd all have paper work to do, questions to try to answer before they could start the impossible task of erasing this image from the inside of their eyelids.

In the meantime, as the Hummer tried to evade capture, it was generating a torrent of sparks and then the fireworks display exploded into a raging inferno. The driver was trapped in the Hummer as flames engulfed him. There was little the shocked police officers could do to quench the firestorm. As the fire died down it was obvious that the driver was deceased. All that was left were his charred remains.

The media was all over the fiery crash. They treated it as a spectacular, but routine 'cops versus bad guys' chase that ended in the death of the muggers of a pregnant woman. At least that is what all the reporters did except for one. Chen wanted to know why the woman was beaten up, who she was and what her story was. So instead of getting all the canned quotes from the cops about the car chase and the burning vehicles, she went to the hospital to find the woman. She was surprised when she learned there were two women in the hospital under the name Elliott.

"How is Ms. Elliott doing?"

"Which Ms. Elliott?" responded the elderly volunteer in pink. "Do you want to see Ms. Gisele Elliott or Ms. Azure Elliott? I'm afraid Ms.

Gisele Elliott can't have visitors at this time," the little lady said, with her eyebrows and lips turning down in sync.

"Oh, of course not. I was here to see Azure, anyway. We've been praying for her, you know."

"Of course, dear. She's in room 201. Going home soon, too, I think. Here's your visitors' pass."

Chen was trying to make sense of all of this without letting her surprise show in her face. She smiled as she took the pass and calmly walked toward the elevator to see Ms. Azure Elliott who by this time was feeling pretty well, and was mostly out of danger of miscarrying. She was, of course, terribly upset about the assault on her partner, Gisele. When Chen introduced herself, Azure immediately recognized her name from her bylines. And she looked like what Azure imagined a reporter would look like. She was immediately at ease with Chen.

"I understand that your partner, Gisele Elliott is the woman who was badly beaten tonight. How's she doing?"

"She is in the emergency room and I am scared for her and her babies. Dr. Washington told me about her condition and said that she will be in the intensive care unit for several days."

"She was on the way home from visiting you in the hospital. Azure, why were you in the hospital?"

"A few days ago, a man came to our house imitating a reporter. I am convinced that he was out to get us, so I couldn't sleep or eat, and I started spotting. My doctor put me in the hospital under observation and for bed rest."

"Spotting?" Chen asked, not comprehending what Azure was talking about. Azure had not really started showing her pregnancy yet, unlike Gisele who, pregnant with twins, was obviously showing. And spotting was not a term Chen had heard often in her single, childless life.

Azure immediately felt a little embarrassed. "Spotting, you know, from the babies."

Chen tried not to let the surprise show on her face as she finally picked up on what Azure was telling her. Like her partner, Azure was also pregnant. Then Chen remembered glimpsing the chart on the clipboard at the end of the bed, a quaint custom they still used at Baywater Hospital. The name on the clipboard was Craswell.

Dr. Leslie Craswell, who was the target of the protest demonstration and Mike Wagner's intended victim; the same Dr. Craswell who was conducting reproductive experiments at the clinic. Chen was careful not to let Azure see her excitement and surprise at this revelation. She wished Azure well and told her she was hoping for the best for Gisele too. She also said she'd call in a few days to see how they both were doing.

Once out of the hospital room, she went to the nurse's station and asked if Dr. Craswell was still at the hospital. "Oh yes," the nurse replied. "She's still working on the other girl."

"Where can I wait to see her? Someplace that will be out of the way, but someplace that I'm sure to see the doctor when she leaves intensive care?"

Thinking Chen a member of the family, the nurse showed her to a small waiting room just off the ICU suite. "Wait here and you'll see her come out." That was Chen's ticket to ride. She had some questions for Dr. Craswell. Then she thought to herself, wow, do I have a story!

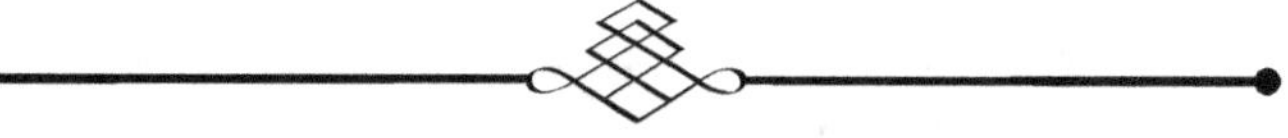

FIFTEEN

DR. LARRY WASHINGTON, EMT call on line 7339, Dr. Larry Washington would you please pick up. The announcement blared out over Baywater Hospital's paging system. Dr. Washington was in the fourteenth hour of his twelve hour shift. He promised his ten year old son that he would take him to a movie that night. With an air of resignation, Dr. Washington picked up the phone. "This is Dr. Washington, may I help you."

As clearly as possible the emergency medical technician stated the facts of the case, "Dr. Washington, this is Jack Waller, EMT. We are on Ocean View Drive, in transport with a thirty- year-old white gravid female. She's just been assaulted. She says she was kicked in the abdomen."

"Do you have vital signs?"

"Yes sir. Blood pressure is 100 over 90, pulse 116, respiration 20."

"How does she look?"

"She's alert and oriented. She seems a little dazed.

I think she is just scared."

"Is she experiencing pain?"

"Yes, she says seven out of ten in the lower abdomen."

"OK, do you have a line started?"

"We are starting a line now, what would you like?"

"Eighteen gauge catheter with normal saline open wide."

"That's what we thought. We have also started her on oxygen, six liters."

"Good. What is your estimated time of arrival?"

"We should be there in about ten minutes. By the way this is a patient of Dr. Craswell; you may want to notify her service. She keeps asking for Dr. Craswell."

"I will ask reception to place the call."

Ten minutes later, the ambulance pulled into the emergency room's reception bay. The paramedics unloaded the gurney with Gisele, who by now seemed anxious, and pushed her into the emergency room straight to bay fifteen.

Dr. Dawn Berman had just come on duty to take over from Dr. Washington, who could not wait to get home to his family. Dr. Berman had just come out of her three-year emergency room residency. She had a particular interest in OB/GYN. She stepped through the closed curtain to assess her patient. Around her the seasoned nurses were busy going through their own algorithms and performing their own steps to prepare the patient. They were busy retaking Gisele's vital signs, attaching the electrodes of the Lifepak 25, checking the intravenous lines and placing a second intravenous line.

Dr Berman looked carefully at her patient. The first assessment is always visual and getting a feel for what might be going on. This woman looks scared. So using her most soothing and sisterly voice, she said to Gisele, "Hello, I can see you've had a rough day. We're going to try to make that better now.? I am Dr. Berman; I am the emergency medical Resident in the ER tonight. What is your name?"

"Gisele Elliott"

"OK Gisele, do you mind if I call you Gisele?"

"No, that's fine."

"Gisele, we are going to take good care of you." "Have you managed to contact Dr. Craswell?"

"We're working on that now. But right now I need to do some assessment. I will need to examine you. Will that be OK?"

"Yes," she had a squeezing pain inside her uterus which was distracting her ability to think straight. She just wanted the doctors to give her something to alleviate the pain.

"Are you feeling any pain?"

"Yes, very painful in my stomach."

"On a scale of one to ten how would you describe your pain?"

"Six or seven doctor," she replied grimacing.

Dr. Berman started her Advanced Trauma Life Support assessment that she had done hundreds of times before. She knew that the first hour is the most important hour for a trauma victim. Of course she had dealt with gun shots numerous times, but she did not think that this woman had been shot, but you just don't know. So the first thing is to disrobe the patient from head to toe with the assistance of her head nurse. Then she felt Gisele's body, starting with her head, and checked her all the way down. But when she examined the introitus of the vagina she noticed a spot of blood. Her experience told her immediately this was bad news.

She turned to her head nurse and asked, "What's her blood pressure now?"

"70 over 40 and her heart rate is 120."

"Look, I want an ultra sound on this woman now.

Has the portable unit been repaired or is it still broken?" "I'll check." The nurse left the examination bay and returned five minutes later pushing a cart with the portable ultra sound machine. Dr. Berman was relieved when she saw the green light indicating it was working.

They positioned the ultra sound machine near the gurney and she smeared the electrolyte gel over Gisele's abdomen. Then using the transducer, she scanned Gisele's belly but what she saw put a chill down her spine.

"Oh shit," She hears a voice right behind her. She turns to see Dr. Leslie Craswell standing there her eyes glued to the ultra sound screen, "That's an abruption."

Dr. Berman had not seen an abruption in real life, except on a simulator, "But this one seems kind of small." "Let's hope it stays that way," Dr. Craswell sounded unconvinced, "I want this woman transported to the intensive care unit stat."

The head nurse said she would arrange a bed and left. But it was the usual problem; there were no beds at the moment. However, they were getting ready to transport a patient to the cardiac department, so his bed would be ready in three hours. She returned to inform Dr. Craswell, who was becoming very worried for her important patient. She got on the phone to the intensive care unit and within minutes they called back to say that they were ready for Gisele.

An orderly came in to move Gisele, and Dr. Craswell accompanied her to intensive care, where she wrote out orders to reevaluate her condition.

Craswell found the duty nurse, Phyllis Lauders, at her station and told Lauders what she wanted for her patient. "I want a complete Blood Count and a complete metabolic profile, urinalysis, type and cross match three units packed red blood cells and find out how many more are available in the blood bank. Hang magnesium sulfate 4 to 6 grams over 15 to 30 minutes, and then a maintenance dose of 2 to 3 grams per hour." She handed her the written orders.

It was two hours later and Chen had just dozed off, when she heard the door open to the waiting room. Dr. Craswell was anxious to see who was asking questions about Gisele and Azure. She didn't think the two women had any living family members. When Chen introduced herself to Craswell, the doctor took a step back. It was too early for reporters. This could be a disaster, not to mention patient privacy issues.

Seeing the doctor's reluctance, Chen started, "Look Dr. Craswell, I've already talked with Azure. I know she's pregnant. And I know she's your patient, just like Gisele is. So you can either help me write a correct story, or I'll just be another reporter getting it wrong."

This wasn't Chen' usual style, but she had no other choice but to show her cards.

Craswell explained that both women were her patients for in vitro fertilization. And yes, she admitted, that it was unusual that they both were pregnant at the same time. What she didn't tell Chen was how they got pregnant. She'd hold that for later, assuming that the women gave live births. Craswell told her about the details of Gisele's wounds and what was done in surgery to save her baby. But then, she asked Chen to downplay the story, promising her an exclusive at the birth of the baby.

"Okay, I'll hold off on printing the whole story, but I have to have something. I'll have to identify Gisele, as her name is in the police reports. I can omit mention of Azure and the fact that she is pregnant, but I'll have to identify Gisele as pregnant and a patient of yours." Craswell reluctantly agreed, realizing she had no choice; this wasn't something she'd be able to control. She'd have to do something she hated more than anything in the world, that is trust another person with her reputation and hope that she was ethical enough to do what she said. She would be on pins and needles until the story came out. If Chen did what she promised and wrote a responsible story, she'd give her the scoop when the babies were born, and she smiled to herself that this reporter had no idea just how big her story would be.

"Libby, if you can be as vague as possible, it will be worth your while. I will have a really big story for you in four months. It will be the story of your lifetime, I promise." Chen agreed.

Both women parted, hating to have to trust each other, but with no other choice.

Chen went off to write her story, focusing on the fiery crash. The photographer from the paper had gotten great photos of the crash, the cops and ambulances. So she had that, at least. And then, she quoted Dr. Craswell on Gisele's condition, and what they'd had to do to save the baby and Gisele's life. She didn't mention Azure's pregnancy, as she had promised, so by keeping Dr. Craswell's trust, she put herself in line for the biggest scoop of her career.

After Chen left the hospital, Dr. Craswell took a deep breath and realized just how tired she felt. She needed to get some sleep, but she couldn't leave the hospital without checking in on Azure. She dreaded seeing Azure and talking to her about what had happened to Gisele. She would have to be very careful. She didn't want to upset Azure and risk another life threatening situation for her baby. She couldn't have been happier than when she peeked in the room and saw that Azure had drifted off to sleep. She wouldn't wake her, now. Tomorrow, she'd have to figure out what to tell Azure about Gisele.

Dr. Craswell barely had the strength to open the door of her Range Rover. She'd go home, try to eat some of Olivia's homemade soup, and try to get some sleep. She slid into the seat of her car, and started uncontrollably shaking. Tears quickly followed. The stress of what she had undertaken had hit her all of a sudden and she began to sob.

Between the demonstrators who attacked her a few months ago, looking down the barrel of a gun, seeing a demonstrator die with the bullet intended for her, the excitement of a possible medical breakthrough, the hospitalization of Azure and now the attack on Gisele, her nerves were coming unraveled. The thought that Azure might need experimental surgery not just to save the babies, but her own life, terrified Craswell. What if this girl died? It would be horrible, and she could easily lose her medical license. Instead of a medical breakthrough, she'd become known as the doctor whose experimentation resulted in the death of her patient. It was all too much to bear.

She had gotten a handgun and a permit to carry a concealed weapon right after the demonstration. She kept it in her glove compartment at all times. As she sat there sobbing, she slowly reached over to the glove compartment. She hit the latch and watched the door of the glove compartment come open; it seemed to come down in slow motion. She reached for the gun. It made her feel sick to her stomach to touch the weapon.

She slowly brought it over to her mouth and put her lips around the barrel. As she did that, it brought back a terrible memory from her childhood. It reminded her of the time that Father Draper had forced her to have oral sex with him; it reminded her of the time she was forced to put her lips around his small penis. The gun barrel, like the priest's penis, felt cold and hard and sickening. All of a sudden, that horrible memory, which had turned her against men altogether, forced her to throw up. She vomited uncontrollably, until she passed out.

She woke up an hour later, smelling of vomit. When she saw the gun in her hand, she began sobbing again. She reached for her car phone. "Olivia, please come to the garage. I'm really sick," she sobbed into the phone. "Please come as soon as you can. I'm afraid I'll hurt myself. I'm so ashamed and afraid."

"Leslie, I'll be right there. Don't hang up," Olivia said. While Olivia seemed to be the more feminine of the two women, when it came to emotional issues, she was a tower of strength. She had seen Leslie in her dark moods. She realized that Leslie was probably stressed because of all that had happened, and all that was expected of her. And she knew just what to say. As she got into her car, Olivia began reassuring her partner. "Leslie, you are doing so much for women. Those girls, Azure and Gisele, are counting on you to help them through their pregnancy. And I could not live one minute on this earth without you. Listen to me, what you have achieved so far is phenomenal. Okay?"

She waited to hear Leslie talk back. "I've made such a mess of everything."

"No, Leslie. You have made my life worth living. And for hundreds of couples, you have given them their greatest gift. You are going to carry Gisele and Azure through this crisis, and they too will have the babies they've always dreamed of. Now tonight, I've made some soup for you. You're going to come home with me, and everything is going to be fine," Olivia said, talking into her cell phone as she pulled up beside Leslie's Range Rover.

Olivia looked at Leslie's face staring out of the car window. Gone was the world renowned researcher. Gone was the confident doctor. Gone was her beautiful partner. Instead, looking at Olivia was a terrified child, her face streaked with tears, and covered in vomit. Olivia didn't hesitate as she opened the car door and pulled Olivia out. She picked her up, as you would do a wounded child, and carried her back to her car, gently placing her on the passenger seat. She got the doctor's handbag, and nearly vomited herself when she saw the gun on the passenger seat. She put it back in the glove compartment, forced herself not to get sick, and quickly got back in her car and drove home.

By the time they arrived home, Leslie was able to walk into the house, with Olivia's help. She got Leslie into the bath tub and washed her from head to toe. As she dried her off with the towel, she kissed her face repeatedly, and then dressed her in her favorite long flannel night gown. Comfort was what Leslie needed and tonight, she'd get that from Olivia. Then Olivia tucked Leslie in bed and brought her homemade soup. She spooned it into her mouth, carefully so as to not let the soup spill down her chin. Olivia then got Leslie to lie down, and rubbed her partner's back until she fell asleep. Olivia turned the bedroom lights down, went into the bathroom and tried to stop the dry heaves that took over her. Leslie would be okay, Olivia knew that. But for tonight, Olivia could not sleep a wink. She laid in bed beside Leslie, listening to her every breath, making sure she was asleep and safe.

Several hours later, when Leslie awoke, it all seemed like a bad dream. She remembered getting sick, she wondered if she had really taken the gun out of the glove compartment. When she asked Olivia what happened, Olivia lied. "You got sick in your car last night and I picked you up. But you look much better today. How do you feel?"

So relieved that she hadn't succeeded in committing suicide, she convinced herself that it was just her fear that led her to believe she had taken the gun out of the glove compartment. Maybe it hadn't really happened.

Leslie brightened, "I think it was your soup, Olivia. I had a good night's sleep and I am much better this morning. Thank you so much. I'm sorry if I worried you. Can you please take me back to the hospital now? I need to see Gisele urgently."

"Yes, in fact, what I'll do is leave my car with you and I'll take your car to get it cleaned. You know you did get sick in it."

"I would hate for you to have to do that."

"No, that's fine," Olivia interjected, "You have work to do to save Gisele." But she really wanted to make sure that damn gun was out of the car and that the car did not bring back any memories of what had almost happened last night.

After Olivia dropped her off and traded cars, Dr. Craswell returned to the intensive care unit. Olivia got into Leslie's car and was almost overcome by the rancid smell of vomit. She would make sure the car was cleaned from top to bottom, and she'd remove the gun. She knew what Leslie had intended. This gun had almost killed her partner, best friend and lover. That gun was as dangerous as any demonstrator. In its place, she would put in a canister of pepper spray, and hope that Leslie would never need to use it.

SIXTEEN

MIKE WAGNER WAITED SILENTLY for the court proceedings to commence. He scowled at the bailiff as he waited for the judge to enter for his sentencing hearing. Once the bailiff was satisfied that everyone was present for this session, he brought the court to order and Judge Burnett entered and took her seat.

"Are you ready to proceed, Mr. Coleman?"

"Yes your honor."

"Mr. Gallagher, are you ready?"

"Yes, your honor."

"We are here to enter a guilty plea to involuntary manslaughter in return for a suspended sentence," Mr. Gallagher started. He stopped somewhat breathless, as he saw the Judge looking askance at him. She was obviously taken aback. She quickly began reading the charge against the defendant.

"Mr. Coleman, it appears that you're dropping the attempted murder charge. What's up?" she said, obviously irritated. She didn't like being surprised. And this surprise was one she particularly didn't like.

"May we approach the bench, your honor?" asked Coleman, appearing to be humble.

"Approach," she said, still obviously irritated.

"Your honor, our two officers were stationed on different sides of the street, and they saw two different things. And we don't have the surveillance tape," Coleman quickly explained in an undertone.

"No tape? I distinctly remember reading that there was a surveillance tape."

"It's missing," Coleman conceded.

"For God's sake," she whispered harshly. Putting her hand over the court microphone so that the court reporter wouldn't pick up on her anger, she added, "What the hell is going on in the police department? How did they lose the tape?" Her brows and face were knitted into one long scowl. It was obvious that she was angry.

"The appropriate people are being reprimanded and the evidence guard has been dismissed. We're dealing with it, but sometimes these things just happen."

"A lot of things just happen, Mr. Coleman. But I don't like it when a lot of things happen in a case that's before my court. You know this could come back to bite you, Mr. Coleman," she warned. Gallagher stood on the side line, not daring to look up. He didn't want to incur Judge Burnett's wrath.

"Yes, your honor." Pressing his luck, Coleman added, "We agree with the defense that if Mr. Wagner brought a gun to the demonstration, he wasn't pointing it intentionally at anyone. And that, unfortunately, his friend and fellow demonstrator was accidentally killed by a stray bullet."

"Oh really! Oh wow! The judge said shaking her head. "Mr. Wagner, it appears this is your lucky day.

Apparently, the surveillance tape had legs and just walked away, just walked out of a locked evidence room. And the best the Commonwealth could do was come up with a plea deal on involuntary manslaughter. So, being this is your lucky day, Mr. Wagner, how do you plead?" It almost looked like smoke was coming out of Judge Burnett's nostrils. Her anger was palpable.

"Guilty, your Honor," he looked down as he said it, trying to look remorseful.

"I am entering your plea of guilty in the record. Mr. Coleman, I want you to have a probation officer prepare a pre-sentence report. I want to make sure that Mr. Wagner is emotionally and mentally stable."

"Yes, your honor. I have already taken the liberty of having a probation officer prepare a presentencing report."

"With the surveillance tape walking, we still have a responsibility to ensure that the doctors at the clinic are safe. And Mr. Coleman, I'm sure you really feel the weight of that responsibility. Don't you?" She dug in.

"Yes, your Honor. The state wishes Mr. Wagner to serve a prison term of ten years." Then he added slowly tugging on his ear, "Suspended for ten years."

"Oh brother," the Judge said, not even attempting to cover up her court microphone.

Coleman adjusted his horn rimmed glasses. This was uncomfortable for him. He didn't like making judges mad. But Coleman knew that if he acted confident, he could pull it off. It's just that he understood what Wagner had been trying to do.

Somebody had to do something to stop people from interfering with the proper social order. And these mad scientists, the in vitro fertilization doctors, were playing God, doing things no man, or woman, had a right to do. While he didn't approve of Wagner taking a gun to the demonstration, he understood that something had to be done. And so, he was putting his credibility as a prosecutor on the line, just this one time.

"I'm stunned that you'd go along with such a plea arrangement. That means he walks out of this court room a free man!"

"Yes, your Honor. The state feels a suspended sentence will be a sufficient deterrent. And after all, Mr. Wagner hasn't had any prior convictions, your Honor."

"He is a church going family man. He had no mal intent." "No mal intent? Well, I've just got to ask this of you gentlemen, especially you, Mr. Coleman. Do you feel comfortable knowing that your reputation is riding on whether Mr. Wagner decides to be a good boy the next time he has a hankering to go to an anti abortion demonstration?" Before he had a chance to respond, she continued, "I mean are you absolutely convinced that Mr. Wagner understands that you don't take a gun to a demonstration?" she spit out the question, and her eyebrows seemed to reach the top of her forehead. Unfortunately for him, Gallagher felt he had to chime in here. "Assuming that Mr. Wagner brought a gun to the demonstration, and that is an assumption, there is no proof of that, and there is no proof that he aimed it intentionally at any one," said Gallagher.

Oh the Judge was pissed!

"You know, I've read all the same law books you read in law school, Mr. Gallagher. But this is not an academic exercise, Mr. Gallagher. This is real life, with real people. So hold the text book stuff, will ya?"

"Yes, your honor. I'm sorry, your honor."

And no, she wasn't going to stop there. She wasn't finished with Coleman. Gallagher was doing his job, and he was green. She wasn't so angry with him. But Coleman, that was another issue. She might give

Coleman what he wanted, but she was going to make him sweat first. Plus, she wanted her comments and Coleman's on the record, just in case this one came back to bite her. "So you are willing to bet your years of law school, your years of practice, your whole career on Mr. Wagner's," she paused and then dragged out the word, "intentions?"

What a bitch, Coleman thought. But looking as sincerely as he could, "Yes, your honor, I have no doubt of it." "Well, I just hope you're not letting your personal feelings get in the way of your better judgment, because honestly, you're putting up a lot of your political collateral on this one." Without giving Coleman a chance to make a comment she turned to the defense attorney.

"Well, Merry Christmas, Mr. Gallagher."

Gallagher wasn't quite sure whether he should thank Judge Burnett, or if it would seem like he was trying to top her sarcasm with his own sarcasm. He decided on silence. There was just so much you didn't learn in law school.

"Well, I have to say again, I think you are being way too lenient, Mr. Coleman, but so be it. Mr. Wagner, do you understand the sentence presented to you?"

"Yes, your honor."

"And do you understand, Mr. Wagner, that you don't take a gun to a demonstration?" Again, not giving the defendant a chance to respond, she continued, "And do you understand that you don't point a gun at anyone's face, whether you think it's loaded or not." This time she waited for his response. But Gallagher piped up, "We're not conceding that point, your Honor, I mean that he pointed a gun at anybody."

"Oh please!" Her look to Gallagher was withering, just as before.

"Yes, your Honor."

Addressing Wagner, she resumed, "Do you understand that your thoughtlessness resulted in a wife losing a husband, and children losing their father?" This time she waited for Wagner to respond.

Gallager nudged Wagner who responded, "Yes, your honor."

"And I wouldn't be surprised if you aren't slapped with a civil suit. So don't go on a spending spree. You may need to save your pennies," she cautioned.

"If you are brought before this court for any crime in the future, the court will look at that crime with a critical eye and in a different light. The court will not show you any mercy for a repeat offense. There will be no plea deal. Do you understand?"

"Yes Ma'am^ your honor."

"I'm afraid your days of demonstrating at the Baywater clinic are over, Mr. Wagner. You are to have no contact with the clinic. Understood?"

"Yes, your honor."

By that I mean, if you have to go to a doctor's appointment in the building beside the Baywater Clinic, or if one million dollars is waiting for you on the same block as the Baywater Clinic, you will have to do it by time travel. Understand? You are to go nowhere near that place."

"Yes, your honor."

"You are to have no contact with Dr. Craswell or anyone who works at the Baywater Clinic. No phone, no in person contact, no letters, no e-mail, no smoke signals. Get it?

"Yes your honor." While Wagner looked contrite when facing the judge, when he turned back to the gallery and caught a glimpse of Sergeant Mila Preston, the bitch cop who arrested him, he glared. His eyes were like daggers. If looks could kill, Mila knew she'd be dead. Then Wagner looked around the courtroom as if he expected to see somebody else here. At first Mila couldn't tell what or who he might be looking for, then she realized, with shock, he was looking for Dr. Craswell. He still wants to do everything he can to get her, Mila thought.

The judge banged her gavel on the bench, "Court will adjourn for a short recess." All rise," said the bailiff. The judge left the courtroom and retired to her chambers. She was disturbed by the outcome of the case presented in her courtroom, but as a judge, she had to remain unbiased. The Commonwealth's Attorney had taken her by surprise. He was always so tough and unforgiving and this defendant was as guilty as sin. She couldn't believe he'd gone for the plea arrangement. She felt he could have put on a strong case, even without the surveillance tape.

And what happened to that tape? She thought she knew, but she just couldn't believe it. Anthony Coleman had always been a straight shooter. But now, she concluded he'd gone to the dark side. She needed to sit for a while to compose herself before hearing any more cases. It was going to be tough to get through the day.

When Wagner walked past Mila, he looked straight ahead but made a clicking sound with his teeth. He was so crude. He made her skin crawl. Even though his defense attorney had him dressed in a suit and tie, Wagner looked rough. It was as if his face was devoid of all emotion except hate. His nostrils seemed permanently flared, as if he were angry all the time. He walked with his fists clenched.

She left the courtroom with a heavy heart. It wasn't that she was disappointed because her eye witness account had no effect on the outcome of the case; and she wasn't so idealistic that she believed justice always triumphed. But she was terrified that this maniac was back out on the street. She didn't believe for a moment that he'd change. The man was on a mission and he wasn't going to stop until that mission was accomplished.

She and Max would have to talk with Dr. Craswell and warn her of the danger this man posed to her and maybe to her loved ones. Perhaps she and Max could drive by her house, just to check on her. At the same time, she and Max would have to be careful so they wouldn't appear to be harassing Wagner. It was ironic but he'd be likely to win a civil case against them, even though he was the one who was had committed a crime.

SEVENTEEN

DR. LESLIE CRASWELL FELT reenergized as she reviewed Gisele's chart. Olivia's love and care had reinstated her confidence and drive. From the life threatening numbers she saw, she knew that Gisele would need her badly today, and she was going to deliver a miracle, if possible. With her blood pressure 90 over 48, pulse 124, Gisele would need a miracle.

She glanced at the labs. Hemoglobin of 6.3. Anxiously, she asked the nurse on duty to get an ultra sound machine and set it up next to Gisele. She watched the nurse as she smeared the obligatory gel on Gisele's belly and started scanning with the transducer. Dr. Craswell was distressed to see that the abruption had widened.

"Do we have the packed cells I ordered?" She was very concerned for both baby and mother.

"Yes, we have them available and can get them within 20 minutes."

She had spent many years in her laboratory experimenting with techniques to operate on rabbits and other small animals in utero. Could she use those surgical procedures to attempt to save Gisele and her babies? She had been involved in research to answer this question for several years now, with her colleague Terry. She did not think twice to pick up the phone and discuss the possibilities with Terry.

"Terry, I am in the ICU at Baywater Hospital with Gisele Elliott. She has a 1.5 cm placental abruption."

There was shocked silence on the other end of the phone. "What are you going to do about it?" She knew very well what Craswell was thinking.

"I want to use the fetoscopic laser," said Craswell.

"But we don't start phase 3 trials on that for another 3 months."

"These fetuses will surely die if we don't attempt this and there is a damn good chance we will lose Gisele as well."

"You know Dr. Bernard will not approve of using experimental procedures." Dr. Colin Bernard sat on the board of the experimental review committee.

"Maybe not, but if we can convince him of the urgency of trying this, he may be able to intervene to get us authorization. You know him better than I do and if you can convince him it would mean the world to embryonic research and it would be important to the future of reproductive medicine."

"OK, I'll try to reach him and I will call you back in a few minutes."

Dr. Craswell returned to Gisele's side and reviewed her vital statistics again. Blood pressure was now 85 over 42 and pulse was 130. She was going to need to do something fast.

The nurse interupped her, "Dr. Craswell, we just got a panic value from the lab, Gisele Elliott's hemoglobin is 6.3, hematocrit is 20."

"Get me those packed cells urgently. We need to transfuse the first unit immediately."

Dr. Craswell decided at that point in time, that the life of her patient was more important than hospital protocol. "Call the OR let them know I need a room within the next 30 minutes." She thought to herself that at this point she had nothing to lose; she had to try to stop the abruption.

While Dr. Craswell was making these life or death decisions, the routine of the hospital continued. And it was up to Patti Taylor, RN, to get the patient's consent. She loved nursing. She got to wear the new white pants uniform that showed her derriere in a most flattering way. Her nails had just been done, and her new push up bra showed off her voluptuous figure. Patti had her eye on several doctors. Married or not, she didn't care. That was the main reason she became a nurse.

Anyway, she had to go down the hall and get a consent form signed from some dyke who had been beaten up. She'd heard that the dyke was pregnant. Now really, that just should not be allowed, dykes and queers should not have babies, it wasn't right. Oh well, there was nothing she could do about that now, she thought. But when she snagged the right doctor, she would raise her babies differently.

When she entered Gisele's room, she was surprised to see how beautiful Gisele was in spite of the fact that she had been beaten up. She didn't look like a dyke. Oh well, you just never know these days, she thought to herself.

"You're Gisele Elliott. Is that right?" And without giving her time to respond she launched into her rapid speech. "We have to get your consent for this surgery. Of course, all operations are dangerous. But you know this one is experimental," she said, extending out the word, experimental, and lifting her eyebrows for emphasis.

"And you know, because you're not married.

Well, I don't know if you and your partner are married," and again she emphasized the words, partner and married, raising her eyebrows at the mention of both words. "But anyway, you're the only one who can give consent. You know you really shouldn't be bringing a baby into this world. I mean, the way you are."

Unbeknownst to Patti, Dr. Craswell had come in and heard her degrading comments. She was incredulous. "Nurse," Craswell paused. "What's your name?" Craswell asked, looking at the cheap little bitch.

"Patti, I'm Patti Taylor," she said nervously.

Maybe she had overstepped her bounds, she thought realizing that the doctor might have heard her unprofessional remarks.

"Well, you might want to start looking for a job, because you won't be back here tomorrow. I'm going to see to that, right after I take care of my patient. Now get out of here." Dr. Craswell dismissed her with a look that would sink a thousand ships and Patti retreated. "Gisele, I'm sorry you had to hear that. But listen to me; you and Azure are going to be the most wonderful parents."

Gisele just shook her head. "I don't care about her. Azure and I faced this bigotry and fanaticism years ago when we decided to get married. We had been in a committed relationship for three years, when we moved to Massachusetts, got new jobs and established residency in order to get married. Our hopes were so high when California finally approved same sex marriages, but they were dashed when that was reversed with the referendum known as Prop 8."

Proposition 8 was approved by 52.3 percent of California voters in November, 2008 to add to the state constitution a section saying "Only marriage between a man and woman is valid or recognized in California." This provision returned same-sex couples to "second-class status."

Even though Gisele said she didn't care about Patti Taylor and her comments, it was obvious that it had upset her. Having a patient emotionally distraught going into surgery was not good. So Dr. Craswell just let Gisele talk, and as she did, the tears began to roll down her cheeks. Gisele was not hysterical. Just hurt. It was obvious that this was an old wound, easy to open.

"Azure and I love each other, we are committed to each other and we want to have children, our own children, like any other couple. What is so ironic about their contention is that these bigots talk about the sanctity of marriage; half the time, they've been married and divorced at least once, or are having affairs on the side, while Azure and I are totally committed to each other," she sobbed while Dr. Craswell stroked her cheek, wiping away some of her tears.

Gisele continued, "Moreover, a lot of people are homophobic because they think homosexuals desire a new partner every day, and yet when gay couples want to commit to a lifetime monogamous relationship, they try to block us at every turn. It doesn't make any sense. It's just bigotry and hatefulness. Azure and I have suffered because of people like this nurse for years."

Dr. Craswell was adamant, "I know and she will lose her job here at the hospital for her indiscretion,"

Staring at the ceiling, Gisele added, "They don't have a right to vote on our civil rights. The majority should never be allowed to vote on any issue that takes away any civil rights of a minority. Marriage itself is part and parcel of everyone's civil rights and cannot be removed without diminishing the whole."

As she stopped to reflect on her thoughts, Dr. Craswell encouraged her to continue.

"At one time in our history, in some states, whites and blacks weren't permitted to marry. These same small minded people said that was against God's law too. Who are they to say who can get married and who can't! It's that kind of thinking that encourages extremists, like my attacker, to take the law into their own hands. Beating me up was his version of a modern day lynching. Well, too bad for him and the Patti Taylors of the world. Azure and I are going to have our babies, and we are going to bring up our daughters in a loving committed marriage for life. The people who don't like it can go to Hell."

Now Dr. Craswell could see that Gisele's sadness had turned to anger. She was happy to see that because Gisele needed to be strong, going into surgery. Dr. Craswell needed a fighter on the operating table, not someone who was sad and defeated. And now Gisele's spirit was upbeat. That would help her and her babies get through this surgery. And on that one point, nurse Patti Taylor was right, this surgery was experimental and potentially very dangerous, not just for the unborn babies, but for Gisele as well. Yet without it, all three would surely die.

"That's my girl," Dr. Craswell said, smiling, lightly patting Gisele on her tummy. "All of us girls, including these two little ones, are going to show them," Dr. Craswell said, "Besides, only small minded people like that poor dumb blonde think that homosexual partners should not be able to get married."

Using bravado to hide her own fears about the upcoming surgery, Dr. Craswell continued, "If only people realized the huge legal consequences that keep gay couples from having a say in the medical welfare of their partners, everyone would vote for same sex marriages. And that hopefully will change in this state, just as it has in twenty six other states across the nation. You wait and see. But meanwhile, let's do what we can now to give your and Azure's babies the best chance in the world. Once they're here, I know you and Azure will do all the rest, giving them the most loving home possible," she smiled, and got Gisele to sign the consent form after assuring her that she'd be safe in her hands.

The head OR nurse began to prep room 7 for surgery. Dr. Craswell had requested the nurse to ensure that the fetoscopic laser unit was available in the room. Gisele was transported from the ICU and gently transferred onto the operating table. Dr. Craswell dressed in her scrubs and while she was scrubbing she was anxiously thinking about whether Terry had managed to get authorization for Gisele's surgery. If not, she was willing to risk her medical license for the sake of her experiment.

The anesthesiologist arrived and after scrubbing up, asked Gisele the usual questions. He explained that he would put her to sleep and gave her the sedative to make her drowsy. He administered the anesthetic.

Just as Dr. Craswell was taking her future practice in her hands, Terry arrived. She quickly scrubbed up and came to tell Craswell that she had her authorization. Craswell was relieved.

Craswell was using a computer-assisted robotic system to carry out the surgery in-utero. The scope was placed into the uterus through a tiny hole in the skin. The small connecting blood vessels could then be visualized and the damaged area closed using laser energy from a small fiber optic passed inside of the scope. Craswell was seated at a computer console a few feet from the operating table. The camera transmitted a high resolution, high magnification image of the inside of her uterus onto the television monitor with excellent depth perception.

She carefully positioned the fetoscopic laser instrument inside the uterus near the placenta. She started cauterizing the placental tissue to the uterine lining. After several minutes of firing the laser on the target and carefully moving the laser around the abruption, Dr. Craswell was satisfied that she had repaired the lesion.

Only then did she relax and move the camera to take a first look at the fetus nestled in Gisele's womb. The fetus seemed to be stressed from the reduction in nutrients, but she was still alive. Then the doctor shifted the camera to look at the other little developing girl. It was a miracle that seemed to meet with opposition every step of the way. She recalled the opposition to the first test tube baby in the early 80's and hoped that the conservative opposition would soon see the error of their ways. She hoped she had done enough to save both of these lives. They looked perfect for this stage of development and Dr. Craswell felt excitement as she retracted the instruments and stitched the incision wound.

Now her next major task, just as delicate as the surgery she'd just performed, would be to tell Azure about her partner's condition and the surgery she'd just been through. She didn't dare not tell her. She'd have to find out sooner or later. And Dr. Craswell wanted to make sure that it came from her so that Azure would not be shocked and risk miscarriage again.

Satisfied that Gisele was as comfortable as she could be, Dr. Craswell left the intensive care to update Azure on Gisele's condition. As she entered the room, Dr. Craswell tried to look cheerful. She could tell Azure was anxious. "How is Giselle doing?" Azure asked before Craswell could say anything, "And how are the babies?"

"And so right now, what I'm about to tell you, might be a little alarming. But I need you to stay focused on your baby. Okay?" Dr. Craswell asked, putting her hand on Azure's. Azure said okay, but Dr. Craswell could see that her eyes were big and she was scared.

"First of all, everything is fine. Everyone is fine. Gisele did have a problem today. The abruption or tear in the placenta was widening, so we did a little repair work. And it looks like mother and babies are doing just fine. I don't want you to worry," Dr. Craswell said, giving Azure a very condensed and simplified version.

She knew that it was vitally important to assure Azure every step of the way. Otherwise, if she got too upset, she could start spotting again, and threaten miscarriage. Because of this, Dr. Craswell decided to omit some very important details about the surgery this morning. Already Azure was starting to tear up. Pregnancy does a number on a lot of women, making them very emotional. And Azure was one of those women.

"I'm kind of tired tonight, so if you can hold off on your questions until tomorrow or so, that would be great. But here are the main points. Gisele will be in the hospital a few days. In fact, I think you two will go home at the same time," she said smiling, again attempting to put Azure at ease.

"I want to see Gisele."

"Of course, but let's let her sleep for today," she said, trying to keep the two women apart as long as possible, so that Azure wouldn't see the extent of Gisele's bruising from the beating she had taken. She wanted to make sure Azure was as rested as possible before she learned the full story and the extent of the beating Gisele had taken. Dr. Craswell was worried that this time she might actually miscarry. "Now tell me this. How are you feeling today?"

"Much better, thank you, doctor. The baby is kicking me. I love the feeling of my little child growing within me. It is wonderful to feel this life inside of me. I am so glad we are both having babies. I never realized what this would be like, never even thought about it. But it's a miracle, a miracle that you made, Dr. Craswell," Azure said, with gratitude and admiration in her eyes for the doctor who had made this possible.

"Azure, I think you and your baby are doing just fine. You are already a good mother. You are doing everything you can to give this baby the perfect home until she decides to join us here in the outside world in a few months," Dr. Craswell said, smiling to reassure Azure. "You just keep resting and relaxing. We'll get you and Gisele together soon. You'll both be going home soon. And everything will be back to normal," Dr. Craswell, said patting Azure's leg.

"Well I am going to go back to Gisele, now. I will come and see you again in a few hours." She smiled at the pretty blond as she left the room. Tomorrow, she'd have to figure a way to tell Azure the extent of what had really happened to Gisele. She and Dr. Washington had been sure to gloss over the gory details. Maybe, it would be best to let Gisele explain everything to Azure. It might be easier once Azure saw Gisele on her feet again.

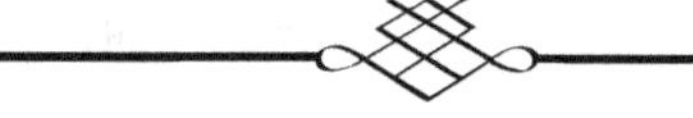

EIGHTEEN

MAX LELAND APPROACHED HIS superior Mila Preston's desk and nervously asked, "Wanna try to grab another hamburger tonight. The last one kind of got ruined and…" he stopped in mid-sentence. "No, let me start again. Mila, I want to take you out on a real date tonight. Maybe we can find a restaurant where there's not likely to be a hold up. And look, talk about us is already all over the station house. So let's give them something good to talk about since they're already talking anyway," he smiled turning on the charm full blast.

Mila liked the way Max just came out and asked her on a date. She also liked the way he handled himself at the hamburger joint. In fact, she liked the way Max handled himself in just about every situation. Just maybe she'd like the way he'd handle himself behind closed doors. She looked up and smiled at him, "I would love that Max. What did you have in mind?"

"Maybe go to a nice French restaurant. I think we both need to unwind. I don't know about you, but the fact that Mike Wagner is walking the streets a free man doesn't let me sleep well at night."

"I feel the same way. He's a loony and needs to be locked up. So your plans sound great to me, I will be ready at seven. See you then." She turned around to tackle the mountain of paper work on her desk, where everything always seemed to be urgent.

The fact that Wagner had gotten off scot free had totally unnerved the police officers. And they were appalled that the Commonwealth's Attorney cared so little about the fact that he had attempted to kill Dr. Craswell in cold blood. It was obvious that Wagner was driven either by religious convictions or radical social ideology. Worse yet, they speculated he could just be mentally ill and feel that he was being called by God to save the universe.

Dr. Craswell arrived at the hospital. She made her way to the fourth floor where Gisele lay confined to bed rest. She wanted Gisele to remain calm and rest for several days to see if the damage to the placentas was repaired successfully.

She tried to sound positive, "Good morning, Gisele. How is my favorite patient this morning?"

"Sore."

"I am so sorry this happened to you." Dr. Craswell looked over her charts and was satisfied that all her vital signs were normal. "We are going to do an ultrasound. I will arrange for you to be taken down to the obstetric department."

She went to the nurse's station and wrote out an order. "Notice anything unusual with my patient?" She asked the nurse on duty.

"No, she seems to be doing well."

A short while later, Dr. Craswell watched as the radiologist positioned Gisele face-up on the examination table. "Are you comfortable?" She asked.

Gisele smiled, "As comfortable as an old shoe," She tried to hide her anxiousness.

They all laughed as she applied a clear gel to Gisele's belly. The radiologist then pressed the transducer firmly against Gisele's skin and swiped it back and forth over her abdomen. Dr. Craswell watched intently as the images appeared on the monitor. Gisele flinched whenever she came close to the incisions.

"Did I hurt you? I am sorry; I will try to avoid the tender spots."

Dr. Craswell pointed to the screen, "Move the transducer over here, please."

She was pleased that it appeared as though her laser surgery had worked and the abrupted placenta seemed to be reattached. She was happy with the results and felt relieved as she reassured Gisele, "I think we may have saved your babies. Continue to rest and give all your bruises time to heal."

"Thank you doctor," she was smiling again.

The radiologist cleaned her up and called the nurse to wheel her back to her ward.

Max was on time for their date. In fact, he had to drive around the block several times because he was early and didn't want to seem too eager. When Mila answered the door, however, he lost his cool. The first thing out of Max's mouth was "Wow!" He hated he'd said that. How stupid, he thought. But she looked beautiful. Her hot pink dress came together in a low cut V in the front, with just the hint of breast showing. And she had on sparkling earrings and a matching necklace. She smelled great. She looked like a cream puff. He wanted to put his hands around her shoulders, pull her close to him and lay one on her. But instead, Max took a deep breath, regained his composure and said, "You look beautiful, Mila." He hoped he hadn't behaved like a horny high school kid.

Mila laughed and actually was pleased that he liked the way she'd dressed. She also liked the bouquet of hot pink tulips Max handed her. This guy just seemed to know what she liked. He helped her on with her jacket and off they went to a fancy restaurant, as promised. It was as different from the hamburger joint as day and night. Max was going all out tonight.

"I've always wanted to try this restaurant. But Max, let's go Dutch. This is a little expensive."

"No, Mila, I'm really looking forward to tonight. We didn't really get to finish our conversation last time, as I recall. I want to make up for that, or you might think that my choice of restaurants is questionable." He flashed that million dollar smile at her, and she melted. They talked nonstop, laughed at funny little things, and Max made what he thought would be the decisive move of the night, he put his hand on Mila's as they laughed over something Mila's station house nemesis, "Pencildick", had done that week. They put off talking about the case until the very end of the evening.

"There's something that's really bothering me. I'm afraid Mike Wagner is going to go after Dr. Craswell until he gets the job done, until he kills her and any other innocent bystanders. He's crazy," Mila said.

"It's bothering me too, Mila. I'll tell you what. It's still early. It's a little before nine. Let's drive by Dr. Craswell's house, which is not far from here. If their lights are still on, let's stop and let them know we are looking in on them. Then after that, we can go to my place for an after dinner drink." And more, he hoped.

"That's a great idea." Mila grabbed her wrap as they headed for the door.

Max and Mila pulled up outside the Craswell home where the lights were blaring. Inside Dr. Leslie Craswell and Olivia Newton were very tense as they sipped a glass of wine. As the two talked, the doorbell rang, jarring them from their intimate conversation. In fact, Olivia literally jumped up from her chair, spilling her wine. Leslie, while she hid her concerns a little better than Olivia, was also scared. She did not feel her usual confidence as she arose from the sofa to answer the door.

"Who's there?" She asked with a quivering voice. "Sergeant Mila Preston and Corporal Max Leland.

We are police officers with the City of Chesapeake and we are checking to make sure you are safe."

Leslie peaked through the curtains to see that it was indeed Mila Preston and was relieved when she saw the officer who had become a familiar face from the courtroom. She was also relieved when she recognized Max Leland as the officer that had interviewed her. She felt particularly close to Mila Preston because she had been present at the riot when Bachmann was killed with the bullet that had her name on it.

"Come on in. Actually, I am so relieved to see both of you. Olivia and I have been quite concerned since court yesterday. Please join us for a glass of wine."

"We would love to," said Mila.

They followed Leslie into the living room and settled down on the comfortable sofa. Olivia left the room and quickly returned with two more glasses. She filled both of them with the excellent Virginia Merlot she and Leslie were already enjoying. The couple liked to tour some of the wineries in Virginia and taste the wines. This Merlot was one that they particularly liked.

Olivia broke the silence, "Leslie and I were talking about the irony of what's been happening at the clinic. The riots and demonstrations over her experimentations are a repeat of what happened last century in the 70's when Dr. Shettles attempted to fertilize an egg."

Leslie added, "That incident in 1980 prompted incoming President Ronald Regan to withdraw all federal funding for embryo research. Sounds familiar doesn't it?"

Max interjected, "There have always been those that resist change and our constitution protects every

body's right to protest. But these crowds at the clinics aren't just protesting, they are taking the law into their own hands. In the case of Mike Wagner, we feel he committed murder. Tell me more about Dr. Shettles; I don't remember reading about him."

"Dr. Shettles secretly agreed to try in-vitro fertilization for a Florida couple, Doris and John Del-Zio. But Dr. Raymond Vande Wiele, the chairman of Dr. Shettles's department, learned about the experiment and destroyed the fertilized egg. Eventually, the Del-Zios were compensated $50,000 in the judgment, but they still lost their chance to have a baby. It was really sad."

Mila asked, "Didn't that set the United States back in the research into in vitro fertilization?"

Thoughtfully, trying to remember the early days of her profession, Leslie replied, "Yes Dr. Shettles was forced to resign, the Del-Zio's sued Columbia Presbyterian Hospital, and in the middle of the trial, the first test tube baby, Louise Brown, was born in Britain. She was a perfectly formed, beautiful baby girl, which swayed the opinion of the court. The Browns' doctors,

Robert Edwards and Patrick Steptoe, went down in history as the first successful practitioners of in-vitro fertilization. But most of all, Louise's birth changed public opinion. The public had been scared off by sensational and speculative articles that said a test tube baby would be a monster. Once baby Louise was born, the fear mongers were squashed. And people wanted to know more about in vitro, especially thousands of couples who hadn't been able to conceive. But the Regan ban left the United States in the dust until private investors realized the potential of the fertilization business. Childless couples were willing to spend enormous sums of money to have a baby. That was how our clinic was built."

Olivia looked worried, "But your life is in danger."

"I know it is. And of course, we also are concerned about the attack on Gisele," said Leslie.

"But I understand mothers and babies are doing okay. Is that correct?" asked Mila.

Leslie looked worried as she replied, "Both women and their babies are recovering, but it was touch and go, to say the least. And we certainly don't know if we have saved Gisele's twins yet."

Olivia pleaded with Leslie, "Can't you stop what you're doing, at least for a little while? You know I support everything you do. But I'm scared for your life, Leslie."

But Leslie was adamant, "No Olivia. I love you for being so concerned about me. But we have to stand for what we believe in. And all scientific research is important to better understand the functioning of our universe. If Copernicus and Galileo had succumbed to the decree of the church, we would not have benefitted from their discoveries that changed our perception of the solar system, which is that the Earth revolves around the Sun, not vice-versa."

Mila backed up Olivia's fear, "If you are murdered, what happens to your research?"

"Mila, my research now consists of three growing babies in two wombs. There's no stopping this experiment until the babies are ready to be born. It's somewhat in Mother Nature's hands now. You might say, the babies are out of the test tube," she laughed attempting to break the tension with some in vitro humor.

Still worried, Olivia said, "These guys are extreme. I'm afraid they will try to pull something deadly. I am very scared. I can't lose you." The couple seemed totally uninhibited about expressing their concern and love for each other in front of Preston and Leland. It was as natural for them as for any married couple.

"Our friends are here from the police department to help keep us safe, Olivia. Please try not to worry so. Sergeant, how do you feel about that demonstrator only getting a suspended sentence?"

"As a matter of fact, I can understand why Olivia is so worried. We are equally concerned that he will make another attempt on your life." Mila was feeling quite apprehensive, but she wanted to find some way to reassure Olivia and Leslie, "I do want you to know that Max and I, and a few other officers, are driving by your house day and night. Even though it's not in an official capacity, we are doing everything we can to make sure you stay safe."

"Wagner is the type of person who will stop at nothing to get his few minutes of fame," Max added.

Mila stood up getting ready to leave, "Thanks for the wine. I'm glad we had a chance to talk. Here is a card with my cell phone number on it. Call me if you need me, day or night."

Max held Mila's hand as they walked down the front path and along the sidewalk back to Max's car. Mila felt much more relaxed as she contemplated an evening of finding out more about Max. She wanted to know him more intimately. They drove the two miles to Spotswood Avenue in just over five minutes.

Max could tell he was a little nervous as they approached his apartment. Then, he had trouble getting the key to work in the lock. Damn, he thought, I need to be cool for this. I don't want Mila to think I'm a loser. At last, the lock worked, and he stood aside to let Mila in first.

"Can I get you an after dinner drink? Wine, liquor, a scotch whiskey or if you prefer, a beer?"

"Well if you have it, I'd like a brandy."

"Coming right up, I'll have one too."

Max selected soft jazz to set the mood and got the brandies and went back to the sofa.

As he handed her the brandy, Mila said, "Here's to getting Wagner off the streets."

Max looked deeply into her eyes, and said "Here's to us."

Max took a sip, and put his glass down on the glass coffee table, then took Mila's glass from her. She couldn't take her eyes off him.

"You know what I like most about brandy?" "What?" she said, breathlessly.

"The way it tastes on a woman's lips." He put his hands on her face, leaned in and lightly kissed her lips. He was tentative at first. Would she want him? How far would she let him go? He whispered her name over and over. Then, without even thinking about it, he began licking the brandy off of Mila's lips. As they groped for each other, their kiss became deep and long.

"You turn me on Mila," he whispered in her ear, "One minute a tough cop, the next a beautiful seductive woman."

She brushed Max's face her long fingers stroking his day old stubble. She smiled, almost breaking Max's heart with love. Her green eyes shimmered with the moon's rays, when Max's lips came to meet her lips once again. Melting into her colleague's embrace, she succumbed to her womanly feelings and allowed herself to get lost in his kiss. Allowing it to wash over her as the dark took over day.

Max broke the kiss and slowly stood taking her hand and softly suggesting they retire to his bedroom. Mila offered no resistance and removed his tie. She slowly started unbuttoning his shirt exposing his powerful chest. Mila was feeling warm as she realized she wanted Max to make love to her.

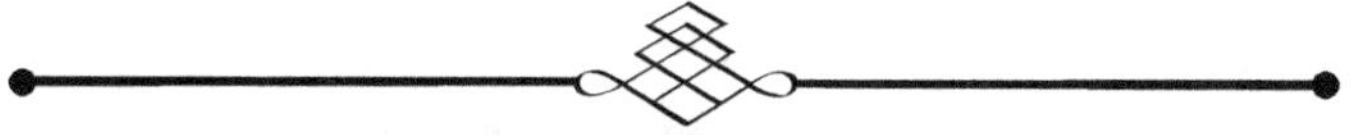

NINETEEN

MIKE WAGNER SHOULD HAVE been thanking his lucky stars that the Commonwealth's Attorney was sympathetic to the anti-abortion cause and all causes geared at stopping experimentation on embryos. But instead, he was fixated on how to stop Dr. Leslie, smug as you please, Craswell. He hated any woman who had achieved success and presented an air of self assurance. And Craswell was the worst, Wagner thought as he lay sprawled on his couch with a beer in his hand. Everybody was saying he was a lucky guy to get off without serving any time. But what was so lucky? He fired right at that bitch Craswell, and then the bullet went and bounced off her windshield and killed poor old Paul, one of his buddies who supported the cause. There was nothing lucky about that. He thought to himself that it did not matter what happened to him, he had to stop Dr. Craswell and her dangerous experiments. She was interfering in God's work.

He finished his first beer and went to the refrigerator to fetch another cold beer. This time he walked out back to his shed and picked up his gasoline containers and threw them in the back of his pickup. As he turned out of his driveway into the street, he did not notice the car parked half a block away. Max Leland was keeping surveillance on him. Leland eased his car onto the road and followed Wagner at a safe distance.

He called Mila on her cell phone, "Sergeant, Wagner is on the move."

Preston asked, "Max, do you know where he is heading."

"Looks like he's turning into a gas station to fill some containers he's got in the back of his truck."

"That sounds ominous. It seems as though our hunch was right. Keep me informed."

Wagner pulled into a filling station and started filling the canisters he had loaded on the back of his truck. When he went in to pay for the gas, he picked up a few quarts of oil. Max was puzzled by his next stop, a drugstore. He went inside with Leland quite close behind him. He went to the feminine products isle and picked up a pack of tampons and paid for the box. He quickly got back into the truck and drove back home.

Leland called Preston again, "I thought you said he wasn't married."

"He's not. He's divorced."

"Okay then, but he just bought some tampons. Either something really strange is going on there or... "

"Or, this guy is going to try again," Preston became very serious, "Max, he is planning to make Molotov cocktails. He will use the tampons as fuses. That is one of the best ways to explode an incendiary device. You tape a gas soaked tampon to the outside of a glass bottle. Then when the bottle smashes, the tampon lights the gas droplets and there is the desired explosion."

"Let's head over to Dr. Craswell's; I'll meet you there. I will assign someone else to keep an eye on Wagner." Sergeant Preston hung up and radioed another officer to take over the observation of Wagner, with strict instructions to notify her if he left his house. A short while later Max Leland and Sergeant Preston parked their own cars a few houses away from the Craswell residence and walked back to the Craswell home.

Leslie answered the door looking tired. Mila began, "Leslie, do you think that Olivia and you can check into a hotel this evening?"

"Why, what's happening?"

"We have reason to believe that our friend is going to attempt to burn your house down. He's been buying some supplies that make us suspicious."

"Can you stop him?"

"Yes, we hope we can, but we want to catch him in the act. That way Coleman will not be able to release him again. And we don't want you or Olivia in harm's way, in case there is trouble."

Mila's cell phone rang, and she answered it immediately. Aware that the women were listening to her every word, she tried to sound as calm as possible. "Just make sure you follow him. Don't let him out of your sight," she told the officer calling on her cell phone. Follow him and let me know where he is headed."

She pressed the end button and turned to the women, "Leslie and Olivia, if my intuition serves me right, Wagner may be on his way here. My officer has spotted him heading in the direction of Woodbury Avenue. I want you both to get out quickly and check into a hotel. Give me your phone number, so that I can contact you when it is all over. Max and I will find a place to hide outside. We want to catch him red handed this time, and then we can put him away for a very long time. Do you have any suggestions on the best place to hide outside?"

Leslie responded immediately. Putting into practice her years of talking calmly to patients in the most tense situations, she kept her voice even, "Behind the crepe myrtles, there is a service area where we keep our trash cans. You can see anyone approaching the house, and they cannot see you because of the Burford Hollies in back of the Crepe Myrtles"

"That sounds perfect. Leave quickly," Leland added, "We're going get this nut case off the street."

Olivia and Leslie quickly packed an overnight case. Leslie grabbed her briefcase and they both headed to their car. As the two women pulled out of the driveway, Mila went to hide behind the trash cans and Max scanned the front of the house for another suitable place where he could conceal himself from the approaching felon, but still remain fairly close to the road. After all, Wagner was a convicted criminal with a suspended sentence. Once again Preston's cell phone rang as the officer pursuing

Wagner reported to her that they were headed towards Craswell's house and would soon turn onto Woodbury Avenue.

As the pickup truck rounded the corner, Max felt his heart thumping in his chest. He felt as though it would soon pound its way out of his body. He stood very still as the truck pulled up right next to him and Wagner climbed out of the cab. He came around and reached into the truck bed to retrieve a glass bottle. Max watched him apprehensively waiting for the right time to pounce. Then he reached into his pocket and pulled out a cigarette lighter and flicked it to light the flame. He lit the tampon fuse on the side of the bottle and drew his arm back as he readied himself to throw the Molotov at the house.

Max lunged at him from out of the shadows taking him completely by surprise. His night stick crashed down on Wagner's arm and you could clearly hear the sickening crack as the ulna in Wagner's forearm broke in two. Wagner let out a scream, but the bottle, a little deflected from its target, was already flying towards the house and hit the side of house bursting into a wild fireball as the oil stuck to the side of the house giving the gasoline time to get started.

The pursuing officer witnessed the whole scene and without delay called the fire department on his radio. The fire engines were dispatched immediately, and by the time the sirens approached the house, it looked like the flames were concentrated on the siding of the bedroom wing of the house.

Apparently, Max's lunge at Wagner had deflected the Molotov cocktail just enough to prevent the whole bedroom wing from going up in flames. The firemen quickly got their gear out and connected the water hoses to the fire hydrant. Firemen always got a huge rush of adrenaline from a real fire and they applied themselves making a big effort to get the blaze under control quickly.

By this time Max had tackled the rogue protestor and pulled him to the ground. Mila was quick to run over to help him. It took them a few seconds to subdue Wagner and handcuff him. He was crying out in pain, with tears streaming down his cheeks, but Mila forced him to stand and told him to shut up. "You got what you deserve and you are now going to think about your cause from behind bars for many years to come."

Max said, "Boy, I'd love to finish him off here and save the taxpayers some money."

"Me too," said Mila, "But I want him to stand in front of Judge Burnett and tell her why he broke the terms of his suspended sentence. Then I want to see Coleman lose his job as Commonwealth's Attorney for putting his personal feelings above his job and the law. It was his refusal to push for a fair trial and a suitable sentence that let this loony back on the street to try to kill Leslie and Olivia. That goes beyond mere bad judgment; Coleman needs to lose his job and his right to practice law."

Mila summoned officers that were on patrol nearby to take the accused into custody. After that she organized her men to gather evidence.

They were amazed that Wagner had five more incendiary devices in the back of his pickup, all complete with a tampon fuse. Wagner had intended to kill Doctor Craswell and her partner and burn their house to the ground.

Just then Mila's phone rang. It was Leslie. "What's happening? I heard on the radio that there is a fire on Woodbury. Is it our house?"

"I'm sorry to tell you this, Leslie, but Wagner threw a fire bomb at your home. It looks bad, but the fire chief says there's not much damage. The siding on one wall took the brunt of it. So you'll need to stay in your hotel for tonight. The fire chief will leave a few men here to make sure that the fire does not re-ignite. By the way, he says you're lucky that the device did not go through a window."

As the last of the flames died down, the firemen were able to assess the damage. They entered the house to make sure the fire was completely out.

"How bad is the damage?" asked Leslie.

"Well, thanks to Officer Leland, Wagner didn't get very far with his fire bombs. Max tried to knock the first Molotov out of his hand, but he managed to lob that moments before Max's night stick broke his arm," Mila stated. "I'm so sorry that we did not manage to stop the attack completely, but he would have destroyed your house completely, if he had managed to throw four or five Molotov's through your windows."

"Where is the murdering bastard?"

"He is at the emergency room under guard getting his broken arm set. He will be in court in the morning for arraignment. His suspended sentence will be withdrawn so he will sit in the state penitentiary until his trial for this crime."

"We'll stay at this hotel for tonight. In fact it might be good to get away for a while," Craswell noted.

"Excuse me." it was Jennifer Granger of the local NBC news channel who interrupted Mila's commands to her subordinates, "Can I get a statement for the news? What happened here tonight?"

"Some maniac threw a fire bomb at that house," replied Sergeant Preston, trying to elude any connection to the demonstration, the murder there and Dr. Craswell. It was just too early to have the press all over this. "But talk to the fire chief, he's handling all the information on this."

Libby Chen joined the throng of reporters swarming around for any information.

"Whose house is it? Was anyone hurt?" she asked.

Preston tried to suppress all her emotions and replied with a flat voice, "All occupants escaped without injury."

"Who owns the house?" she persisted.

"I do not know that yet. Check back later."

Granger butted in with a question, "Did you catch the person responsible for this arson?"

"Yes, he is under arrest and has been taken to the city jail for processing. I do not have any more information at this time. Check back with me later. Please keep out of the way of the investigating officers. Thank you for your co-operation. Excuse me, I have work to do."

Soon the front yard was full of reporters sniffing around for some information. They tried to hound the police officers and the firemen; but they could not tell them much. Libby sauntered over to the street side mail box, and opened the lid enough to read the name on the mail, still waiting to be picked up. Dr. Leslie Craswell. Holy shit, she thought. Libby Chen immediately realized that this was no ordinary arson attempt. She also realized that within the hour, all the reporters would figure out what she already knew that it was Dr. Leslie Craswell's house. They'd all quickly realize this was connected with the demonstrations at the clinic and the doctor's work there. If only she could get an exclusive interview with Dr. Craswell, who obviously was stowed somewhere in a safe house.

She stood back a little and took in the whole scene, noting a man and a woman standing off to the side. They were in deep conversation. One of them looked so familiar. It took Libby a minute before she placed her. The woman was Sergeant Mila Preston, who arrested Mike Wagner following the shooting at the clinic demonstration and later testified against him in court. That's where Libby had seen her. And it was obvious in court that Sergeant Preston was terribly upset about the suspended

sentence that Wagner got. Libby decided to try to win Preston over using a straight forward approach.

"Sergeant Preston, I'm Libby Chen, a reporter for the Virginian Pilot," she said, extending her hand. Preston reluctantly shook the reporter's hand,

and immediately responded, "The fire chief is dealing with reporters, Libby. I'm sorry I cannot make a statement."

"I think you might want to talk with me for a moment. I am already working with Dr. Craswell. She has promised me an exclusive if I downplayed the attack on Gisele Elliott. I know both women are her patients and that they are due to give birth within a few months. I am honoring that deal with her. She has promised me there is a twist to their pregnancies that will make it worth my while to soft pedal this story. I feel certain, she'd want me to break this one and you know a well written story that is factually correct and compelling often helps convict criminals. I want to get the best story I can on Wagner. He's a loose cannon and needs to be put away for life."

She barely took a breath and kept talking, "I have her private cell phone number, and I've called it several times, but it's turned off. I have a suspicion that you might know where she is and how to reach her. Please call her and tell her I want to do a story about Wagner and how he tried to harm her today. Can you do that? I think she'll want to talk with me. Please ask her to call me on my cell," she said, handing Mila her card.

Chen's confidence threw Mila off. She thought Chen was a good reporter from the articles she'd read. But she didn't like being boxed into a corner. On the other hand, a good story from Libby Chen couldn't hurt their chances of putting Wagner away for life. Judges aren't supposed to care about public opinion or read the papers. But that's a joke. Everybody knew they are influenced by the court of public opinion.

"Wait a minute, let me see what I can do," Preston said, looking like she had a fish bone stuck in her throat. Preston walked away, leaving Libby with Max Leland. It was awkward for both of them; the silence between them was deafening.

Sergeant Preston returned shortly and told Libby that Dr. Craswell wanted to meet with her. Then she added, "Max and I would like to be present at the interview, but please promise me that you will not quote us in any report. We want to be present for background only, and to make sure that Dr. Craswell doesn't say anything that would compromise our case against Wagner."

Libby agreed, "That sounds fair enough," Her success as a reporter had been her ability to make good contacts, and negotiate what she'd report and what she'd hold back. Eventually the whole story would unfold, but delaying important details for a few months is smart when you want to win the story of a lifetime.

Mila arranged for them all to meet at the hotel where Craswell and Newton were spending the night. Libby followed Preston and Leland in their unmarked car to the Princess Anne hotel. There they spoke in the hotel restaurant for three hours. Libby had her story, with quotes from Craswell about how terrified she and her partner, Olivia Newton, had been when they realized that Wagner was a free man. Without letting Libby know that Mila Preston had asked her to leave the house in case of trouble, Craswell said that she and Olivia had decided to leave their home, to take a break and that they were lucky not to be home when the firebombing happened.

Dr. Craswell said that thugs like Wagner were not going to disrupt the clinic's work of helping women bear children. Libby's story came out as a human interest article, with a large photo of Craswell and Newton. It would outrage any citizen that Mike Wagner, who was just a thug and a murderer, was out on the street with only a suspended sentence. Preston and Leland were thrilled. This would not only help keep Wagner in the slammer, but they hoped it would also be a nail in the coffin of the deceitful Commonwealth Attorney's undistinguished career.

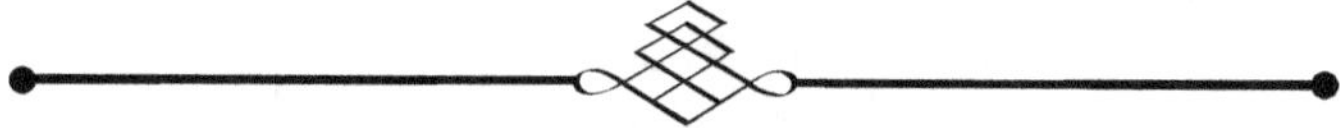

TWENTY

MIKE WAGNER WAS BROUGHT into court, his arm in a cast and flanked on each side by a police officer. He looked disheveled, his hair was a mess and he was dressed in the orange jumpsuit of a prisoner. He was told to sit next to his attorney, Robert Gallagher.

Wagner leaned over to his attorney, "Why didn't you come to see me last night?"

Gallagher turned to his client and looked him over with disgust. Before he could answer the Bailiff came into the courtroom shouting his usual announcement. "All rise, court is now in session. The Honorable Judge Carol Burnett now presiding over the Chesapeake Circuit Court..." Judge Burnett entered the court room and made her way to her usual place in the center of the bench and sat down. "You may be seated."

"Mr. Wagner, I did not expect to see you back in my court room in so soon," She started, "Mr. Gallagher approach the bench."

Gallagher walked over to the Judge and handed her a brief, "This is my resignation as Mr. Wagner's attorney. I would like to withdraw from this case."

Judge Burnett read the motion in silence and then asked, "Has this decision got anything do with getting your bills paid?"

"No, your Honor, there is a difference of opinion that I cannot reconcile. Defending my client fairly has become untenable. And the recommendations of the prosecutor have disturbed me."

"Wait a minute, are you suggesting that the Commonwealth's Attorney has not acted in good faith?"

"Yes."

"Mr. Coleman, approach the bench."

Coleman, suspecting that his troubles were just about to begin, approached the bench, tugging at his ear.

"Mr. Gallagher is suggesting that you have not acted in good faith."

"I object, your honor. This is ridiculous."

Judge Burnett simply said, "Attorneys, I want to see both of you in my chambers immediately. Mr. Wagner, the suspension of your sentence is hereby revoked. You will be incarcerated immediately. Bailiff, please escort him into the holding cell in the court house. Court is adjoined until 2 p.m.," she banged her gavel and rose to leave the court room.

Gallagher and Coleman followed her into her chambers, where she proceeded to admonish Gallagher for his conduct in her court.

"I am sorry, your Honor, but the events of last night were so unexpected that I did not have the time to prepare the proper motion and file it in time for today's proceedings. I cannot continue to defend this man with a clear conscience and I cannot provide my client with an unbiased defense."

"Mr. Coleman, your leniency with this defendant was inexcusable. How do you defend your recommendation to release this prisoner now that he has committed another dastardly deed?"

"Your honor, Wagner has always been a pillar of the community. Something must have snapped in his mind to make him do something like this. I believe we need to have him examined by a psychiatrist to see if he is insane."

"Mr. Coleman, at this point, the only thing I am recommending is your removal from the office of the Commonwealth's Attorney."

"But Your honor, I have done nothing wrong."

Gallagher interjected, "During our conference into a plea bargain, you were adamant that you wanted Wagner to be released because it was all an accident. You gave him a get out of jail free card."

Coleman pointed his finger at Gallagher, "What are you insinuating? You agreed to the terms and conditions of his release," he shouted.

"Of course I did, I am.. .was... Wagner's defense attorney. The truth is that you are so supportive of his views that you would kill Dr. Craswell yourself, if you thought you could get away with it."

"That's slanderous! But Dr. Craswell is doing research into fertilizing eggs with other woman's eggs. It's not natural; she's playing God and His great intentions for his children."

"Has she broken any laws? Can you arrest her for any criminal act?"

"No, but if not for Roe vs. Wade, I am sure she could be convicted of killing babies."

"Well, in the first place, you idiot, she's not even performing abortions. And in the second place, she's creating life. But most importantly, she is protected by the constitution of the United States of America. Maybe you have forgotten where you live, Mr. Coleman," Gallagher shouted.

Judge Burnett intervened, "Gentlemen, calm down. Mr. Coleman, you will stand down from prosecuting this case. I intend to contact the Justice Department to have you investigated for allowing your personal views to interfere with your duties. Mr. Gallagher you are relieved from this case, but you might consider taking the job of Commonwealth's Attorney to replace Mr. Coleman."

The two men left the Judge's chambers and did not even glance at each other as they went their separate ways.

Dr. Craswell was apprehensive as she pulled into a parking space in the garage. She was alert to anyone around that might be a danger as she walked towards the entrance. As soon as she was safely inside the hospital, she composed herself and quickly made her way to the fourth floor to check on Gisele first. She greeted the nurses cheerfully as she entered the ward and made her way to Gisele's room. Her patient looked much better and a quick review of the vital signs on her charts made her feel much better.

"You look well this morning."

"I feel much better, thank you doctor. It was lovely to feel my babies kicking inside me again," Gisele was smiling.

"Oh that is good news. You can go home today, but I want you and Azure to both to stay in bed for a least another week. I will write out your discharge orders. Do you need a ride home?"

"Yes doctor, remember Azure is also in hospital." "You know I think I will give you two ladies a ride home myself."

"Let me go and see how Azure is doing."

When she entered Azure's room, she found a much different scene. Azure was in tears. "Azure, what's wrong?" Dr. Craswell inquired.

"I feel ugly, I feel fat, and I don't know why we're doing this. It's crazy. Are we always going to have people jumping out of the bushes at us, and at our children?" And then she stopped talking and just sobbed.

Oh no, Dr. Craswell thought. She had seen this kind of pregnancy blues before, and while in most cases, it wasn't serious, it was the last thing Azure needed. She had already threatened to miscarry. Dr. Craswell realized she had to put on her best face. "You're doing this because you and Gisele love each other. You're doing this because you wanted to start a family, and you will have a beautiful family," Dr. Craswell said, sitting on the side of Azure's hospital bed, reaching for a Kleenex, and wiping Azure's eyes. "Listen, what I want you to do now is get dressed, so that I can discharge you," Dr. Craswell said as cheerfully as she could. "I'm giving you and Gisele a ride home, and I've got a little proposal for you. But that will have to wait until we're in the car. Now cheer up. You look beautiful, you have a radiant glow, and you are carrying a beautiful baby. Okay?" she said, more as a command than a question, as she looked deeply into Azure's eyes.

Dr. Craswell made a quick call to Olivia to tell her what had happened. She also discussed a plan with Olivia to see if she had Olivia's support. Olivia, as always, was sympathetic and welcomed her partner's suggestion. Dr. Craswell then headed back to Gisele's room to let her know about Azure's blues, and she said, "I want you two to think about something I have to say in the car. I'm going to give you an advance preview. I think it's important that we do everything we can to shake Azure's blues."

"What's up doc?" Gisele asked.

"I want you two to come home and stay with Olivia and me for a few weeks. It will give Azure time to get over her miscarriage threat, and also to stop fixating on what happened at your condo. Once she and you are fully rested, you can go back home. I've talked with my partner, Olivia, and she can't wait to start making homemade chicken soup. I will warn you, she loves to mother, so both of you may have more care and concern than you could possibly want. But it will be good for you. She's pulled me through many a blue streak. What do you say?"

Gisele was thrilled. She dreaded going back to the front porch where she was beaten up. She just didn't feel strong enough for that yet. And she was concerned about Azure. "I'd love to stay with you two for a little while; let's see if we can talk Azure into it. But I think she'll be thrilled too as she was really scared when that guy came to the house posing as a reporter. By the way, did the police catch him?"

"Well yes, it was a wild car chase through the streets of Chesapeake, ending in a fiery crash with both assailants dead."

"That's a relief now that there are a couple more lunatics off the streets."

And Dr. Craswell, even though she didn't say it, was relieved too. She liked the idea of having someone at home with Olivia during the day while she was at work. After all, there is, as they say, strength in numbers. "I am going to hire a security guard for our house, so that we can be as safe as Fort Knox," she said, "Now let's give our best sales presentation to Azure, and then let me take you home."

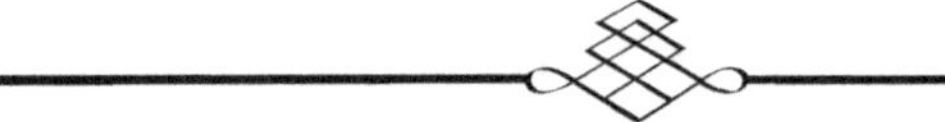

TWENTY-ONE

The National Association of Investors Corporation (NAIC), the umbrella and resource organization for investment clubs, reported in 1998 that 50.2 percent of its clubs were women-only clubs. And the clubs' reported results showed that women's clubs had an average return rate of 32.1 percent annually -- better than the 23.2 percent average return rate for all-male clubs and 27.4 percent for coed clubs.

TANYA JACKSON STARTED THE club 16 years ago with friends and acquaintances. During a recent newspaper interview Tanya reminisced about forming Silk Purse, a women-only investment club. She was one of the founders of Women Investor's Group, an international powerhouse that helped promote the new generation of female headed corporations and banking institutions. "I met some of our members in college, and several others after I started working in the banking industry. I feel that every investor is a personal friend. Our club forces us to get together on a regular basis. It is a major source of strength for all of us," she said.

Well, that was only part of Tanya's story. As it turned out, she had worked at AmeriBank and absorbed everything she saw and heard. Like all the other new hires, Tanya started out as a teller. She had no money to go to college, but graduated at the top of her high school class. She was bright as a shiny penny. She had risen the hard way, but she managed to work her way into the best social circles in high school. She was a cheerleader and achieved acclaim when she was voted class president.

She had big ideas about what she would become, and she knew she'd go places, even if it meant running over her best friend to get there. Nothing would stand in her way. She just knew she wasn't going to be dirt poor like her mother and grandmother. She knew she did not want to raise a passel of kids with no man in sight. She wouldn't live in a cold house where the wind blew through cracks in the walls. She wouldn't live on the wrong side of the tracks. She'd use anybody or anything to get where she was going, all the way to the top.

With all of this ambition tucked under her belt and more than a willingness to work long hours, she was surprised when the male hires were moved along quickly, up the ladder at the bank, leaving her behind in her teller's cage. Some of the men who got advanced were dolts and lazy to boot. Then she got it. They were men and she wasn't. So if sex was the key, she decided she'd use hers. She had a good body and no scruples about using it.

It had served her well in high school when she slammed into the hard cold wall of chemistry. She got extra tutoring after school, and she paid her chemistry teacher in flesh. She got an A and he got off. Then after she finished chemistry at the end of the year, she told him a sob story about needing cash, indicating that if he didn't pay, she was afraid his wife would find out that he wasn't faithful. Tanya figured he owed her. So she got money for cheerleading camp and lots of new clothes, more than a fair trade, she figured.

So now, she would see what the bank manager, Mr. Charles Fortner, might like in the way of after work recreation. One evening Tanya followed Fortner to the Full Shilling for a drink. This authentic Irish bar is over a hundred years old and apparently the whole interior of the bar was shipped over from Ireland. It was a popular drinking spot for Wall Street executives in the good old days.

As he ordered himself a drink, she sidled next to him and as she tried to catch the barman's attention, she casually looked over towards Fortner and said, "Fancy meeting you here. Do you drink here often?"

Fortner was startled but replied, "Yes, this is my favorite drinking hole in the area."

As the barman handed Fortner his beer, she quickly asked him for a gin and tonic, acting like they were together. The barman returned with her drink and asked if they wanted a separate tab. Tanya said in her sweetest voice, "If the gentleman wants, that is fine."

Suitably embarrassed Fortner told the barman, "Put it all on my tab."

Tanya smiled to herself as she chalked up her first victory. They took their drinks and went to find a table. With the cunning of a fox, Tanya ensnared her quarry and Charles soon succumbed to her sexual advances. After a few drinks at the Full Shilling, Charles took her to a midlevel hotel in Manhattan, and began a torrid and lengthy affair with her.

Tanya quickly found out that Charles liked a little fellatio with his brandy before bed. And she learned that after sex, instead of smoking or snoring, Charles liked to brag about his exploits at the bank. She had to assume, or at least she hoped, that he was more successful at the bank than in the bedroom, where he was a total bore.

Over the next several months, the more Tanya acted like a dumb blond, the more comfortable and trusting Charles became. He told her how easy it was to fool the auditors, the shareholders and the board of directors, and explained in some detail about the funds he had embezzled at the bank. Tanya never asked him a question and never seemed overly interested in what he had to say about his bank exploits. But Tanya had an audiogenic memory. She didn't forget a thing she heard. And she filed it all away for a day in which she'd have to remind poor Charles of his indiscretions, both sexual and financial.

Meanwhile, her adulterous affair with Charles led to successive pay increases, some of them pretty hefty, and most importantly, Tanya rose to the senior management level at the AmeriBank New York City office.

Her promotion to senior bank management was her entre to networking with some bigger fish than poor Charles. She volunteered to attend every bank wide conference and convinced Charles to let her serve as the secretary for the meetings. She always managed to look professional, but sexy too. Whether she wore a suit with a slightly plunging neckline or whether she wore fishnet stockings, there was always the suggestion that this package would have a surprise inside. And that's how she met Matthew Gomney, her next sexual target. Gomney was President and

CEO of AmeriBank National. As such, he was one of the most powerful banking executives in the United States.

"Mr. Gomney," she said, extending her hand at a regional bank meeting. "I am so pleased to meet you. I have heard that you are the genius that has led AmeriBank to be the number one bank in this great country." She smiled at him, and as they shook hands, she leaned over slightly and kissed his cheek. Tanya was so glad she had worn her zebra striped Wonderbra. The effort was not missed on Gomney. At day's end, Gomney asked Tanya if she'd be available to help him prepare a power point presentation that night. And yes, of course, she was available.

They started with dinner in his hotel room, and that quickly escalated to sex. But he liked to play rough. As he threw her over the arm of the hotel chair, grabbed her hair and pulled her head back while he entered her from behind, Tanya vowed she ruin this guy. That she'd not only rise to the top of the bank, she make sure he left without a penny and maybe if she could prove that he liked to double dip, she'd see he got jail time.

But Tanya was a trooper. So time after time, when Mr. Gomney invited her to his room, she'd go, partially afraid, partially curious to see what variation he'd have on the rape theme. There were no variations. He just got rougher. The rougher he got, the more determined Tanya was to ruin him. The payoff for her was that from nine to five, he was a prince. And he saw that she got promoted to senior management of AmeriBank Nationwide. As she ascended the ranks of the bank on a national level, she left poor Charles in her dust and focused all of her available time on Mr. Gomney.

As an aside, Tanya started the Silk Purse, an investment club. She did it for one simple reason, she needed money. After all, she had to find a way to pay for her expensive suits and accessories that she needed to play the part of femme fatal and banking maven. She ran the club, and unbeknownst to any of its members, all her friends, she turned it into her own little Ponzi scheme. She would invest in what they wanted to invest in, but would keep some of their money. However, unlike a lot of Ponzi schemes, she made real returns, so the group never knew what was happening. In fact, all the members of the investment club were thrilled with the return on their money.

Tanya also used some of the siphoned money for her own investments on the side. She made a killing doing this and built up a substantial nest egg for any future business she might want to start in addition to Tanya's smart money management, the Silk Purse was lucky. When the Silk Purse started, they rode the crest of the boom just before the housing crisis led to the credit freeze and the financial institutions of the world started collapsing. But the club, under Tanya's guidance, quickly converted its holdings into money market accounts which meant that the members were able to limit their losses. And an added bonus for Tanya was that this presented her with a way to cover her tracks in case any of the Silk Purse members started digging around in the accounts. With all these transactions, she kept her little secret silk purse safely tucked away.

The Silk Purse met every other month to make decisions on joint investments. All the members were professional women and each member invested at least a couple of hundred dollars every month. Their objective was to provide for themselves in retirement, without relying on fund managers. But Tanya, of course, was using some of their funds to dress like a millionaire and to lure in a higher class of man to achieve her real goals. In addition to all of that, studies had shown that women naturally made good investors because they have a modest inclination towards risk and a more calculated approach toward buying and selling. The women who owned the Silk Purse and other similar investment groups had what it took to weather the storm of the Second Great Depression. Tanya could weather any storm; her life as a child had been a tropical hurricane. What was a little financial storm to her?

Concerned by the enormous drop in the value of investments around the world and deciding to enlarge her queendom, Jackson contacted Claire Ritchie founder of the Diamond Gatherers, another investment club run by women. Tanya knew of Claire because of the reputation she had built as a mover and shaker among women's investment club circles. They met at Grey Dog coffeehouse and Clair ordered a macchiato while Tanya sipped on a cappuccino. Once settled they got down to business. Tanya could tell at first sight that Claire was her kind of gal. She knew they'd see eye to eye, and if their partnership deepened, she might even share the Ponzi scheme with her. Or maybe not. She'd see what would work best for her.

"We need to run the companies we invest in," stated Tanya quite matter-of-factly.

"Obviously the board of directors and senior management of the corporations are incompetent," Claire agreed. Oh, Tanya liked this woman.

"They can only make money when times are easy," Tanya said scorning the current economic crisis.

"Do you really think we can take advantage of the downturned economy to improve our fortunes?" Claire asked.

Tanya, looking straight ahead replied, "Oh, yeah! Our investment club is making a better than average return now. And I am personally not doing badly," she said, hinting at her own personal profit from her investment club. Just to be on the safe side, she added. "Besides we believe in socially responsible fiscal policy, something most of my male counterparts at the bank have never heard of. The corporations of America and Europe need to reduce the pay to top executives and increase wages for the workers and middle management. If you pay the middle class more, they will spend all their earnings on toasters, televisions and cars, things the rich already have. The economy will get an instant boost."

In addition to being two peas in a pod, it turned out that Tanya and Claire also had the same social agenda and philosophy. Claire was a successful professional woman at an investment firm, and Tanya wondered if she had climbed the ladder on the back of some sucker the way she had done. The two women chatted for hours during that first meeting. They discussed their friends that belonged to their investment clubs and discussed some of the other investment clubs that they knew. They formulated a plan to invite several clubs to send representatives to come together to discuss the seriousness of the world economies and their possible solutions.

Within two months Jackson and Ritchie had convened the first Women's Investment Group Convention. Jackson stood amid a round of applause and took her place at the podium looking very smart in her blue suit. Her skirt fell just below her knees and her shoes shouted out her love of being a woman. Even though she was a successful banker and investor, she never lost any of her femininity.

"Ladies welcome to the first meeting of the Women's Investment Group or WIG as we will be called.

All of you are concerned about the state of the economies around the world. We all agree that it is the direct result of the incompetence and greed of management that has led us into this mess since the beginning of this century. It is also evident that the politicians in power now cannot reverse the depression because those running the corporations are still trying to feather their nests. We need to become players, real players, in big business and government if we care about our future."

There was applause as she finished her opening address. Then Claire Ritchie stepped up to the podium. "We represent investment clubs run by women. Statistically we have been more successful than men in growing our portfolios and we collectively own more than half the large corporations in the United States. What we are proposing is that we pool our stock and then plan to vote our investment club members onto the boards of the corporations we can control."

She smiled, what to Tanya looked a little too cunningly, but then regained her serious face and said, "We obviously need new leadership. And I know so many hardworking, smart and ethical women in this very room today who will make wonderful executives," she took a minute to look around the room, searching the faces of the women before her. To each woman, it looked like she was staring straight at her. They were thrilled at the individual attention.

Then Claire resumed, "For starters, Tanya, as most of you know, is a talented and gifted leader," and she looked at Tanya. She smiled and sealed the deal with her for life, "While our plan may cause some upheaval, and we do hate to displace some of these executives, who are in leadership positions now. But it's for the good of our nation, our families, and most importantly, to our most precious resources, our dear little children. If we don't do something now, our children will grow up in poverty and stay that way forever. And I don't know about any of you, but I came from a background of poverty, and that is a condition that neither I nor any of my family ever wish to return to. We ladies in this room are going to make sure that our children will grow up in a better world, a better United States of America," and at that she slowed her speech down and again looked around the room, "No matter what it takes, so help us God!"

And at that the room burst into a thunderous applause. At that moment, at that day, in that room, two leaders were born, complete with an army of devotees to follow them. They would grow WIG into financial leadership not just in the United States, but eventually worldwide, uniting women investors in a common cause.

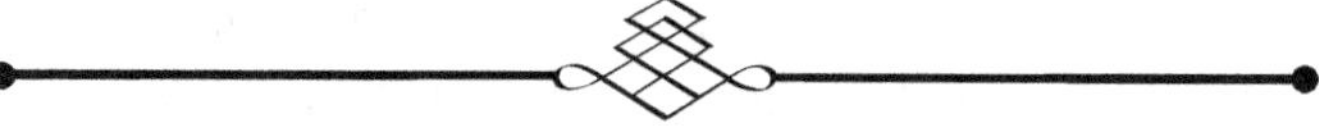

TWENTY-TWO

RACHEL T. CASEY WAS an up and coming lawyer in the Attorney General's office when Judge Burnett called to report prosecutorial misconduct by the Commonwealth's Attorney. The judge outlined the Commonwealth's Attorney's actions in the attempted murder case that had come before her in court and had been plea bargained out to involuntary manslaughter. She described her concern about Coleman's ethics and possible conflict of interest. She told Casey that she felt he had violated the Virginia rules of professional conduct.

Casey opened a case file and proceeded to document everything the Judge had told her. This was an unusual case and she was the fortunate one to answer the phone and get the case. She had heard about the violent demonstrations in the local news and she had read something about how the case had kind of evaporated because of a missing surveillance tape and contradicting reports from police officers at the scene.

Now, Wagner had tried to harm the clinic doctor again, this time by firebombing her house. Wagner, of course, would have to answer for that. But it would seem as though the Commonwealth's Attorney in the City of Chesapeake had some explaining to do.

Within a couple of days Casey headed to Chesapeake to interview the defense attorney, Mr. Gallagher. It was a two hour drive from her Richmond office. During the drive she reflected on the details of the past couple of months and went over the sequence of events in her mind. She wanted to be clear on the facts of the case when she asked questions.

The facts were: in early April, Mike Wagner originally had been charged with attempted murder. Sergeant Mila Preston had reported that he had aimed a gun at a doctor, point blank, aiming at her face, as she drove out of the parking garage connected to the Baywater Clinic. The doctor was fortunate enough to be driving a car with a reinforced windshield, and the bullet ricocheted, killing another demonstrator. That was the involuntary manslaughter charge. Police officer Preston said the surveillance tape would substantiate everything she said. But then the tape went missing. And the second police officer at the scene had a different account from Preston's.

Unbelievably, the Commonwealth's Attorney had agreed to a plea deal where Wagner got off with ten years suspended. To top it all off, in spite of this unbelievable deal, Wagner wasted no time in trying to kill the doctor again by firebombing her house. Yeah, she had some questions for the Commonwealth's Attorney and the defense attorney. Her main question was how in the world was Gallagher able to pull off such a plea bargain.

Arriving a little early for her meeting, she had time to buy a cup of coffee and sit for a minute to unwind. Then she went up to Gallagher's office and announced herself to the receptionist, "Mr. Gallagher is down the hall on your left, last door on your right," she was very efficient. "I will let him know you are on your way."

As she entered Gallagher's office, he approached her with his hand extended and a cordial smile, "I am pleased to meet you, Ms. Casey. Please, have a seat."

"Likewise, Mr. Gallagher. Let's get down to business. You defended Mike Wagner against charges of involuntary manslaughter and attempted murder."

"That is correct."

"My understanding is that Mr. Coleman was very quick to accede to a plea bargain that was very favorable for your client. How in the world did you get him to agree to that?"

"Well, actually, when we met, he was the first to suggest that he had a weak case because of the missing tape and contradictory reports from the police. I have to admit, even at the time, it seemed almost too easy."

Casey liked that Gallagher admitted it was puzzling. He was young, just out of law school, and she recalled that just three years ago, she was in the same position. You have mountains of academic knowledge and enthusiasm to change the world, but very little experience to create a comfort level. Yes, she decided she liked Gallagher.

"Did he offer any explanation?"

"He kind of threw in the towel the minute the tape went missing and he didn't seem to be able to corral the officers so that their stories were compatible. I guess the problem is compounded by the fact that Coleman and Wagner go to the same church."

"Oh really, then why didn't he recuse himself? He should have been disqualified because of possible bias or personal interest."

"I wondered about that, myself. But Coleman said he didn't really know Wagner, that's it's a big church. I don't know and quite frankly, it is not my responsibility to expose a conflict of interest."

Casey was troubled by the evidence she was gathering. It seemed as though the Commonwealth's Attorney allowed his personal bias to influence his decisions in this case. And now the accused had committed arson. He easily could have succeeded in killing the clinic doctor this time.

If Coleman had colluded to get the man released because of his personal bias, maybe even because he also wanted to see women's clinics shut down, then at the minimum, he should be disbarred from practicing law.

Casey next headed to the courtroom where she met with the Judge and made extensive notes of her interview with Burnett. The record spoke for itself. What had seemed to be a judge's tirade during the hearing was now prophetic and clearly outlined the Commonwealth's Attorney's responsibility in the matter. It was obvious that the Judge didn't like the plea deal any more than Casey did.

Then she met with the investigating officers, who were very damning of Coleman's performance. Her interview with Dr. Craswell confirmed that the activities of the group of demonstrators were connected to the various attacks. She connected Coleman to the activist group through their membership in the same church. Soon she would be ready to release her report.

That evening Craswell discussed her interview with Olivia, Gisele and Azure. "It seems as though justice might still work in this country. I am encouraged by Casey's investigation. But of course, it would take a woman to get justice done and cut this man down to size."

Olivia mused, "She should cut his manhood down to size too. Maybe we can apprehend him and bring him in for surgery."

Craswell laughed and scolded, "Now, now Olivia, we are above vengeance of that sort. Gisele, how are you feeling tonight?"

Gisele looked serene. "Much better and thank you for taking such good care of us. My baby girls are kicking wildly. It feels like they are playing jump rope with the umbilical cord.

"We like jumping; those must be athletic girls you've got in there." Craswell turned to Azure, "And you, Azure?"

Now that they felt safe and secure, Azure was quite calm, "My baby has also been kicking my bladder and making me run to the toilet every few minutes it seems."

"Kicking, I like kicking. Kicking is great," Dr. Craswell said with delight. "Kicking and jumping. That's what we like to hear. Go to it girls," the doctor said, leaning toward the bellies of Azure and Gisele.

Gisele suggested, "Let's watch some television. It's just time for the Daily Show and the Colbert Report. And since laughter is the best medicine, let's see who they will fillet tonight."

"Oh Jon Stewart and Stephen Colbert are so funny. They are really good at exposing a politician's handling of facts to suit their arguments. Maybe even our own Commonwealth's Attorney will make the spotlight one of these days," said Olivia.

No sooner said, than done. They turned on the Colbert Report, just in time to hear: "Okay, Nation. You've heard about the trial in Virginia where a demonstrator against a reproductive clinic and its doctors, just had to make the cocktail hour at one of the doctor's homes. It was a Molotov cocktail without an olive."

They were all amazed that the story had made the national comedy circuit. They all howled as Stephen Colbert continued to poke fun at Wagner and Coleman. Laughter was good after so many weeks of tension. It truly was the best medicine.

"Olivia, please make me a cocktail. We'll call this the Coleman-Wagner Memorial Cocktail," they all laughed.

"I am sorry; you girls cannot have any alcohol. We want the very best for your babies. What about a cranberry juice cocktail so we can all toast Colbert?" Olivia slipped out to make the drinks.

Leslie said, "Do you remember when Colbert ran in the South Carolina primary in 2008 for President? That was so funny."

Azure laughing said, "No, I think I was still in elementary school during that election."

Gisele chipped in, "Did you see the episode when Heidi Susman appeared on the Colbert Report? It was very funny. I think Stephen was at his best."

"Yes and Stephen was quick to point out that she received the Colbert bump, when she increased her lead in the polls the following week," Azure added.

Olivia returned, handed a drink to everyone and then said, "I wonder if Coleman will receive the Colbert bump," somewhat uncharacteristic for her, but humor was just what they all needed.

They all settled down to an evening of laughter.

Upon reviewing the evidence filed by the Attorney General's Office, the Virginia Bar got involved, filing a formal ethics complaint against Coleman.

Rachel T. Casey made a statement to the press, "The overwhelming majority of law enforcement officials and prosecutors perform their duties with honor and professionalism, but when officers abuse their authority, and prey upon the public instead of protecting it, this office will prosecute them to the fullest extent of the law."

After a brief pause, she continued, "I would like to thank the Chesapeake Police Department and the Circuit Court Judge for cooperating with this investigation. The alleged conduct is troubling, especially given that the person charged was an elected official. There is no place for abuse in the American justice system. No person is above the law and no person is beneath its protection."

A disciplinary panel, on the third day of an ethics hearing, said the evidence showed that Coleman had deliberately ignored crucial evidence when determining sentencing of the demonstrator in the Baywater clinic that led to the perpetrator committing another crime within days of being released. They found that he had engaged in "dishonesty, fraud, deceit or misrepresentation" during his prosecution of the case.

Hours after he was found guilty of ethics violations, Chesapeake Commonwealth's Attorney Anthony Coleman surrendered his law license to the state bar. His career in ruins, he began the long journey of becoming an embittered old man who wanted somehow to get revenge. He still did not see the error of his ways and he believed more than ever that the doctors, who think they are God, must eventually be stopped.

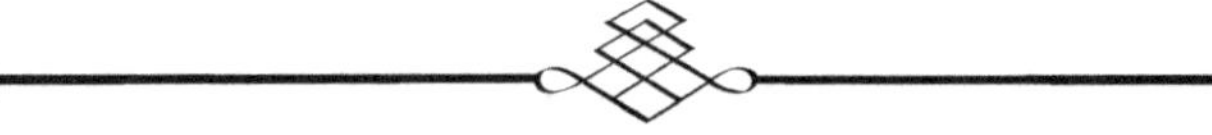

TWENTY-THREE

GISELE AND AZURE ELLIOTT had enjoyed living with Dr. Craswell and her partner, Olivia For the past two months. They felt safe there, and thrived under Olivia's mothering. But they were also anxious to get settled back at their condominium once the babies came and they were safe from threats from fanatics.

They had been living with Olivia and Dr. Craswell since Azure and Gisele came home from the hospital; Azure because of the threat of miscarriage and Giselle, after emergency surgery to save her life and that of her babies following an attack by an extremist who apparently had learned of Dr. Craswell's reproductive experiment, and wanted to stop it in utero.

July 17 was circled in red on the wall calendar. It was a red letter day because that was the date scheduled for Gisele Elliott's Caesarian section, when medical history would be made, one way or the other. Because of her complications from the attack and because she was having twins, Gisele was going to deliver by C section, two weeks before her expected due date.

As the seventeenth approached, everyone was getting a little nervous. Dr. Craswell tried to act calm, but you could see she was worried. Would these babies be healthy, would they even survive? Or could they be freaks or still births? Dr. Craswell's reputation was on the line, not to mention her care and concern for the Elliotts.

Gisele, of course, was anxious about her babies and about the whole procedure. Olivia was fussing over everybody even more than usual, and while appreciated, her fussing made everyone a little more self conscious about the risky business of what was about to happen.

And as for Azure, everyone was walking on egg shells to keep her calm and stay out of her way. The last month had been especially difficult for Azure; in fact, she was acting more like a menopausal shrew than an expectant mother. But for some women, the last month can be especially difficult and have that effect. Gisele was assured that this generally went away once the baby arrived.

Everyone, especially Gisele, was hoping that would be the case for Azure.

Craswell had picked the best ob/gyn she knew to perform Gisele's Caesarian section. Dr. John Shaw was skilled, had a wonderful reputation, and as is often the case with doctors, an ego to match. They'd overlooked his ego, just to make sure Gisele had the best doctor available.

The first procedure was to insert an epidural catheter into Gisele's spinal canal and then administer the anesthetic so that Gisele could remain awake during the operation. She was brought into the operating room and positioned on the table. The nurses waltzed around preparing for surgery like a well-choreographed dance. They knew their assignments and made sure the patient was comfortable. Then Dr. Shaw made his grand appearance and under the watchful eye of Dr. Craswell, made the first incision through the mother's abdomen and uterus.

As she watched, Dr. Craswell thought to herself, no matter how many times you see it, when you cut into the mother and literally pull a new human being into the world, it is always overwhelming. And to do this with two baby girls, babies that would forever make medical history, it reduced Craswell to tears. She knew once Dr. Shaw pulled the first of those babies out, there would be a major commotion as the medical team went into action and waited to hear the baby girls' healthy cries of protest.

"Well, hello there," Dr. Shaw said to the first baby with his hands firmly on her head, inching it out of the bikini incision. "We have a very pretty girl here," he said to the anxious team of health professionals.

Even though time was of the essence, Dr. Shaw did something Dr. Craswell never dreamed he'd do. Before pulling the first baby girl out completely, he called Dr. Craswell over, "This baby is the product of your life's work, isn't it. Come on over here, Leslie and pull this baby out of her mother's womb and into the world," he said to her.

Even though he was a man, she could have kissed his bald head at that moment, but Dr. Craswell was originally trained as an OB/Gyn before she specialized in reproductive medicine. She stepped up and completed the job of working the baby's shoulders out of her mother's womb and into the history books.

History recorded that Dr. Craswell delivered the first baby girl, born as the result of egg-to-egg fertilization. As Dr. Craswell gazed lovingly at the baby she held, Dr. Shaw went back and delivered the second beautiful girl out of her cozy home for nine months.

All the medical staff had known what was precious about their upcoming deliveries. In fact the entire room burst into applause as the first beautiful baby girl yelled her dismay at leaving the security of her mother's womb. Then Dr. Shaw placed the second baby in Dr. Craswell's arms that soon joined the screaming chorus with her sister. When everyone present saw the healthy baby girls, they were jubilant. Beaming from ear to ear, she held Brigid and Jasmine proudly for the cameras to record this special moment in history.

The babies were healthy, weighed six pounds two ounces and five pounds ten ounces respectively. Their APGAR scores were high. But Dr. Shaw ordered the added precaution of placing them in the neonatal intensive care unit because the twins were delivered early, had surgery in utero and of course, they were conceived in a very special way. They would need to be watched and monitored at least for a few days.

In addition to the delivering medical team, Dr. Craswell, and Gisele, there were four other people in the room. Azure, of course, was there holding Gisele's hand the entire time. A medical photographer was quietly but busily walking around the room taking photos and a camerawoman took digital of the whole procedure. This was, after all, medical history.

The fourth person was a reporter, Libby Chen, who would write a story that would that would be featured in magazines and newspapers around the world, and of course, on the web. These twin babies were making history, and Chen would be the first to write about them. In addition, she had a series of articles already underway about why the new medical breakthrough was needed and certainly wanted.

The nurses brought the babies back to their mothers and informed Azure, "Both girls have inherited your beautiful azure eyes."

As the applause died down, the room quieted for a short while as Azure and Gisele shared some time with their baby girls before the babies were to be placed in the Neonatal Intensive Care Unit.

As Azure looked at her and Gisele's daughters, she let out a cry. It was not a cry of pain, but a cry of surprise. Everyone else in the delivery room knew exactly what had happened, even if Azure was still figuring it out. Azure's water had broken. And it was a gusher. The water hitting the delivery room floor sounded like a water balloon breaking. Splat! And there was no rest for the weary as Dr. Shaw began issuing orders.

"Get her prepped. Let's use room E for this vaginal delivery, depending on how dilated she is," Dr. Shaw commanded. Then he named the members of his team who would continue the exciting task of delivering the Elliott's third baby girl.

Azure didn't seem to grasp what was happening as she was put in a wheel chair and taken back to a hospital room to be examined. It was all happening so fast. She was eight centimeters dilated. That meant they would most likely have a third baby tonight.

From Azure's point of view, the sensation of pain began to register itself quickly. The pain seemed to come in waves. It was like a fine piano piece; it would crescendo and then dissipate. Azure decided she could handle this. She could deliver naturally. This wasn't all that bad. And so when they asked if she wanted a spinal block, she bravely said, "No, I'm going to deliver this baby without any drugs."

In one hour's time, she'd regret that decision. She just couldn't dream of the pain she was about to experience. It would turn out to be a roller coaster ride she'd never want to repeat. But for now, she was excited.

As the dilation process continued, Azure began to rethink her decision, and a little after five that afternoon, she called in the nurse and said she believed she would have some pain killing drugs.

"I'm sorry, honey. You're already nine centimeters. If we gave you anything now, it would interfere with the delivery. It wouldn't be good for you or the baby."

Oh shit, she thought. When she was taken to a little room outside the actual delivery room, Azure realized that while Gisele had her for moral support, Azure had nobody. She was so happy to see Olivia waiting for her.

She needed someone's hand to hold. Someone that would help her focus and breathe as they had learned in the delivery prep classes.

The pain now was almost circular. It was as if someone had stuck a knife right in the middle of her belly and was turning it slowly. It was so excruciating that she thought she would scream out, something she'd never done in her life. Instead she held on to Olivia's hand. Sweat poured down her face and breasts. As her pain increased, she began to think of her mother and long for her, even though she'd been dead for years. Olivia was a good substitute.

Just as she had this incredible desire to double over and push, Dr. Shaw came in, checked her again, and said,

"It's time for us to have a baby. Come on folks. Let's see if number three is a beautiful as one and two."

He put his hand on Azure's sheeted leg, smiled, and said reassuringly in a lower voice, "Of course, she will be just as beautiful; she is after all one of three in a matching set." He winked and dashed ahead to the delivery room. What a night, he thought. One for the books.

In between the huge spotlights in the delivery room, Azure felt like she was swimming in a sea of pain. She could no longer see any break between the cutting stabs of pain. It was just there all the time. At times, it doubled her over, and she felt better when she pushed. That was a relief. But once in the delivery room, Dr. Shaw was getting her attention again.

"Azure, listen to me. Push when I say push. Stop pushing when I say stop. It's really important. When you feel like pushing, and I don't want you to, breathe out instead. Remember that from your Lamaze classes?" She shook her head in agreement, although at the moment she didn't remember anything.

How had she gotten in this situation, she asked herself. Then she remembered, it was all Gisele's fault. It was Gisele who wanted to do this. She'd kill Gisele the next time she saw her. At the moment, Azure hated Gisele. She hated Dr. Craswell too, and she would really like to kill Dr. Shaw... but only after the little bald headed guy delivered her baby.

Dr. Shaw could tell he had lost Azure's attention. This always happened for first timers, he thought.

"Azure, soon you're going to have your beautiful baby in your arms. You need to listen to me. Look at me." And for the first time she did. She looked between her legs, and all she could see was his shiny bald head.

The humor of it all distracted her for about half a second. But the pain got her attention again.

"Don't push Azure. I want you to breathe and blow out. Blow out, blow out. Come on now, don't push." Azure did what he said, irritated that she had to resist this most powerful urge to push. While she was breathing out, Dr. Shaw was busy removing the umbilical cord that had wrapped itself around her baby's neck. He was so glad

Azure was able to cooperate. Otherwise, by pushing the umbilical cord would have strangled her baby to death. As he quickly worked, he was able to free the baby from the cord.

"Now, Azure, give it all you've got. Push as hard as you can."

That was all he had to say, she was pushing and squeezing Olivia's hand as hard as she could. For the first time during the night, she screamed as she pushed. "Hey, I see your baby's beautiful face, Azure. Now, one more big push, your baby's shoulders will come out, and we'll catch her. She'll be in your arms in minutes."

As he saw the wave of contractions start again, he said, "Push, push, push."

She did push, the pain was so severe she couldn't even scream this time. But then she felt her baby's shoulder push through, and it was almost instant relief. She laid back down, with tears coming out of her eyes. She could hear her baby crying. And in a moment's time, there was a baby on her belly. A very quiet baby, a smart baby, she could tell.

The baby seemed to be taking everything in, looking first at her, and then it seemed that this beautiful little baby was looking around the room. The baby's hair was still matted with blood, Azure's blood. She was beautiful. Her eyes were ice blue. It struck Azure that this baby looked like her. It was the baby she had always wanted and dreamed of, but never thought she'd have. This was her baby, her's and Gisele's baby. She wept with joy. The pain of labor and delivery... it was gone. The only pain she felt now was Gisele's absence. She had to see her and share this moment with her. She longed to thank Dr. Craswell for what she'd made possible. And oh yeah, baldy wasn't such a bad guy after all.

Then she did what was natural for any new mother; she put the baby to her breast, and she was in love. She forgot about Gisele not being there. She forgot about everything except for this beautiful baby suckling on her breast. She would name her Toni.

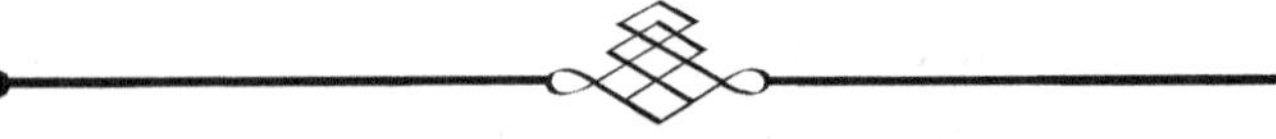

TWENTY-FOUR

TANYA JACKSON'S FIRST TARGET for a takeover by WIG was AmeriBank, which was where she was steadily and rather quickly rising to the top through hard work and after hours sex with the boss. She had a strong foothold there and knew all the key players. And AmeriBank was easy pickings for her, since she had already managed to amass a large stake in the corporation. With the additional resources of her supporting investor club's she should be able to acquire enough votes to pull off her coup d'etat.

Formed in 1923, when a group of hometown businessmen felt there was room for another bank in the community, AmeriBank became one of the most respected, but staid banks in the U.S. It's true that its meteoric rise was amazing. Starting with an authorized capital of fifty thousand dollars in a rented room in the old Pendleton Building located at the alley on Columbus Avenue between Seventy and Seventy First Streets, the bank opened for business after a vault and counters were installed.

But since it became big and successful, the bank had forgotten some of its founding principles. The concept of customer service no longer existed and the bank had initiated no new innovations in the past decade. Most of all, it was a bastion of old boy conservatives. Jackson saw ways it could greatly expand, secure customer loyalty, and make changes that would reap huge financial rewards.

And most of all, Jackson couldn't wait to do to the bank's president what Gomney had been doing to her in lavish hotel rooms throughout New York City over the past several months. Instead of being thrown over the arm of a chair or across a bed, having her head pulled back by her hair and being brutalized in what passed for sex, she would enter Mr. Gomney's office, go around to the back of his leather swivel chair, grab him by the hair, pull his head back, and whisper in his ear, "You, Matt Gomney, have just been fucked, oops, I mean fired."

The only thing that disappointed her about this prospect was that she wouldn't be able to see the look on his face when he got his rough treatment. Oh well, she rationalized, you cannot always orchestrate events exactly how you want them, and you just can't get everything you want.

The member clubs of WIG started buying shares in AmeriBank, while Jackson leaked rumors to the press about AmeriBank's "problems", which had the effect of depressing the share price. Each time a report appeared the investment clubs were ready to pounce and buy shares at the lower price. Of course, soon after when the gossip was denied, the share price rebounded.

Many women attended the shareholders' meetings, and nobody paid any attention to these lovely little ladies who became well known by the executives. WIG members waited until they had their ducks in a row. Then at the annual general meeting of the shareholders, they nominated several women as replacement directors including Ms. Tanya Jackson. The outcome was a peaceful but unquestionable board takeover. And with Jackson and Ritchie at the helm, they changed many of the bank's policies and transformed the way customers and employees were treated.

Using WIG's resources and AmeriBank's creditworthiness, the ladies prepared to stage their next takeover, even bigger than the first. They targeted Martway, one of the largest retailers in the U.S. The way it happened at Martway followed the pattern of the takeover at of AmeriBank. When the change of control occurred at Martway, the Wall Street Journal did a front page feature story on the audacity of these women.

The chairman and chief executive officer of Martway, Mr. Norman Gates, did not suspect anything was amiss, at the annual shareholders meeting. Gates came into the conference room and addressed the shareholders. He noticed that there seemed to be a lot of women there, but dismissed it as unimportant. After all shareholders did not have democratic representation of one man one vote, their votes were based on the number of shares they owned. Little did he know of the shock he was about to receive.

There were nominations for alternative directors on the ballot. That was normal, but nobody knew any of these people. All the names seemed to be women's names, but Gates was still not worried. But once the voting started for the appointment of directors, Gates stuttered as he realized that all his directors, his entire good old boy network, had been ousted. All of them had been replaced by women, it appeared.

As is customary, the new board convenes at the end of the shareholders' meeting to confirm the executive positions. Gates found himself facing a hostile board who demanded his resignation. Ritchie was nominated to be the new Chairman and Chief Executive Officer and the board unanimously elected her to take over the reins from Gates.

Ritchie informed him, "I will give you one hour to pack up your personal belongings in your office and leave." The rest of his board had no idea that they would leave the meeting relieved of their responsibilities and unemployed.

Gates asked, "What about severance pay for the departing directors?"

Ritchie enjoyed replying, "What about severance pay for all the workers you laid off last year and the year before that? Did you care about them?"

Gates stammered, "But we were trying to keep this company viable in the worst recession this country has ever experienced."

Jackson shot back at him, "While paying yourself millions in compensation and taking bonuses in spite of losses." She enjoyed this so much. It was worth all the years she had to screw her bosses to get ahead, and all the lousy cheap perfume she had to wear to get men's attention.

"We have enormous responsibilities," retorted Gates.

Ritchie replied, "You have no responsibilities now and we will discuss your remuneration at our next board meeting. The new Chief Financial Officer will be scanning the accounting system for any irregularities. Trust me, if we find anything suspicious, you will be going to jail along with all the members of your board. Maybe you can form a bank behind bars. Oh! And by the way, you will refund all the bonuses you were paid while the company was posting losses."

The consensus of public opinion was that Gates was greedy and had gotten what he deserved. Gates had taken millions in stock options, while none of Martway's employees had even the most basic health care benefits or any benefits at all, for that matter. In addition, Martway was noted for buying goods in developing countries where children worked in awful conditions. The list of grievances against Martway was long. So no one cared what happened to Gates. The public supported the new management under Claire Ritchie.

The day of the takeover, Jackson stood back in the hushed boardroom, admiring her accomplice. Ritchie was tough as nails and sounded righteous. She was ruthless, but nevertheless what difference did it make that they had to cut a few corners to get where they were. Business, after all, is business, and no matter what it takes, you have to bite the bullet and plow ahead, she thought.

Jackson and Ritchie lifted their Champaign glasses to celebrate their success at the Perle French Brasserie around the corner, as Gates solemnly packed a few personal items before leaving the building, a defeated man.

Mr. Gates headed up the inevitable group of men that met behind closed doors to plan how they could gain control of their fortunes once again. The plans involved buying up large blocks of shares in both AmeriBank and Martway, and then confront the boards of directors of Martway and AmeriBank to reinstate the former management team. They had brokers out buying stocks at a feverish pace, driving the prices higher and higher. The stock market was booming and the politicians, mostly women now, were receiving all the credit.

It was not long before a group of men led by Gates and Gomney headed down to the head quarters of Martway in New York and demanded an audience with the board. As they were shown into the board room, they looked at the directors who were all women.

"How can we help you?" the Chairman, Ms. Claire Ritchie asked sweetly.

Mr. Norman Gates stated firmly, "We have purchased a majority of shares in the company and we wish to exercise our right to nominate the directors on the board."

Ritchie stood and walked around the conference table to stand in front of the men. She looked them straight in the eye and asked, "Please present the share certificates you own. We would like to verify your claim." As it turned out, she had to stoop a little to look Gates right in the eye. Ritchie had suffered all of her life because of her six foot tall stature. Now, she thanked God for every inch he had given her. She could see her height was stunting Mr. Gate's confidence. I guess even just a couple of inches makes a big difference, size does count, she thought to herself, smiling inwardly, but keeping a straight face for the sake of professionalism.

Gates placed his briefcase on the table and clicked the lock. He withdrew a pile of papers and handed them to Ritchie. As she looked them over she turned to her assistant and said, "Please bring these gentlemen the resolution passed at the last annual general meeting regarding voting rights."

Gates stammered, "What do you mean?"

Ritchie answered with a smile on her face, "These shares do not have any voting rights. We have limited voting rights to the original holders of current stock. You see we had to protect the investment of our shareholders to stop interlopers." Ritchie had to force herself not to say the word, men, "from taking over and destroying the viability of our firm."

Gates took the copy of the resolution from Ritchie's assistant and read it over. Then he went pale. After consideration, he got angry, "You haven't heard the last of us, and we will sue you."

"Well, yes, I guess you will sue, but that will take several years. You might be able to find some more other productive work during that time," she said, trying to look sympathetic.

"You and all your dyke friends are discriminating against us, the businessmen of America!" he spluttered.

"Oh dear, I'm so sorry you feel that way," she said, again trying to look sympathetic. "I remember all the times in the past that I felt that way and how awful it was to feel that you had been denied opportunity because of your gender. You must just feel terrible now that the shoe is on the other foot but it has high heels." She shrugged her shoulders and pressed her lips together in a sad little grin. It was so difficult to suppress the gales of laughter she felt coming on.

She watched with amusement as Gates followed by Gomney and Fortner left the board room and made their way to the elevator. As the doors closed she waved at them with a big smile on her face.

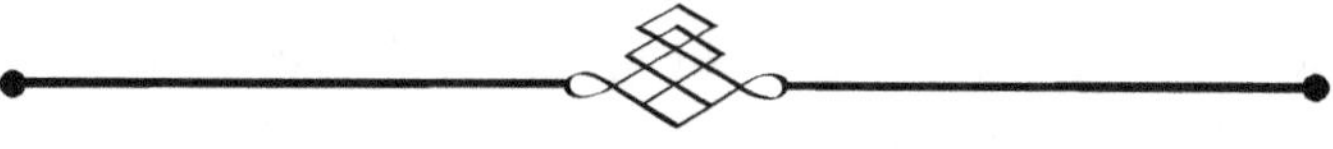

TWENTY-FIVE

LIBBY CHEN SAT DOWN at the computer to write her big story. Her mind was a whirl with all she had seen that night, and all that Dr. Craswell told her afterwards. She did a quick review of all the facts and the scenes in the delivery rooms. As she sat at her computer keyboard, her hands began to tremble. She realized this was the biggest break of her life. And she had to do it right. She knew it would go all over the world and that every media outlet would try to follow up. Maybe even she would be interviewed and her stories would be challenged by other reporters eager to tear them down.

Sometimes when she started writing and her brain could not keep everything straight, she would just starting typing. And that's what she did tonight. As she typed the story, she wrote it as a first person account, something she'd never done before, but this was so different. After all she had been present at this amazing occasion.

"This afternoon in the delivery room at Baywater Hospital in Chesapeake, Virginia, I saw something I'd never seen before, and something that no one had ever seen. I saw two baby girls taken from their mother's womb by Caesarian section, an unbelievably stunning event, in and of itself. And even though it was certainly not the first time the delivering doctors and attending medical staff had seen twins delivered in this way, it was the first time that any of us, or any one in the world, had seen the birth of beautiful baby girls created in vitro, not with a female egg and male sperm, but with two female eggs. It was a first for the human race," Chen wrote.

"Our hearts stopped as Dr. Leslie Craswell and Dr. John Shaw pulled the babies from their mother's womb. The entire room held its breath as we

waited to hear the girls give that triumphant cry that signals a healthy baby. Both girls, Brigid at six pounds two ounces and Jasmine at five pounds ten ounces, gave their victory shouts two minutes apart shortly before four thirty on July 17, 2019, a date that will be remembered in all of history," she
continued in her first person account of the birth of the twins.

"These babies appear to be as normal as any babies conceived through ordinary methods from a man and woman," said Dr. Shaw one of the delivering doctors. "Dr. Leslie Craswell appears to have pioneered a procedure that will enable lesbian couples to have children exclusively from their own flesh and blood. It also could have other positive implications for heterosexual couples who are unable to conceive children as a result of male infertility. Potentially, a man could ask his sister to donate eggs that could be used to fertilize his wife's eggs, replicating as closely as possible his own genes. For a lot of couples, this is a most blessed event."

Libby had been surprised that Dr. Shaw had been so generous in crediting Dr. Craswell for the miraculous birth. But of course, she realized that his success and fame would ride on Dr. Craswell's coattails. She continued typing, getting lost in the excitement of her account.

"The twin girls were born to Gisele E. Elliott of Chesapeake, as her partner, Azure P. Elliott looked on, holding her partner's hand and encouraging her through the procedure. The two women were married in Massachusetts ten years ago, and have always wanted children. And what they wanted more than anything, babies conceived and born as a result of their union, seemed impossible until Dr. Craswell's research and experimentation at the Baywater clinic made their hopes and dreams come true tonight.

"This most amazing story, which just months ago would have sounded like science fiction, but is now as factual and documented as in vitro fertilization itself, didn't stop there. Within an hour and twenty minutes after the Caesarean section was performed, I witnessed the birth of the couple's third baby girl as Azure gave birth by vaginal delivery at five forty five. Azure's baby was named Antoinette, who will be known as Toni, and weighed six pounds four ounces. All three sisters are technically fraternal triplets, since the eggs used at conception came from the same parents."

Chen continued her story, giving the account of Azure's water breaking, the delivery and the need for Dr. Shaw to halt the process to save the baby by untangling the umbilical cord that had wrapped itself around Toni's neck. Her first person account was genius as readers immediately identified with the reporter and what she had witnessed.

"I know reporters aren't supposed to become personally involved in their stories. But I must confess I lost all objectively tonight when Dr. Craswell placed Toni in my arms, after the baby's first attempt at breast feeding and before they placed her in an incubator headed for the Neonatal Intensive Care Unit," she wrote. "This baby is so alert, such a beautiful new creation that I think she would bring tears to the eyes of any hardened sailor. I only got to hold her for a minute, but in that time she melted my heart as she stared quietly at me, intent on figuring out who I was, figuring out this new place she found herself in, and this new warmth of human contact, sight and sound."

In addition to this report, Chen wrote a sidebar which included a factual account of Dr. Craswell's work and how this type of in vitro fertilization was scientifically possible. Tomorrow, she'd follow up with a tie in story about the demonstration and Mike Wagner's attempt to kill Craswell.

On the third day, she brought back the story about the attack on Dr. Craswell's home and the attack on Gisele. Chen kept this story rolling for three weeks, as all the other reporters in the world ran behind her picking up rewrites. She was featured in talk show after talk show, as were Dr. Craswell, Dr. Shaw and of course, the parents, Azure and Gisele Elliott. Within three weeks, the babies made their debut in the newspaper, with photos and stories by Chen. The Today Show got the exclusive rights to the television debut of the babies.

At the end of the year, Chen won not only the Pulitzer for her newspaper series, she was also honored to be asked to be Toni's godmother. While Chen was thrilled to get the Pulitzer at such a young age, she was equally thrilled at being Toni's godmother and later her mentor.

She had bonded with that baby, just as she had said in her story, and through the years, she encouraged her in every way. Her fondest hope was that Toni would follow in her footsteps and become a journalist. Chen knew she would never get married, since her career was everything to her. So Toni became the daughter she would never have.

At the triplets' first birthday party, she brought the cakes and howled with joy as the little girls practically dived into the cakes head first, joyfully getting icing on their hands and faces. The little girls had never tasted sweets before, and once a dollop of icing was held to their lips, they loved it, and didn't hesitate to show their pleasure.

As the first day of school approached, Chen waited anxiously with Gisele and Azure for the school bus that would take the girls away from their mommies to their next big adventure in life. When Brigid, Jasmine and Toni climbed onto the bus and turned simultaneously to throw kisses and wave good bye, Chen cried along with Gisele and Azure.

Chen was there for every birthday, every school event, every graduation, and was even able to share with Gisele and Azure special times such as Toni's district championship basketball game. At each event, there was another series of stories. And each story showed the sensitivity and love that Chen felt for all three children and for Azure, Gisele and Dr. Craswell.

And so it went, as the years passed by and the children reached milestone after milestone until they were no longer children, but young women on their own. One of Chen' happiest moments was when her godchild, Toni, attended the Columbia School of Journalism, following in her footsteps. Chen really loved Toni as much as she would have loved her own flesh and blood. And Toni loved her back. Toni considered Libby her third mother. And amazingly, Gisele and Azure were happy to share her with Libby.

Chen was so proud of Toni. And she knew she'd be a great reporter one day, a day not too far off, and ironically enough, it would be a day connected with the egg-to-egg fertilization technique that brought her into the world.

TWENTY-SIX

MR. NORMAN GATES WAS steaming as he left AmeriBank's head office and led his entourage into the Bourgeois Pig for a drink. Unlike the old days, when these former tycoons would have clinked glasses together to celebrate their good fortunes, the toast this time consisted of Gates banging his glass on the bar. He cursed, "Goddamnit, we are outmaneuvered for now. But don't worry gentlemen if we put our heads together, we will come up with a plan to undo this idiocy."

Charles Fortner was still unemployed after Jackson seized the bank and retrenched all the men in senior management. He was especially bitter. "Maybe we could sell off our stock holdings and depress the price of the stock."

Gates thought about this proposal and replied, "No, they will simply use the lower price to increase their stockholding making it even more difficult for us to gain control back."

Not to be swayed Fortner retorted with, "Well then maybe we can somehow buy voting stock disguised as women."

Gates rebuffed that with, "No that will make them look like an excellent management team as the share price skyrockets."

Mathew Gomney interjected with his own suggestion, "The most destructive thing for any bank is a massive withdrawal of deposits. A run on the bank makes management look bad and causes the share prices to tumble." Gomney was proud that he, at last, had been able to harness his rage and come up with a plan to win back his empire. He smiled and now offered a toast, raising his glass and clinking it with his cohorts, "Cheers, my friends! We now have a plan."

Fortner asked, "How do we start a run on AmeriBank?"

Gomney replied gaining confidence in his scheme, "We get all our colleagues to go into the New York City branch office, stand in line and demand to withdraw all the cash in our accounts. Once that happens, panic will spread, and the other branches will be swamped with frightened customers."

Gates added, "But first we need to float a new bank that we control to deposit our money."

Ever the public relations man, Fortner added, "We need to arrange for the media to cover our withdrawals to start a panic."

After that night, the scheming partnership of angry old men started putting their plan into action. Within weeks, they registered their bank under the name of Manhattan Bank of New York. Within their circle of disenfranchised men, they nicknamed it ManBank, an ironic and yet symbolic nickname. They signed a lease for their first and as it turned out, only branch.

As the pre-determined day got nearer Fortner informed the media that they were concerned about fraud at AmeriBank and that they thought that the bank was in worse shape than the current management was prepared to admit. The reporters arrived with their camera crews and interviewed the men waiting in a queue for the bank to open. The queue was impressive and stretched around the city block and almost back to where it began. When the doors opened, each man withdrew large sums of cash and deposited it into Manhattan Bank. It did not take long before other anxious customers joined the line and the run on AmeriBank was out of control.

Jackson was seated in her office when the news broke that AmeriBank was under siege. Her personal assistant came rushing in, "Ms. Jackson, you need to turn on the news and watch what is happening down at our Wall Street Branch. It's chaos there."

Jackson opened her armoire and switched on the television to be confronted by an unruly crowd of men outside a branch of AmeriBank.

"What is going on?" she asked.

"I believe they are demanding to withdraw their cash from the bank."

"Get Jennifer Warren on the line."

Within seconds, Warren was talking with Jackson. "What is going on down there?"

"It is a run on our bank. It just started minutes ago. The line wraps around the block and I am afraid they will draw down most of our cash reserves. And they keep coming. We are very afraid about what will happen when we have to tell them that we have run out of cash."

"Jennifer, don't worry about this. Stay on the line while I call the feds." On another line, Jackson calmly contacted the bank's auditor at the FDIC, "Have you seen that there is a full scale run on our bank at one of our branches? Maybe you would like to send in a team of auditors to verify the accuracy of our books of account. There has not been any fraud since I took over as Chairman."

"You can shut down all branches of your bank," noted Jonathan Trimble, "Then we will announce that customers can calm down as their money is safe since it is insured up to two hundred and fifty thousand dollars. Then we'll work without delay to determine what is causing this. Do you have any thoughts? Do you think that maybe this run was started artificially by a disgruntled employee or possibly a competitor?"

"I have an idea, but let me get back to you on that. I have my branch manager on the other line. Let me tell her what we've just discussed. I'll be waiting for your auditors."

Meanwhile, Jackson got back to her call with Warren. She could almost feel Warren sweating. "Close the bank down. The auditors will be there within minutes. We will announce that all the depositors' money is safe as it is FDIC insured. This will stop the run on the bank, and we'll figure out who is causing this." She could hear an audible sigh of relief on the other end of the line.

Jackson had a pretty good idea that somehow this run was caused by Gomney, the former President, and Fortner, the New York Office president. She didn't realize that the ousted men had formed an alliance with Gates and that they had launched a concerted effort to win back their empires. She asked Ritchie to come over and together they examined the withdrawals. They immediately noticed that the first few withdrawals were in fact made by Gomney, Fortner and other members of the board of directors of a relatively new and unknown bank, Manchester Bank of New York.

Jackson had already found and uncovered the embezzlements that Fortner and Gomney had committed during their tenure as management of the AmeriBank. As soon as she took control of the bank, she called in a team of forensic auditors to scrutinize the boasts of her former lover, Charles Fortner. Claims he told her during sex.

She outlined everything that Fortner and Gomney had told her leaving out the steamy particulars of how she got the information. Then the auditors spent a couple of months combining advanced computer investigation techniques and traditional auditing and accounting procedures to investigate the alleged fraud. They uncovered over two million dollars of misappropriated funds in Fortner's accounts and over seven million in Gomney's.

They were experts and had to employ some unusual tricks to discover how they pulled their schemes off. Both men had covered their tracks expertly, but when auditors begin with the result and work their way back, they can start to see the racket unfold. The one thing that gave them away was the enormous amounts of money in their investment accounts. Once they had their evidence, the auditors called in the FBI to take over from there.

The FDIC inspectors sent a team to Manhattan Bank together with FBI agents to investigate possible fraud there and arrest the men.

Jackson called a press conference to announce that AmeriBank was stable and secure and that the run on her bank was started by a competitor bank for nefarious reasons. She alluded to embezzlement and that charges would be brought against the directors of Manhattan Bank.

Within minutes Manhattan Bank's stock price tumbled to just a few dollars. Gomney, Gates, Fortner and their cronies were ruined financially and would eventually go to jail for their scheme to cause the crash of AmeriBank, while Jackson quickly bought up the small bank for pennies on the dollar.

Then Jackson and Ritchie met in her office to discuss the crisis. "It is amazing what one can find out in bed," she told Ritchie.

Ritchie laughed, "You sure know how to buy and use an insurance policy. I am impressed with your smooth exploits. Those men are going to spend a long time behind bars and good riddance."

Getting back to the present crisis, Jackson said, "But now we need to find a way to restore confidence in AmeriBank. We need our customers to deposit their money back in the bank."

"That's easy," replied Ritchie.

"Really?"

"As chairman of the Martway's board, I can easily put out a directive to transfer all our bank accounts to AmeriBank. We were going to make this move anyway. I can just do it sooner. It might have a devastating effect on the other banks, since our accounts are spread among many banks. But most importantly, it will immediately boost AmeriBank."

Jackson knew that would restore their deposits and reserves, "That is a brilliant plan that should restore confidence to our customers."

Jackson's shrewd play and her partnership with Ritchie once again led to her success.

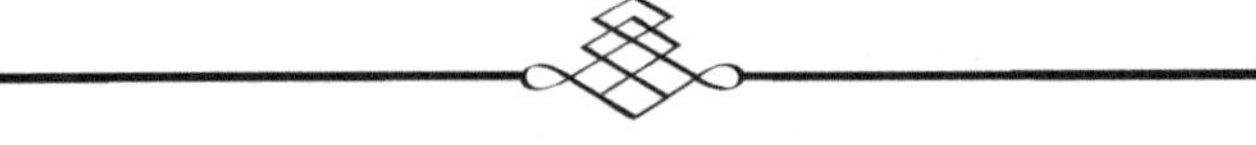

TWENTY-SEVEN

SUSAN THOMAS WAS A political cheerleader, who worked the crowd, getting waves of chanting to fill the arena. She joined Heidi Susman's campaign soon after she announced her candidacy. Heidi, Heidi, Heidi, Heidi, Heidi, the word filled the circular building so that it was one long Hi.. .Dee. This went on for 10 minutes.

Then more crowd motivators came on and primed the pump. "Who's going to break the backs of corporate lobbyists?" asked one adorable young blond with a megaphone and a cheerleader outfit. Of course both the megaphone and the red and white short skirt and top were for effect only. And she got the effect she wanted when the crowd answered back, "Ieidi!"

"Who?" She yelled back, "I can't hear you. Who is it going to be?" On cue, the crowd screamed in excited unison, "Ieidi!" This time the crowd shouted much louder. She repeated her questions again, this time motivating the crowd to even louder screeches.

The political choreography wasn't over yet. Rally participants in each section of the arena were given giant letters to hold up. Each section stood on cue. The effect was a giant graphic of Heidi, Heidi, Heidi, Heidi, Heidi.

Last but not least, a rock and roll group came on with a new version of a 1960s rock and roll song. "Heidi, Heidi, Heidi Ho," and the crowd echoed in unison. "Heidi, Heidi, Heidi Ho".

"Who's gonna make the greedy bosses go?" "Heidi, Heidi, Heidi Ho," the crowd roared back.

At that the rockers came back with another round of "Heidi, Heidi, Heidi Ho." This was followed by a rousing hot metal beat. By this time the crowd was as sweaty and excited as any politician could hope for.

At last Heidi Susman came on stage. She was dressed in a white cashmere sweater and knit skirt, with the hint of a silver sequin here and there. Her blond hair gave the look of a supernatural being, maybe even an angel. Every detail had been thought out by Heidi, her mother and other advisors. The crowd audibly gasped when they saw this vision of loveliness. Heidi always kept her speeches short, emotional and yet oddly enough, she'd manage to discuss one major issue and nail it every time. The combination was a winner with every audience. By the end of her speech, Heidi had some in the crowd in tears.

The media loved Heidi Susman. She looked like an angel, and was the master of the thirty second sound bite. The media's only problem was which angle to tape her from. She was like a visual orgy. The media, like the crowd, couldn't get enough of her.

"Harry, get that camera over there, get a profile. No, now get her full face, shoot in on her full face, and..."

The producer for NBC news was interrupted mid sentence by the lead grip, who by this time was frustrated with the conflicting directions. "Alex, for God's sakes, shut the fuck up; you're driving me up the wall. We'll get it all. Just back off."

"Sorry, Harry. This is just so spectacular. Of course, you guys always get your shot. I'll just have to trust you. But I feel like an angel has descended from heaven."

"Yeah, I know," Harry said, lowering the cherry picker to get a better angle.

And so it went at every rally. The media was falling all over itself to get a piece of Heidi Susman. And then there were the crowds to film, and the pre speech spectaculars. Heidi Susman was like a made for TV special. And she virtually took over the internet for her big rallies.

The crowd was filled with young people in their twenties and early thirties, both male and female. That demographic formed the ground swell of Heidi's supporters. The next largest group was women from forty to sixty. Some middle age men were present too, but by far and away the majority of middle age supporters were women.

They were tired of getting passed over for promotion to top positions. They were tired of getting groped by the boss and keeping their mouths shut for the sake of job security. These women were ready to elect a woman. They had given a lot of promising men an opportunity to make a difference, and while some had improved things, no one did a thorough spring cleaning. And that's what women in America wanted. And besides, the political future of the United States in general was shifting toward women, and now it was time to claim their place in the halls of power. It was long overdue, they thought, to get a woman in the white house. Women, at last, were beginning to trust women.

As well as media support, Heidi got lots of support from her mentors in the House and the Senate. Everyone was taking her seriously; everyone was taking her party, the Progressive party, seriously. And as the presidential campaign moved forward, even the most established and respected Congressmen watched in awe as she drew incredible crowds. Her rallies were choreographed like an intricate ballet. Always the media was there in full force to show the ardent supporters, the crowd frenzy and the fact that Heidi Susman was starting to look a lot like the first woman President of the United States of America.

After the huge success of Barack Obama to raise campaign finance from small donors and completely swamp his opposition, large corporate donors and special interest groups became marginalized in United States politics. Lobbying members of congress became inappropriate when the real money was coming from the general public. And woman's issues were becoming more relevant as more women were taking over jobs once held by men, forcing men into the unemployment lines or into the kitchen to take care of the kids, do the housework, grocery shop; in short, making them househusbands.

Heidi rallied many congresswomen and female senators to join her in creating a political party that would be true to Thomas Jefferson's creed that the purpose of government "Is to allow for the preservation of life, liberty and the pursuit of happiness." There were an unprecedented number of elected politicians who joined Heidi's cry to implement a new set of values.

As the elections approached, the polls showed that Heidi Susman's Progressive Party was poised to take control of the house and possibly even the senate. That would be a bonus for her once she won the election and became president. It would mean that she wouldn't have to battle for every bill, every reform. She'd have a team to work with in Congress.

On the economy Heidi vowed she would expand her already popular Corporate Responsibility and Workers' Reform bill to limit the power of corporate executives. "It's time to give the greedy corporate executives of this country a one way ticket out of Washington," Heidi would tell cheering crowds at rallies throughout the United States. "Our founding fathers and mothers didn't intend for the United States to be run by corporations. And now, some of our corporations are as powerful as small governments.

This has got to stop or the people, you folks right out here," she said looking around the auditorium, "You folks will never get your say in Congress. Your voice will always be hushed by the big corporate giants."

She repeated her claim at every campaign stop that the executives running the large corporations were greedy and they must surrender their unreasonably large remuneration packages for a structure that helped build the nation's overall wealth. She wanted laws to regulate how these corporate executives who were at the helm of publically traded companies were paid. Her suggestions were extremely popular and despite cries that her policies were simply a redistribution of wealth from the rich to the poor. The only voters who disagreed with her seemed to be wealthy executives.

But not all executives withheld their support. In fact, two very prominent executives contributed generously to Heidi's campaign. They were Claire Ritchie, president and CEO of Martway, the largest retail establishment in the United States, and Tanya Jackson, president and CEO of AmeriBank, one of the largest banks in the world. Both CEOs applauded Heidi Susman's effort to reform corporate America with legislation limiting the power of corporate executives.

Not only did Ritchie and Jackson give large financial contributions, they also schooled Heidi in techniques to motivate big crowds. She had gotten to know them through her participation in local investment clubs and in WIG International, a worldwide investment club for women. At every rally, she'd be sure to look straight at different areas of whatever rally hall she'd be appearing in. It always had the same effect; it looked like she was looking straight at each of the adoring members of the crowd. That personal touch is what usually brought tears to the eyes of those so inclined.

In addition to the theatricality of her rallies, Heidi was truly trying to introduce some new ways of doing business that would be good for America, especially for working class America. The proposed legislation would limit the power and wealth of corporate executives in companies listed on any stock exchange. The bill mandated that all senior executives with decision making capacity could receive a maximum remuneration package that was tied to the actual salaries of the whole work force of the company. The way in which the average was calculated was clearly defined in the legislation. Then the factor for the multiplier would be adjusted from time to time by congress. It was intended that profitability allowed for a higher multiplier and when a corporation was trading at a loss, the multiplier would be low.

This gave the executives incentive to ensure that their employees were paid higher salaries to enable themselves to be receiving higher pay and bonuses. There were disincentives for retrenching workers but when expanding and hiring new workers, they could really earn big bonuses. This bold new control over the private sector was expected to boost the economy after years of slow growth and recessions.

One of the biggest problems that led to the collapse of the economy was that many financial institutions were considered too big to fail. Well Heidi's solution was to limit the size of a company to a small percentage of the total market in its sector. That way a company would never again be too large to fail and free market forces would work to correct bad management decisions.

Another issue Heidi liked to talk about was the need for reforms by utilities. Some of her proposals were more complicated like multiplex of energy streams, and how that could be ecologically sound as well as financially prudent. Some simpler suggestions, which the utilities fought tooth and nail, was for the utility companies to bury all the overhead electric cables. The opposition was rowdy with the spokesmen for the utilities claiming that the costs would bankrupt them.

But Heidi had all the answers. Every hurricane and winter storm wrecked havoc on the economy. Billions were lost when power lines were damaged and businesses had to shut down for several days or weeks until power could be restored. She intended to pass legislation to allow the residents and businesses that were dependant on power to seek compensation for their lost production from their local utility.

Utilities would then have to include their costs to repair downed power lines as well as all the associated costs incurred by their customers. One bad winter would finance burying all the power lines. The legislation included a provision that utilities that were taking appropriate steps would be allowed to use that for an exemption during the transition over to the new technologies.

Even though all of her suggestions for change to corporate America and to the utilities were challenged by traditional big donors, the issues were popular with average working class people, and special interest groups found themselves marginalized into a small minority bleating their usual mantra that the world would end if Heidi Susman were elected.

Low and behold, it appeared that the world did not end when Heidi won 62 percent of the popular vote and overwhelmed the Electoral College vote to become the United States' first female president.

TWENTY-EIGHT

THE NEXT TWENTY YEARS saw a social, economic and political revolution which started in the United States and then spread worldwide. The balance of power was definitely shifting to women in politics and business. And the structure of the American family changed dramatically. Movements that started from very humble beginnings, maybe seemingly inconsequential at first, exploded into recognizable trends.

On the business front, two self made women had become household names. Tanya Jackson and Claire Ritchie became business tycoons in their own right. They orchestrated many corporate takeovers after their first two successes with AmeriBank and Martway. They now had the financial resources to help more women executives take the leadership chairs in board rooms across the United States and in Europe. The scenarios played out over and over as corporation after corporation fell to the onslaught of these powerhouse women who started out by forming women's investment clubs. It was the beginning of a revolution of enormous magnitude and history would eventually teach that this era was the largest transition of power in the history of mankind.

As women took over leadership of corporate America, they implemented a strategy of reducing excessive executive remuneration, which had gotten egregiously out of line with multimillion dollar corporate bonuses, extensive perks and outlandish salaries. They used the resulting enormous savings to increase earnings for middle management and they brought worker's wages up to fair levels.

Whenever asked about this revolutionary financial policy shift, the new corporate matriarchy was fond of quoting Henry Ford, "It is not the employer who pays the wages. Employers only handle the money. It is the customer who pays the wages." Ford, in the nineteen twenties, increased the minimum wage to five dollars a day for his factory workers. The industry standard was half that. Wall Street was very critical of his wage increases and when Ford was asked about it, he said, "One's own employees ought to be one's own best customers. Paying high wages is behind the prosperity of this country." By the end of that decade, Henry Ford was the most successful industrialist in the world.

Implementing Ford's philosophy, the female entrepreneurs helped rejuvenate America's ailing and crippled corporate structure, reviving the country's economy. Reganomics or the 'trickle down' ideology expounded by former President Ronald Regan was discredited, replaced by the 'trickle up' approach that was considered not only socially responsible but a boon to big business.

As other countries witnessed America in the midst of business resurgence, the trend spread. The European economies started to revive as businesses in Europe were able to hire more workers and pay them much higher wages. The effect was astronomical as consumers started to gain confidence spending their hard earned wages on goods they had postponed buying for years.

There was also a side effect. Because of improved efficiencies by the new management of women owned businesses following the takeovers, other companies began looking at their talented women more closely. Instead of being bypassed for promotion, as had often happened in the past, women began getting the edge over men. More and more corporations were managed by women. At first, the change seemed almost imperceptible. By the time the media picked up on it, it was a fait accompli.

Politically, the balance of power worldwide also shifted to women. Again, it started in the United States. In the elections of 2020, Heidi Suskin became the first woman President of the United States defeating a very conservative President who had tried to revive Reganomics and the laissez faire pro business attitude of the second Bush dynasty. Suskin's presidency and her concern for middle class America ushered in a new era in politics, one that focused on the stability and health of the American family, however that might be constituted.

She implemented her platform policies within the first one hundred days of her presidency and the economies of the world started their biggest recovery in recent history. She ushered in new boom times. She got Congress to institute stringent controls to prevent the old style bosses from taking over corporate America again. Congress and the public began to realize that business in America was important to the health of the whole country, not just a past time for a few old men in the good old boys' network.

Politically, the public's perception of what it wanted from its lawmakers began to shift. More and more women were elected to public office because the public seemed to have shifted its trust away from males to the female sex. Voters liked the fact that women were not perceived to be power hungry, that women seemed to have empathy for families in trouble, and that women seemed to be more in touch with the needs of middle class America.

There was also a huge shift in the make-up of the typical American family. Females were dominant, same sex egg fertilization became commonplace, and the make-up of the typical American family changed. No longer did the public embrace the belief that a typical family was a mommy, daddy and two children. In fact, if anything, that became the atypical American family.

With the decline of fertility in men, women who wanted to have a baby readily accepted the same sex reproductive technique. As the male sperm declined in potency, it became the preferred method, cheaper and often more successful way to get pregnant. Of course, this led to the unprecedented birth of female babies, as there was no Y chromosome present in egg-to-egg fertilization.

It wasn't unusual for women to live together in Israeli style Kibbutzs. There were frequently up to twenty or more women with up to thirty or forty children living in large dormitory style homes. Most of the women had traditional jobs outside the home, while a few remained at home to provide nurturing and education to the growing girls.

Dr. Leslie Craswell, long recognized as the world's leading authority in same sex procreation, was excited when she received an invitation to deliver the keynote address at the Global Association of Reproductive Medicine conference in Singapore. It always amazed her partner, Olivia, at how excited she got with each new invitation, even though she was in demand for speaking assignments all around the world.

Dr. Craswell was booked to teach her specialized techniques to the doctors at all the major reproductive clinics in the world. Fertilizing an egg with another egg would prove to be a very lucrative service for those clinics to offer as the procedure became routine. She held seminars' teaching the reproductive doctors how to perform her technique of removing the nucleus from one woman's egg and then injecting the nucleus into another woman's egg. But the Singapore conference was something special because it was bringing together not only western scientists and doctors, but also scientists and doctors from Asia, Africa and even the Middle East. It was truly a global conference, the biggest of its kind.

"Olivia, this is such an important conference. We want to make same sex reproduction available to all women worldwide. And so far, our techniques have for the most part been squandered on women in the West and on those elite who can afford it in third world countries. For the rest, male infertility has meant many women have had to remain childless." Craswell was animated as she continued, "So I'm really excited about this speaking engagement. The ability to bear children shouldn't be limited to the rich and educated only."

"I know, Leslie. I admire what you are doing. It is a fundamental right of every human to have offspring and it should not be a privilege of the few. Who would have thought when you pioneered the first same-sex conception thirteen years ago that the technique would become standard and would actually help keep the world's human population from going extinct?"

"It is ironic, Olivia. Sad to say, but because the scientific community ignored warnings about estrogen levels in the water, the results now are almost irreversible, and the health of the male sperm pool is so greatly compromised. It's of great concern to me and other scientists. Our focus for so many years was concentrated so narrowly on the dangers of antibiotics in the water. Scientists just did not see estrogen as a threat, and here it is becoming the biggest threat to the viability of mankind. It's all the more important that I teach as many young medical students, scientists and researchers as possible egg-to-egg fertilization techniques."

"Speaking of thirteen years ago, you know our little triplets are going to have their birthdays just about the time of the conference in two months and we always celebrate their birthdays with them." Olivia pointed out. Olivia loved acting as a kind of grandmother to the triplets, who were the first babies conceived and born as the result of Dr. Leslie Craswell's pioneering, same sex egg-to-egg fertilization technique. Even though we are going to be out of the country, I would hate to miss their birthdays. What are we going to give them this year? Thirteen is a very special birthday."

"You know what I'd love to give them for their birthdays?" Craswell hesitated for a second, and then continued, "I'd love to invite them and their mothers to travel with us to Singapore. It would be amazing for all of them, and what better proof of the success of this technique than these girls? They are so beautiful, smart and charming. What do you think? Should we phone Azure and Gisele to see if the five of them would like to travel with us on this adventure?"

"Oh yes, let's invite them. I think they will love the experience. And this would make the trip so much fun for me," Olivia said. She immediately tried to rephrase what she had just said, so as not to hurt her partner's feelings. "Well what I mean is, while you're at the conference all day, I'd be able to sight see with the Elliott family to see the tourist attractions."

"I'm sorry my meetings can be boring for you, darling. I'd love for you have the Elliott's for company. It means so much to me that you come on my trips, since you make my trips to faraway places feel like home for me. I'm afraid I'd get terribly lonely if I had to go alone. Besides, it would be fun to have the Elliott girls with us. I will phone and invite them now."

Azure answered the phone when Leslie called. Their family maintained a close bond with the doctor and Olivia, so Azure was thrilled when she heard Leslie's voice. When Leslie proposed they all travel together with the Elliott family as guests of the Craswell Foundation Fund, Azure was speechless at first. Then, she was overwhelmed.

"Oh, my gosh! Wow! That would be wonderful. Let me talk with Gisele sind the girls and get back with you. I am so excited at the prospect of such a fabulous trip. But let me talk with the rest of the family," her high pitched voice exuded excitement. "You know how teenagers are; these girls have quite a social calendar. Hopefully two months notice in advance will be enough warning. But let me see. Oh, Leslie, you are once again a fairy godmother to us. Thank you so much and I'll talk with you later tonight."

The Elliott triplets were truly amazing young women. They were smart, beautiful, full of fun, sparkling with ideas, and eager to take life on head first. They squealed with delight when Azure and Gisele presented Dr. Craswell's proposal to them. If the girls had anything on their social agenda, they eagerly scuttled it for a trip to Singapore.

"Do you think we will be able to talk with some of the scientists attending the conference?" Jasmine asked.

Both Jasmine and Brigid loved science. They just couldn't decide which field of endeavor they wanted to go into.

"Well, I have a feeling Dr. Craswell can arrange something," said Azure.

"Maybe I can meet some journalists," Toni piped up. Her interest was in journalism and her adopted aunt, Libby Chen, a Pulitzer Prize winning reporter, mentored Toni every chance she got.

"Well, let's ask Aunt Libby if she has any ideas." And so the decision was made with much excitement. The Elliott family was going to Singapore. It's what got Jasmine and Brigid interested in the field of astronomy as they met Dr. Raj Pavit, one of the world's leading astronomers specializing in the study of sunspots. They received a personal invitation to visit his laboratory at the Khureltogot Observatory in Mongolia. Seeing the keen interest of these young women, Dr. Pavit took them under his wing. Under his tutelage, they quickly refined their scientific interests and set their sights on astronomy.

At the same conference, thanks to encouragement from Aunt Libby, Toni reported on the highlights of the conference for CNN World News. The opportunities available to these girls were amazing, and they thrived in the public spotlight, which was a good thing because as the world's first same sex test-tube babies, they were never far from it.

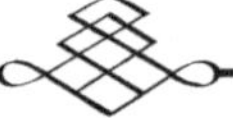

TWENTY-NINE

ST. JOHN, New Brunswick, February 18, 2008 - A study by Dr. Karen Kidd, of the University of New Brunswick and the Canadian Rivers Institute, found that estrogen from birth control pills flooding into the water system through sewage adversely affects fish populations. "We've known for some time that estrogen can adversely affect the reproductive health of fish, but ours was the first study to show the long-term impact on the sustainability of wild fish populations," explains Kidd.

"What we demonstrated is that estrogen can wipe out entire populations of small fish - a key food source for larger fish whose survival could in turn be threatened over the longer term." Health authorities estimate that 100 million women worldwide take some form of hormonal contraceptives; but there is still little media attention given to the growing concerns of scientists about its environmental impact. However, studies are leaking out into the mainstream press more frequently as public interest in the environment grows.

The Pill, along with numerous other commonly used chemicals, ends up in the water system as estrogen. At a conference on breast cancer in Toronto in 1998, author and cancer surgeon Dr. Susan Love said, "Pollutants are

metabolized in our bodies as estrogen. And it is lifetime
exposure to estrogen that has increased world cancer rates
by 26% since 1980 We live in a toxic soup of chemicals".

TONI PUT DOWN THE thirty three-year-old newspaper article that
confirmed what she already knew. She was a pretty twenty two-year-old
journalist reporting on the drop in male births and other societal changes
that had occurred as a result of the imbalance in the male-female ratio.

She found references to several studies that were not available using her
wireless reading device; to access the archives, she had to visit one of the
public libraries. These facilities made available to the public the old paper
versions of books, magazines and newspapers that dated back before the
device was invented.

Actually she was already familiar with the technique that enabled two
women to conceive a baby, using no male sperm. After all, she was the first
baby born to two mothers using this reproductive method.

Her twin sisters were the same age as herself, but born to her other
mother. She tended to be more of a loner as the other two acted like
identical twins, even though they were fraternal twins. But they loved
and cared for each other just like any other sisters. They were a close knit
family and their mothers were still very much in love.

This article from about thirty years ago foretold what was now taking
place. She thought to herself that maybe no one had taken the threat as
seriously as it should have been taken back then; maybe it was taken as
an over exaggeration, a "Chicken Little" doomsday scenario that was just
too fantastic to take seriously. But the results were now very clear. The
high levels of estrogen in the drinking water were having a huge impact
on human reproduction.

The beat of Toni's favorite hit song broke the silence in the library
when her cell phone rang. "Hello, Toni Elliott here. How may I help you?"

"It's me," said Crystal, Toni's best friend and lover, "What time will
you be home?"

"I'm nearly finished. I was going to stop soon but became engrossed
in my research project and forgot the time. Sorry."

"What did you find?"

"It's exciting. I found what I think is one of the first articles predicting that the sperm count in the human male was already dropping back in 2008 and would continue to drop significantly unless drastic action was taken. Although many scientists knew that this was happening, no one took them seriously. This thirty year old article clearly predicts our present day reality. What might have been considered scientific speculation just three decades ago is painfully obvious now."

"Do come home quickly. I'd love to hear about it" "OK".

When Toni got home, she was hardly in the door before Crystal accosted her. "Alright then, what has caused this trend?" demanded Crystal.

"Women started taking birth control pills almost a century ago. Although it was known that excess estrogen passed through our bodies when we urinate," Toni explained, "the water utilities made no attempt to remove the estrogen during water purification; so it cycled back into the water supply."

Crystal was amused, "Perhaps this spike in estrogen in public water will help men understand women better."

Toni laughed and continued, "Maybe, but as water was consumed again, the estrogen was absorbed and passed back into the waste water with more estrogen added each time, steadily increasing the concentration of estrogen in our drinking water. The authorities just didn't realize the extent of the damage that was caused to the urban water supplies, and that is still happening to this day."

Crystal quipped, "Maybe it will permit the male population to get in touch with their feminine side."

"Doubtful, men seem to be slow learners. Now they can't even do the one thing they used to be really good at." They both laughed at the male bashing jab and Toni continued, "As we all know now, it's rare for a man to impregnate his wife without assistance from a fertility clinic."

"It's a good thing we don't need men to make babies anymore," Crystal asserted.

Toni added, "Various studies in scientific journals suggest that the human population is ingesting a cocktail of drugs from the urban drinking water throughout the world. But the increase in the levels of estrogen is quite alarming causing the level of estrogen detected in men to rise significantly. This also causes early puberty in girls."

Crystal added thoughtfully, "I remember my first period in the fourth grade because I was so embarrassed. But some of my girlfriends started going through puberty as early as six or seven. Some of them had beautifully developed breasts by third grade and most had started their periods before their tenth birthdays."

"But the effects on the boys is much more dramatic, since they also develop breasts and look pudgy," said Toni. "The condition is known as gynecomastia, which in adolescent boys is often a source of distress. When a boy is taken to a doctor, the cause of common gynecomastia is rarely determined. So the main culprit, estrogen in the drinking water, gets a pass, while the condition is generally attributed to an imbalance of sex hormones. But nobody blamed our water supplies, even though it was becoming increasing clear that it was the main culprit."

"Do you think the astronomical increase in the gay population is linked to these high estrogen levels?" asked Crystal.

Toni answered, "The rightwing conservatives believe that liberals are converting all men into sissies, but no, I don't think so. I think that sexual orientation is like any physical trait. You're born with either a heterosexual orientation or a homosexual orientation. It's not something you acquire or choose."

In fact, the truth about estrogen in the drinking water was alarming; the human male was in danger of fading away. Had it not been for the then groundbreaking research of Dr. Leslie Craswell more than twenty years ago, which made it possible to conceive a baby using two female eggs, the whole human population might have been in danger of extinction. Multiple regional wars did not help, so that by 2040 women outnumbered men by a significant ratio.

It had become totally acceptable, even fashionable, for women the world over to conceive their babies with other women. They would consult with fertilization specialists trained in the techniques of Doctor Craswell. This reproductive technique had led to an increase in the ratio of baby girls to boys.

Sometimes single heterosexual women would live together to raise their daughters in a kibbutz style community. Ironically, married lesbian couples became the socially accepted parental model. Their children were their genetic progeny and they provided a loving and stable home life for their growing girls. These marriages were similar to what might have been considered a traditional two parent household with a stay-at-home mother.

Of course, there were still some heterosexual relationships, even though they were now in the minority. But even in those cases, the husbands were most often stayat-home Mr. Moms. Toni wanted to do a feature story on heterosexual couples showing how the husband was now the parent providing the nurturing and "mothering" to his daughters. In fact, she decided to go out on Halloween night to interview some of the Mr. Mom's taking their daughters trick or treating. It might be a cute angle to illustrate the changing marriage roles within the dwindling ranks of husbands.

The biggest change in society was the change in the governments of the world. Women were starting to gain total control of the governments of most of the countries on planet Earth. The United Nations was firmly in the control of the hands that rocked the cradles. The matriarchal society that overtook the planet was having an amazing effect on all nations as peace reigned.

Aggression in both men and women was reduced, and somehow the need to control and have power over others was taking second place to helping make the world a better place for all. It was no longer acceptable for aggressive men or alpha males to hold public office.

Toni's research substantiated what was already becoming apparent; the paternal age was dying out and it appeared that Homo sapiens was entering a new phase: the Maternal Age.

This change in society was causing consternation in the hearts and minds of those with the most power and wealth. The men of the world suddenly seemed at a disadvantage and they felt the power of discrimination against them. There seemed to be a disruption in the balance of power among nations, this matriarchal direction was muddling every established and accepted mores of marriage.

But most importantly, once powerful men were losing power and control of the world's resources. It was time to reverse the direction of this matriarchal trend. The very existence of the male was in jeopardy and the wealthy barons were afraid that their fortunes would be sacrificed by the women who were taking over the reins of civilization.

The "Group of Eight" as they liked to call themselves, fashioned after the political alliances of countries that ruled the world at the turn of the century, met regularly to formulate various schemes to change the direction in which the world was moving. They were a group of the eight most powerful men left in the world, and they came from countries around the globe. They repeatedly tried to come up with schemes to change the balance of power back and restore men to their "rightful" place in the world. Every attempt had failed so far.

The Group's attempt to create a banking calamity in the 2020's fizzled out when women leaders managed to outmaneuver their male counterparts and solve that crisis quickly by seizing control of the management of the financial institutions.

They tried fanning the flames of religious fervor. But even the fundamentalist religious movements, which usually enabled manipulation of the masses, had steadily lost public support and collapsed. In their desperation to reestablish the policies of the former leaders, they were again willing to kill in order to regain their influence.

The Group's latest conspiracy involved poisoning the water supply of the world's largest cities. The reasoning for this sabotage was threefold: to stop the ingestion of estrogen by men; force governments to clean up their water supplies and to throw the governments of the world into chaos. They believed the resulting loss of confidence would bring the women-led governments into doubt.

Most importantly, it was unlikely that the Group of Eight members would be suspected of such a heinous crime as they would never get their hands dirty. They would find more than enough disenfranchised men, angry and disempowered, who would be willing to carry out their conspiracy.

And in fact, they had one group ready to go in America where bigots and religious extremists were willing to come together to restore the old macho ways. They had picked Halloween night as the time when they'd poison the water supply in Chesapeake, Virginia, which was chosen as the first city in honor of Dr. Leslie Craswell, whom one activist described as "the bitch who started this mess."

Although Dr. Craswell had died a long time ago, they wanted to make sure the world had not forgotten who was to blame for this ungodly situation, in which children were now conceived by egg-to-egg fertilization, women were taking control of industry, and where men were no longer head of the family.

In the target city of Chesapeake, six men were meeting to plan the Halloween plot. Two men watched from the shadows. The old man in a wheelchair looked angry as the Reverend Josiah Marsh opened their meeting with a call to prayer. "Gentlemen, let us pray." When Rev. Marsh heard a low grumble from three of the men in the room, he added, "Don't think we can do this on our own, men. We will need God's help to staunch this ungodliness, to stop this unholy society that has taken over, to vanquish our enemies and the enemies of Our Lord and Savior. We are Christian soldiers, and we'll need God's help to carry out his will," he said, casting a stern eye toward the three ruffians.

Marsh wished that he had all church goers working for him, but unfortunately, his flock was small and definitely unskilled in the area of crime. While his band of criminals would be breaking laws, he knew they were righteous in doing so. They would kill if they had to in order to ensure that God's will be done.

They had to restore the traditional family to its righteous place; they had to restore men as the head of the family and the head of governments. It was men who had to rule the world, run governments and see that women kept their rightful place at home. Things had to be changed.

And besides, Marsh had received one million dollars to carry out this task. When he first got the money after anonymous communications with someone describing himself as a Sheik, he thought it was a hoax, until he found his bank account was bloated with all that money. Of course, he wouldn't keep the money for himself. He was sure he'd use it to help the poor, but lately he had started thinking about where he might chose to live, and most recently, he was thinking he'd move to South Africa, buy an estate there, and from there, do all he could to help the poor, as time and resources permitted.

He silently cursed himself for letting his mind wander from the prayer that would corral these lowlifes. He asked God to please let that one rogue stop farting long enough for him to get his prayer out. That guy was sick or something. He was killing Marsh with his stinky farts. Marsh thought, God, you sure did make all types in your almighty wisdom, and please help me accept that asshole as my brother at least for tonight. Then Marsh began his prayer in the revival tone of voice that was his trademark.

"Lord, God, help us vanquish our enemies. They are making a mockery of your mandate that Adam, not Eve, lead the world. Eve was the weak vessel you created. She was the one that forced us out of the Garden of Eden. It was because of her sin that mankind has been disgraced and made to live a life of toil and pain. Now, the dykes and fairies have created a Sodom and Gomorrah of our world. There is nothing holy left. And so we pray, help us skillfully poison the water supply here in Chesapeake, this city where this inequity originated. This will force mankind to abandon the drinking water that is turning men into queers and sissies. We are in your hands tonight Lord, and everything we do, we do in your name. In Jesus name, we pray."

"Amen," managed the three ruffians, none of whom had ever stepped inside a church in their pitiful lives. They were here to receive the payout that was promised.

"Now men, remember you are Christian soldiers working in God's name. Conduct yourselves with the holy demeanor this task calls for." This caused a nervous shuffle among the five, as these dullards had no idea what demeanor meant, and they definitely knew they weren't holy. Seeing this unease, Marsh realized he needed some old fashioned magic to make these men stronger in their task. He needed to lay hands on them. The only problem with that was that he'd actually have to touch each man, and he hated to put his hands on their greasy heads. He silently prayed for strength.

"Men, I'm going to do what we call laying hands on you. This will convey God's strength from my hands to you. Bow your heads to receive the Lord."

The greasers obeyed. Marsh went from man to man. Damn, he thought, this is when I wish I was a high Roman fish eater, and then I could use Latin mumbo jumbo and wouldn't have to think of anything sensible to say. He focused, as he laid his hands on the farter: "Lord, this man is your vessel, please enter his body." (Oh, Lord, something surely has entered his body, Rev, Marsh thought to himself).

Then he focused again, "Lord enter the body of (what's his name, he thought in a panic. It's important to say his name.. .oh) Igor Webster (of course that was an alias, he obviously needed to retain his anonymity). Make him your strong servant. Lord, you destroyed the world with water once; help us destroy it again with water, so that it can be remade in your image. Use this man, Lord, to do your holy will. Come into him, Jesus," he shouted and tightened his grip on Igor Webster's head. "Amen," he said again loudly. "Say Amen, Igor, accept the Lord has your God and captain."

"Amen, Lord." Igor screamed loudly.

Oh, my God, Marsh thought. Do I see tears rolling down the cheeks of this redneck? Damn, I'm good, he thought as he went to the next man.

After saying a similar fiery benediction for all the men, he went over the plan once more with them. They had the plans for the treatment plant, and the idea was to kidnap someone who was a former employee of the water plant. Marsh had been stalking the guy they needed to carry out their plans. The Reverend thought this guy was a schlub, one of those freak stay-at-home Moms who used to handle the computer operations for the plant, until there were forced layoffs.

Now he had turned into such a sissy and wasn't earning an honest living any more, but was taking care of his daughter. His wife was obviously the one with the balls in the family. They'd kidnap this guy and get him to cooperate. They might have to kidnap his daughter too.. .which was unfortunate, Marsh thought, but people had to suffer so that God's will could be done.

"Okay, men. On Halloween night, you are to pick up Yale Freeman and Yale's four-year-old daughter as they go trick or treating. Yale isn't that a queer name, though," he said as an aside. "Yale knows the layout of the treatment plant. See, that's how you'll get to the water supply." Reverend Marsh forgot to mention that Yale was a man. And the five ruffians had never heard that name before.

They just knew that they had to follow Yale and the daughter from their home on Oak Ave; they'd start waiting outside their house around 5 p.m. and follow them when they left the house. And when the two got to an out-of-the- way location, they'd nab them. That sounded easy enough. "And men, it's God's will that there be no witnesses left to tell police what happened or why. Understand?" Reverend Marsh said, looking each ruffian in the eye. They all shook their heads. They didn't care. They'd all done worse in the past, so doing away with Yale and Tandy would be no big deal.

There were two men that watched the Reverend Marsh carry out his cynical prayer convincing these hooligans that what they were doing was God's will. The younger man pushed the wheelchair out the door and back to the car. They would report back to the Group of Eight that the plan would be executed. The men carrying out the orders were expendable.

THIRTY

Washington-Post
Sunday, June 17, 2007

With their wives as breadwinners, the fathers are part of a small but growing group of men who are quitting or retooling their careers to stay home with their children.
On Father's Day, an estimated 159,000 stay-at- home dads, or 2.7 percent of the country's stay-at- home parents -almost tripled the percentage from a decade ago -will celebrate what has become a full-time job, according to the U.S. Census Bureau.
Stay-at-home dads now have Web sites, blogs such as "A Man among Mommies," support groups and an annual convention. They are showing up in "Mommy and Me" classes and PTA meetings. Many men's restrooms now have diaper-changing tables, and companies' market souped-up strollers with brand names such as "the Bob."
Those in the Washington region who have lived elsewhere say they sense more of their kind here because of the prevalence of high-powered working women. DCMetroDads, a group started nine years ago, has 325 members.

Men tell stories of being excluded from mothers' groups and hearing of police questioning fathers seen hanging around the playground.

Some have found close friends among stay-at- home mothers, while others say they don't feel comfortable with such socialization or fear their wives would disapprove.

Most stay-at-home fathers say the decision boiled down to money: Their wives had fatter paychecks or more promising careers. Many say relying on one income has *meant a more* modest home, older cars and fewer vacations. Few opt out *completely; many say they work part-time from* home.

Jeff Miller and his wife, Shawn *Brennan, both worked from their Silver Spring home after their first child was born. When they needed more* money, Brennan took a full-time Montgomery County government job. Miller, 40, could continue as a lower-paid, parttime business professor at the University of Maryland, while his flexible home consulting business let him care for Burnett, now 7, and Megan, 5. Miller said he knows four other stayat-home dads in his neighborhood. "Today when I get back, I'll make a pot roast," he said Wednesday morning as he boiled pasta for Megan's picnic lunch with some preschool friends. After mixing Megan's "mystery cereal" -- his own concoction of three cereals and nuts for extra protein -- Miller pulled her hair into a ponytail, pointed her toward a flowered sundress to put on and loaded her into his Chrysler convertible.

"DADDY I WANT TO be a princess for Halloween tonight," said an eager four year old Tandy as she climbed up onto Yale's lap and laid her head on his chest. She knew how to manipulate her stay-at-home father.

Ever since the Second Great Depression of three decades ago, it had become increasingly difficult for men to get work. Studies showed that a large number of companies, now owned and run by women for the most part, were discriminating against men. Ironically, it was as if the same old problems were cropping up in society, but just with a different cast of characters.

"So we need to find a dress fit for a princess then," Tandy's dad said in a falsetto voice playing the part for his daughter.

"Daddy, please dress up as well?" Tandy oozed sweetness.

"What do you have in mind, Tandy?"

"I want you to dress up as my mommy for Halloween," she kissed him on the cheek.

Yale was especially fond of his daughter and would do anything she asked, "What do you want me wear?"

"Will you wear a pretty dress, please, please, please," Tandy pleaded with her dad holding her hands demurely in front of her.

"Wouldn't it be strange for me to dress up as your mommy?"

"Most of my friends have two mommies. I love you daddy, but it would be so much more fun if you were also my mommy. We could do so many things that girls like to do."

Tandy loved her real mom, but she seldom saw her. Her mother left for work before she woke up in the morning and frequently arrived home after she was asleep at night. She related to her father as she would to her mother. Yale's wife, Harper, had received several promotions since she first started work at the bank. Now she was a senior Vice President and brought home a sizable salary which was great since Yale had been laid off.

"Like what?" Yale asked feeling a warm glow from his daughter's spontaneous expression of love.

"Will you let we put make up on you?" She looked at her father pleadingly.

"Sure if it makes you happy my darling."

"Oh yes, let's go to the mall to buy some girly stuff."

Before budget cuts forced him out, Yale was the manager of computer operations for the city water treatment plant. And since Yale did not need to supplement his wife's ample paycheck any longer, he assumed the role of house-husband and was actually starting to enjoy it.

The financial crisis of '08 was started by greed and attributed to corporate executives, bankers, Wall Street tycoons and others who stood to profit from the unscrupulous and risky business dealings. Their greed was fueled by an administration which removed most of the regulations that controlled large corporations.

In fact, when the credit crunch occurred and the financial markets seized up, the government provided funds to help prop up the ailing financial institutions. However, the male dominated Boards of Directors still paid themselves huge bonuses from the taxpayer's money in spite of enormous losses to their corporations.

Popular opinion turned against this unacceptable corporate behavior and demanded changes. Because of their sheer numbers and a new look at their capabilities, women often replaced ousted Boards of Directors and senior management. Now under this new management, the large corporations took on the task of undoing the unfair practices and "business as usual."

The bottom line for Yale Freeman and other dads like him was that he now got to be both mom and dad, and he found, much to his surprise, he loved the role. Tandy also loved having her dad be both mom and dad, even though she missed her mother's touch. He did what he could to make up for that.

He turned and pointed upstairs, "Go and get dressed. We will go to the store and see what we can find."

Tandy ran to her room very energized as only a four year old could be and quickly pulled on a dress. She found a sweater, as the days were starting to get colder, and put that on as well.

Yale drove to their local mall where the two spent several hours having a lot of fun shopping for appropriate dresses. It was a little awkward for Yale, but his daughter's excitement infected him with enthusiasm and even patience. Tandy encouraged her daddy to choose a very feminine dress.

It was burnt orange in gauzy chiffon over a satin lining. The hem was asymmetrical and the bodice wrapped around and gathered in the waist where a silver applique held it together. The spaghetti straps would mean that he would need to buy a strapless bra to finish off his new look. Oh, this was going to be embarrassing, but Yale would do anything for Tandy.

"Can I wear makeup with my princess outfit?" Tandy was jumping up and down with excitement, holding the frothy ivory taffeta dress they had just purchased.

"I think we can make an exception for Halloween." "You too, Daddy, you too."

Yale reluctantly sought out the cosmetics counter. As he tried to explain that he was only dressing up for Halloween at his daughter's request, the consultant took it all in her stride. These guys all had reasons why they were buying cosmetics. But the consultant was not surprised to do a complete makeover on a man. It was a common occurrence now. She began by showing him how to put on foundation and seal it with powder, and then she worked on his eyes. She explained how to use blusher sparingly and how to apply lipstick.

"And for the little princess you are already beautiful, so we will use some eye shadow and a little lipstick to highlight your pretty lips," the beauty consultant gushed, as she smeared the light pink color to Tandy's lips. The girl smiled as she gazed at herself in the mirror.

"Can you put all of those products together, we will buy them," said Yale as he took his wallet out to pay for it.

It was still early, so Yale drove to the play circle, where Tandy could tell her friends all about her new dress. As he walked in, he noticed that the group of adults was all men. All of them in the same situation as himself, they commiserated with each other about their relatively new roles as they watched their offspring run around happy and noisy. "Where have you been?"

"Oh just buying Tandy a Halloween outfit. What is Chalice wearing tomorrow night?"

"She is going as Dorothy from the Wonderful Wizard of Oz."

"And you? Are you dressing up?"

Erling's face went bright red and he looked away from his friend, "Chalice begged me to dress up with her. Are you dressing up?"

"Yes I am. Tandy asked me to, using her finest devious approach and I succumbed. These girls learn at a very young age how to manipulate their dads."

"What are you going as?"

"You first."

"OK, I am going as the Good Witch of the North. And you?"

"Very appropriate. I have bought a dress that Tandy picked out for me. I guess she wants me to be her Mommy for a day, even though I am being her Mommy all day and every day. And if the truth be told, sometimes it drives me completely bonkers!"

Erling leaned back in his chair and let out an audible sigh, "I suppose that is what society is turning us into. We are becoming the mother figures as the women have become the bread winners. I wonder if things will ever turn back, you know, like when we were in control." He laughed and the other fathers all laughed with him although they felt irritated, just as women in the same predicament, decades earlier had felt.

Yale looked at his friend and said, "When it does, we will probably not be able to resuscitate our careers. I think I am doomed to being Mr. Mom for the rest of my life. Got to run, I have to make dinner for my family. Let's meet up tomorrow night and we can accompany our daughters together."

"OK, have a good evening, bye." Erling extended his hand as they shook hands in the last display of their masculinity.

That evening after Tandy was in bed and asleep, Harper arrived home, "Do you have anything for me to eat?" She kissed him lightly on the cheek.

"It's in the warming drawer, I hope it's not dried out," he replied with some concern, emphasizing the reversal of roles in this household.

"How was your day, sweetheart?" She enquired affectionately. He proceeded to tell her about Tandy's Halloween costume, but he was reticent to tell her that Tandy wanted him to dress up as a woman and be her Mommy for trick-or-treat.

"Are you going to dress up with your daughter?" Harper sensed that he was holding back some important news.

"Actually, she asked me to dress as a woman tomorrow night."

Harper laughed as she realized that her macho husband was becoming very well adapted to the role reversal in their marriage. "Did you buy an outfit?"

"Yes."

"Please model it for me."

"Only if you promise that you will not laugh."

"Darling, I would love to help you if you want my help."

Yale retired to the bedroom and quickly undressed. Then he carefully put on the new lingerie he had purchased earlier and when his wife entered, she helped him into the dress zipping him up at the back.

"Well you do look like an attractive woman. Come and sit down so that I can do your makeup for you."

It was not long before the loving couple retired with the wife taking the lead in their love making and the husband obliging her in the submissive role.

THIRTY-ONE

TANDY AND YALE SPENT many hours during the day of Halloween preparing for trick-or-treat. It started with a bubble bath, which Tandy loved. By night fall Yale had completed his transition and looked in character as the princess's mother. Harper arrived home early to see her family. She took lots of photos of her smiling girls before they departed for their trick-or-treat adventure.

"Have fun girls," she said as her husband took hold of Tandy's free hand, the other clutching a treat bag.

Yale stood on the front porch in the fading light considering his new persona. Much to his surprise, he was feeling quite flush about the whole adventure and he was surprised at how comfortable he felt in the silky underwear as he walked. It was new to him and yet somewhat enticing.

Lucky for Tandy, her dad only looked like a willowy woman because later that night, to save their lives, he'd have to call on all of his masculine strength, which for the moment was cleverly disguised for Halloween trick or treat. Yale was no push over since he was well versed in the techniques of the martial arts; in fact he was a black belt in karate.

As he left the porch, and stepped rather demurely onto the sidewalk, he noticed something at once strange and exciting. No one noticed him as being out of place. He was actually pulling this off. He was just a mother out with her daughter, nothing unusual. They walked the five blocks to where Tandy's friends and their fathers had arranged to meet.

Many of them were dressed in various female costumes. Of course all the children were girls and they were as happy as they could be with their daddies dressed up for Halloween. The group planned their route and began going from house to house. The fathers stayed close to their daughters and some of the group lagged behind a little while others went ahead. Yale and Erling walked together, chatting away as Tandy and Chalice collected a large bounty of candy.

As they were talking, a young woman, Toni Elliott, walked up to them and asked if she could interview them. "I am a reporter for the Virginian-Pilot and I'm writing a story on fathers who stay at home, look after their children and take them out on special events such as Halloween trick or treating. I thought that would be kind of a cute angle to the-stay at-home dad story. Will you guys talk to me please?"

"Well, yeah, but how did you know we were the dads. Most other people seem to not notice."

She laughed, "At first I thought you were a mom, for sure, until I heard you start talking to these other fellows. Otherwise, you would have fooled me, Mr.... What did you say your name was?"

"Freeman, Yale Freeman." He looked a little embarrassed, but kind of tickled too that he had fooled the reporter. "Sure, I have a good sense of humor. We would love to talk to you for the story," Yale said, after seeing the other guys didn't mind.

"You both look very convincing as mothers out with their daughters," singling out Yale and Erling.

"Oh yes, it is more fun than I thought it would be," said Erling.

"I love your witch's costume. What is your name?" Toni asked.

He relied sheepishly, "Erling Baker, and thanks for the compliment. If it makes Chalice happy, I am happy." The girls skipped happily from one house to the next.

"Well tell me, how did you guys assume the role of Mr. Mom? I mean, not just tonight, but day in and day out," Toni asked, taking notes the old fashioned way, with pen and pad in hand. She found that writing down her notes seemed less threatening than using a computer and that people actually talked more. She just hoped she'd be able to read her notes later this evening when she compiled the first of four stories she'd be doing on the increasingly common role of husbands as the nurturing mother figure and wives as the breadwinners.

This would be a great story, she thought, with the two darling little girls. She had already snapped their photo with big grins on their faces. Tandy was so darling with her front tooth missing. She was the perfect four-year-old, going on fourteen year old. And her Mr. Mom dad was darling, if you were into men. The other dad and daughter were cute too.

Both men took their turn explaining how they had been laid off and not been able to find work again. Erling explained how he had lost his job as a financial analyst. And Yale told how the county water treatment plant had cut back, outsourcing the staff in his department and then making his job as manager of computer operations redundant.

Yale and Erling were deep in conversation with Toni and were distracted from watching their charges as they gathered fists full of candy. It seemed to Yale that Tandy had separated from Chalice. He could not see her. "Wait up for me, I am going back to find Tandy." There was considerable anxiousness in his voice and Erling and Toni stopped into the road to watch him until the darkness engulfed him.

Luckily, when the thugs had asked Tandy to show them her mother, Yale, she pointed to the figure

approaching the car and said "That's my mommy coming to save me. I don't have a daddy anymore."

Suddenly, a voice behind him said, "If you want to see your daughter alive again, don't scream or do anything stupid. She is safely in our car and my buddy, Damein, over there has a gun pointed at her head. We need a little help from you so get into the car nice and quietly."

As soon as Yale saw Tandy in the car, he put his finger to his mouth, indicating to Tandy she should not say anything. Yale complied with the thug's order and climbed into the car as gracefully as he could under the circumstances. Yale saw Tandy in the back seat with another thug who held a gun pointed at her head. Her hands were tied behind her back and it appeared as though her legs were strapped together with duct tape.

The thug, Webster, got into the driver's seat but just as he was about to drive off, Yale yelled out that his dress was caught. He opened the car door and without revealing what he was doing, made sure that a part of the hem of his dress was hanging outside the car.

"Where are you taking us and why?" He tried to sound like the woman he was supposed to be.

Igor Webster sneered at him, "Look lady, you're going to help us with our plan to change the world back to its normal state."

"This is Yale?" said Petersen, the other kidnapper.

Webster snapped back at his partner, "Yeah, just shut up and let's get to the treatment plant. What kind of a name is Yale anyway?" Yale again looked at his daughter, giving her a look that signaled her to not say anything. He closed the door, hoping that he had caused enough delay for someone to see them.

Meanwhile after a few minutes, Erling and Toni started to get anxious and followed in Yale's footsteps. They made sure that Chalice stayed close to them. Pretty soon they became worried that Yale and Tandy were nowhere to be seen.

Toni starting to panic about the father and daughter's safety. She felt a little guilty because she had diverted Yale's attention from Tandy. She reached for her cell phone to call 911, "I want to report a lost child and her father. Please activate the Amber Alert system. We were trick or treating in the Ventosa neighborhood and these two people disappeared into thin air a short time ago. I fear they have been kidnapped."

"Can you give me their names and do you have a description of them, what they are wearing? Can you get us photos?"

"Yes, we can. The father's name is Yale Freeman and he is dressed in an orange dress and looks like a woman. The child is Tandy Freeman and she is dressed as a princess for Halloween."

"We will dispatch a police cruiser to meet you and get details. What is your address now?"

"We are standing on the street outside 856 Oak Ave."

"Did you see anything suspicious?"

"No. We were all together and then we noticed that the young girl was not in our group. Her father, Yale, went back to find her and also vanished. We are worried that something terrible has happened to both of them."

Toni realized that not only did she have a good feature story; she could have the breaking story of the year if the dad and his kid had actually been kidnapped. But what in the world could it be? She remembered he had said he worked at the water treatment plant. And that wasn't far from here. Those guys worked all day every day, or at least they used to. Maybe she could go around and interview them to see if any of them remembered their fellow coworker.

Toni told Erling where she was going and told him to call Harper Freeman to find out if they are home. "Wait for the police here to make a statement and then go home and let me know if Yale or Tandy shows up."

Erling called Yale's home to make sure they hadn't returned home. When Harper answered the phone, Erling tried to sound as casual as possible. "Hey Harper, listen have Tandy and Yale gotten home yet? We've gotten separated."

"No, not yet, Erling. I think they'll stay out a while longer. Are you all having a good time?" Harper asked.

"Oh, yes. I kind of like dressing as a mom. Well, I'll talk to you later."

Meanwhile Toni ran to her car and quickly pulled out heading in the direction of the water works. She soon spotted a car driving rather erratically and drove a little faster to catch up to it. Then she spotted the orange cloth from the dress flapping outside the door and grinned to herself as she recognized the fabric of Yale's dress and realized she had found the kidnappers.

She took her cell phone off the seat next her and dialed 911 once again.

"911, what is your emergency?"

"This is Toni Elliott again. I reported a father and daughter missing a few minutes ago. I think I am driving behind the kidnapper's car."

"What is your position and direction of travel?"

"I am on Riverside Drive heading north."

"Keep your phone on and we can find you on the GPS tracking system. Pull back from the suspects; you don't want them to think that they are being followed."

As Erling and Chalice waited for the police to arrive, they became more anxious about the disappearance of their friends. As soon as the cops arrived, they went to the Freeman residence to get photos and descriptions. When Harper was told about the disappearance of her daughter and husband, she was distraught and had to be tranquilized.

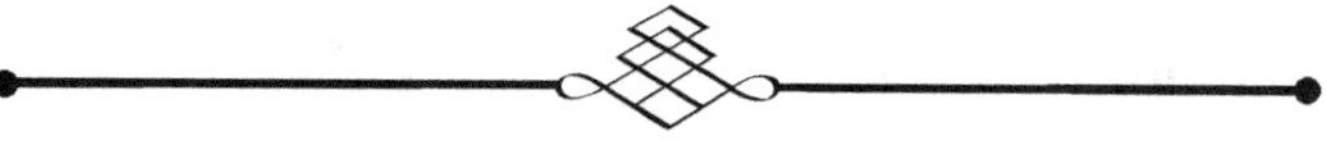

THIRTY-TWO

IGOR WEBSTER DROVE THE car to a quite location near a golf course. Yale Freeman felt helpless but he recognized the roads leading to the Lake Wright, one of the nine reservoirs that supply drinking water to the residents of Hampton Roads. He had worked for water resources for many years before he was laid off. Did they intend to drown his daughter and him? He was frightened, but he managed to maintain his demeanor. He watched the two thugs closely, looking for weaknesses that he might be able to turn into a slight advantage.

"What do you want with my daughter and me?" Yale asked with a trembling falsetto voice.

"Just a little help and if you are a good girl, nothing will happen to your little girl," Webster sneered.

"If I cooperate what are your intentions with us? Will you let us go?"

"Sure honey, once you have done everything we ask of you, we will leave you both alone," Igor said rather unconvincing.

The other gangster, Damein Petersen, watched Tandy as she squirmed in her seat.

"Why don't you untie her, she can't do you any harm," Yale pleaded with Jason.

"She is our insurance policy that you will do your part for us, baby doll," Damein smirked.

"I will not do anything until you untie her," Yale was gaining some confidence that he could outsmart these ruffians. He wanted his daughter to be in a position to run as soon as he got his chance.

The car came to a stop outside the high security fencing that surrounded the water reservoir. Even though terrorists had made threats to contaminate water supplies at the beginning of this century, they were not considered to be main targets. Therefore security was not as high as for other infrastructures and not worth a full scale security contingent.

"Now angel, you are a lovely lady with a lovely daughter that you want to continue to hold and love. You are going to show us how we can get into this facility and shut down the water supply to the city. Then we will tell you what's next."

"Are you going to bring Tandy with us?" Yale asked as sincerely as he could, realizing that these ruffians still thought he was a woman. Maybe he could use that to his advantage.

"Yes. Damein, get the kid out of the car and remove the duct tape from her legs," he instructed his crony.

As Damein complied with his buddy's request, Yale watched waiting for a suitable moment to pull off an attack.

"Tell him to remove the ties around her wrists or I won't do what you want," Yale looked over at Igor.

"OK, OK. Damein untie her wrists."

"That's better," Yale said as they cut the wire ties that bound her wrists together." Tandy rubbed her wrists as soon as she was freed.

"Now you keep your word. How do we get inside without alerting the control room?"

"It's simple really. If they have not purged the database, then the computer should remember me."

Yale stepped up to the retina scanner and placed his eye on the detector. The computer scanned his eyes and immediately released the lock to the gate. Yale secretly cursed the security of the system for being so lax that it hadn't even removed him as an acceptable entrant. He opened the gate and the four of them entered the enclosure.

"Stay clear of the camera over there. If you walk there then you will be spotted." He pointed to a path and then signaled them to walk down that way to the entrance. He knew that the control room would be watching them and tried to make it obvious that he and his daughter were in danger. The control room was over twenty miles away, but he hoped that someone there was watching the monitor and would call the police to investigate.

They entered the facility and walked towards the reservoir. The villains prodded them to walk quicker, but Yale thought that if he could walk slower he might give the police an improved chance to apprehend these ruffians. On the lake's shore, the thugs took off their backpacks and threw the contents of the bags into the water.

They then turned to Yale and Tandy and said, "OK, now you two can go for a swim. I am sure you will enjoy the flavor we just added to the water." He waved the gun at them and started coming towards them.

"Wait, what did you just throw into the water? What are you trying to do?" Yale was stalling for time.

Igor replied somewhat proudly, "Since you will be dead soon, I guess I can tell you. These waters are already contaminated with estrogen. We are adding anthrax and other biological agents, such as brucellosis and the bubonic plague to counteract the effects of the estrogen."

Yale looked aghast at him, "How do these biological agents change the effects of estrogen?"

Igor rather impatiently said, "Cities will be forced to purify their water sources once they discover what we have pulled off. Then a side effect will be to remove all the estrogen from the water. The sissies will all die and we can get the real men back in power to fix those women's libbers."

Just as Yale thought he was going to lose any opportunity for a counter attack, a bright flash went off in their eyes. It took Yale a moment to realize someone had taken a photo using a flash and since the camera was behind him, he was not blinded. But the flash distracted the thugs long enough to give Yale the opening he needed. He reacted swiftly and spun around executing the roundhouse kick perfectly to catch Damien in the groin with his stiletto heel. This was a classic karate kick and easy to execute for Yale, who had earned his black belt in the martial arts.

Damien's eyes bulged as he dropped the gun and clutched his private parts. He doubled over in pain, and let out a cry of agony. Then Yale performed a precise follow up kick in his rear causing him to plunge headlong into the anthrax laced water. He floundered around in the water kicking and splashing and trying to get to the side to get back out. Toni was there and every time he reached up to try to get out, she kicked his hands and pushed him back. She was holding Tandy's hand at the same time, trying to assure her that her dad would save them all.

By this time Igor had recovered from the shock of the camera flash and lunged at Yale. Yale blocked his kick and executed a downward chop to the side of his neck. Igor managed to block Yale's blow and tried to land a punch of his own to Yale's solar plexus, but once again Yale was too quick and side stepped him. Yale seized his neck in a vice like grip. Then Yale maneuvered himself behind Igor and wrapped one arm under Igor's armpit and then placed his hand behind Igor's head. Yale then pulled back with that side of his body while he pushed forward with his hand. He bent Igor's shoulder back and pressed his chin against his chest. Yale had him in a half nelson head lock and this immobilized Igor temporarily.

He had a moment to look around to see who was there. "Tandy, where are you?"

"She's here with me," called Toni in the semi dark.

"Who are you?" shouted Yale.

"I'm the reporter who was talking to you earlier. I followed the car and waited for a suitable moment to try to help." Yale was never so happy to see a reporter in his life. He was so thankful this young woman had happened along.

She had probably saved their lives by bravely using the only weapons she had, her brains and her camera flash to distract the kidnappers.

"Let me go, you are killing me," cried Igor.

"Shut up, you moron," said Yale as he stomped the heel of his shoe into the thugs foot. He could feel the man slump from the pain and tightened his grip.

"Hey lady, how come you are so strong?" he was blubbering by now.

Yale gloated over his domination of the situation, "I am not a woman, and you are a fool. It is after all Halloween when people dress up as something they aren't, genius," Yale was mad and therefore uncharacteristically cruel to this idiot.

Just then a couple of police arrived on the scene and ran over to help Yale. As soon as they had Igor restrained, they turned to Yale, "What's going on in here?"

Yale straightened his dress and told them, "You need to get a hazmat team to haul that other guy out of the reservoir before he drowns. These guys threw anthrax into the water so he will die from contamination in a few days.

Then contact the control room and get them to shut off all valves immediately. My guess is that it has already infiltrated the water supplies to the city."

The police threw a rope out to Damein and pulled him out of the water. Then with Tandy by her side, Toni never missed an opportunity for a story, "Who do you work for?" she asked the thugs.

"Reverend Marsh of the Jesus Fellowship Church told us that we are carrying out God's will. He said that God does not want all the real men in the world to die out."

The police overheard the interview and called in a request to arrest Reverend Marsh and bring him in for questioning.

Toni turned to Yale white faced, "That is the modern Jesus Army, a radical evangelical Christian church."

"They were talking about the estrogen in the water supply and killing all the sissies. I guess that's me."

"You are no sissy, Yale and by the way, where did you learn to fight like that?"

"I have my black belt in karate and train for an hour every day. But this guy was no push over and with the gun pointing at Tandy, I had to be patient and wait for a suitable opportunity to disarm him."

"And you still look like the beautiful mother that set out this evening with her daughter. You did not even mess up your hairdo? Maybe a bit disheveled, but let me help you touch up your makeup," she said, using a tissue to wipe his smeared lipstick. "You make a very impressive woman; maybe you should think about switch hitting," she said. Yale cringed. Smiling, Toni walked on to catch up with the cops. There was a much bigger story here and she wanted to cover all of it.

When he saw what happened with the flash camera, Coleman cursed silently, and ordered his driver to quietly move out. Their car headlights had been off the whole time, and they were far enough away from the skirmish that neither the thugs nor Yale knew they had observers.

Coleman couldn't be caught at the scene. He pounded on the driver's back seat with his fists, furious at this apparent failure of these men. If his legs hadn't been paralyzed, he'd have gotten out of the car and beat that girl, who foiled everything, beat her to a pulp. He finally regained his composure as the car rolled away.

At least, they had succeeded in poisoning the water supply. But now, he was concerned that this clumsy attempt would put other cities on notice and alert officials to the danger to their own water supplies. He'd have to get back to the Group of Eight immediately and make sure their plans were well underway. He hated stupid people, and yet he seemed to be surrounded by them.

For Coleman, ever since he was disbarred for helping Wagner out, he'd been foiled every time he sought revenge. He wouldn't be foiled this time. Damn that reporter! He'd find out who she was and she'd get hers. He'd see to that. Damn the world! Damn everybody! He was so frustrated he started to howl and cry.

His driver was used to these outrageous antics from his employer. He just steered straight ahead, turning on his driving lights as they reached the paved highway, making sure to obey the speed limit so they wouldn't get stopped for anything. He couldn't have anybody see Coleman this way. Otherwise, they'd know something was wrong and maybe even connect him to the crimes at the city reservoir. As they drove down the highway, cop cars with sirens blaring flew passed them going at a hundred miles an hour. He just kept on going at a slow steady pace, smugly thinking how funny this had been.

Yes, Mike Wagner had been a good driver and aid to Coleman, ever since he got out of the penitentiary three years ago. In a way, he felt like he was still serving his sentence. But at least he and Coleman could get their revenge together.

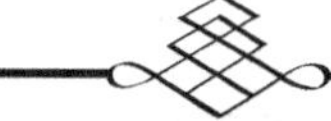

THIRTY-THREE

Norfolk, Virginia,

November 1, 2040 by Staff Reporter Toni Elliott -Two water men supply *were arrested and charged with kidnapping, assault and attempting to poison the Tidewater area last night.* Police arrived upon the scene after Norfolk resident Yale Freeman fought the two men in an effort to free his four-year- old daughter, Tandy and save the water supply. Freeman, who was a black belt in the martial arts, apparently convincingly dressed as a woman for Halloween trick or treating, dropped his demure appearance and used his karate skills to throw the suspected kidnappers off. In addition, a reporter's camera flash blinded the men *as they were about to shoot Freeman and* his daughter Tandy. *The two men have been identified as* Igor Webster and Damien Petersen, of Chesapeake.
Traces of *anthrax were found in the water. The* reason for their ttempt to poison the *water was*unknown.
The city has stepped up security at all area reservoirs which supply Chesapeake, Virginia Beach, Norfolk, *Hampton, and James City County. In addition, a* nationwide alert has been issued to all utility and water treatment plants. All valves leading from the reservoir into the water supply lines

have been shut off. And residents have been urged to stop drinking city water until further notice. The American Red Cross is distributing water at all the high school parking lots in the Tidewater area until the emergency is over.

ARNIA DEVLIN, CHIEF MAINTENANCE supervisor, was in the control room when the commotion at the reservoir broke out. She quickly shut off all valves leading from the reservoir into the water supply lines. Her quick action probably helped to contain the poisoned water.

In addition, Devlin activated the emergency broadcast system and within thirty minutes, Chesapeake officials made an announcement urging the public to stop drinking water from the city water system until further notice. It would be a slow process to identify the toxins that were thrown into the water. Purifying the water to make it safe to drink again could take weeks.

FBI and CIA experts in biological warfare and homeland security were flown in to help with the tests. They also wanted to trace the biological agents to their source. They were determined to make arrests and they were looking for any clues as to whether the two were part of a national or even global conspiracy.

FBI Special Agent Velma Kenyon was one of the first special unit forces on the scene. She was quirky, no doubt about that, but she was good at her job. Kenyon joined the FBI as a graduate of the College of Criminal Justice & Criminology with a Bachelor of Science degree in Applied Police Science and a Masters Degree in Homeland Security. She was a standout student of Terrorism and Threat Assessment. That's why the FBI cut her a wide swath. They didn't stop her from wearing safari pants and jacket everywhere she went. Oddly enough, she seemed to use all the pockets in the jacket for weird little pieces of equipment, made by her, to collect clues at the scene of any offbeat incident. And this definitely classified as offbeat.

An investigation like this was not carried out frequently. A hit on drinking water supplies was a terrorist attack that was always considered difficult to accomplish. And so most of the regular FBI were baffled; they just didn't have any experience in dealing with this type of attack.

Kenyon, on the other hand, seemed to see what the others were blind to. She immediately took samples from the water in the reservoir and sealed the containers, labeling them carefully and noting each sample on her notebook computer. She listed where it was taken, date, time and every important detail that may need to be recalled later. She placed the samples in the evidence case to be sent to laboratories for analysis.

After careful review of the procedures and satisfied that her team was carrying out their search thoroughly, she left the reservoir to go to the detention center where the prisoners were being held.

Kenyon interviewed each of the suspects separately. They seemed overwhelmingly stupid to her, but she hoped that she didn't let her feelings show. She learned a long time ago that no one will give up information if he or she thinks you're looking down on them. Kenyon was also fighting to keep her tick under control. She had a bad habit of blinking her eyes repeatedly when she was handling an exciting case like this. While the tick was unattractive, it was also distracting to suspects.

"Damien, I understand you were at the reservoir tonight. You were seen, in fact, you were videoed on the surveillance cameras, putting a harmful substance in the water. You can help yourself by answering a series of questions."

Petersen thought for a minute. "We was doing God's work."

"Really? God's work, you say. What do you mean?"

"Reverend Marsh said that we was doing God's work, that we need to stop the way things are going in this country. He explained to us that the water is turning us men into sissies."

The terrorist attack was starting to become clear to Kenyon now. The pieces of the puzzle were all falling into place. She realized that one, these guys who were arrested knew nothing about why they were trying to destroy the water supply. And two, they would only parrot what they had been told, apparently by Reverend Josiah Marsh, a local pastor.

Marsh might be able to lead the FBI to the big fish financing this group. But the chances were that he was paid through some devious third party route that left the brains behind the conspiracy anonymous and protected from detection. There were still powerful and wealthy men who did not accept the new political reality that women were now in control of politics, business and even the household.

Kenyon spent about twenty more minutes interrogating the second suspect, Igor Webster. Then she reported to command central, a combined unit of FBI, CIA and local law enforcement. Interpol was also kept up to date about new findings in this case.

"I think we have an international group that is calling the shots here. One of the men we've arrested is pretty talkative and he's mentioned a local bible thumper. But you can be sure that this minister, Reverend Josiah Marsh, is not the instigator behind this scheme. I would be willing to bet my prize fly fishing lure that he's taken a big check and received his orders from some untraceable communication. Probably some international businessmen have created an underground organization to carry out this hit."

"What so you want us to do?"

"Can you pick up Rev. Marsh, and audit his bank account. Let's face it, he is probably only the middle man, and we're looking for the big fish in this pond. We need to recruit someone to be a spy, a man," and she looked around the room at this point, making sure that no one would contradict her. Her tick was going wild. "A man that we can trust to infiltrate this group and find out how big it is, how it is financed and what plans they might be forming for future terrorist attacks," Kenyon said, twisting one of the fly fish lures she had pinned to her safari jacket.

Where does the FBI get these weirdoes from, thought Police Commissioner Joe Higgins? But he reminded himself that weird or not, this Kenyon was pretty darn smart. She had worked out the plot in a matter of hours. But why can't she stop twitching her eyes? It's downright unnerving.

They had excluded the Commonwealth's Attorney and the police chief from the circle of trusted local officials for the task force. Instead, they went to Commissioner Higgins, a by-the- book kind of guy who could be trusted with your life.

"I got a man who can do the job," Higgins spoke up. "Retired police chief, Max Leland, would be a good candidate. He can mix it up with these guys."

Higgins set up a meeting with Leland within a few hours and they discussed the events of the previous day and the findings of the FBI agent.

"So are you willing to infiltrate this group?" Higgins asked.

"Sure." Max was always confident of his abilities as a policeman. And he missed detective work.

Meanwhile, when the special taskforce cops got to the home of Josiah Marsh, he was just about ready to leave his house with a hastily packed suitcase. Apparently he had plans to take a quick Caribbean vacation with a one way ticket. Did he take us for fools?

As he walked out the door, Agent Kenyon walked up beside him and asked, "Can I take the bag for you sir?" She gripped his bag with her left hand.

Marsh was a little confused. He didn't remember calling a cab. But he was under stress, realizing the attempt at the water plant had failed. "That's okay. I can handle this bag," he smiled his sappy preacher's smile.

"No, actually you can't," Kenyon said, bringing her right hand with her service revolver from behind her back to a resting place beside the Reverend's right temple. "FBI Special Agent Velma Kenyon. You're under arrest. You know what your rights are, you've seen it on television often enough." God, she loved this job! And this was one of her favorite parts, seeing how confused and surprised these jerks get when the FBI has the audacity to arrest them.

She proceeded with reading him his Miranda rights, "You have the right to remain silent, anything you say can and will be held against you in a court of law. You have the right to an attorney. If you cannot afford an attorney, one will be appointed for you. Do you wish to give up these rights?" At last her tick had stopped. It had been driving her crazy all night.

Kenyon didn't wait until they got to the station to quiz Marsh. "It's like this, Reverend. The only choir we got here is you, and you're going to have to start singing or you'll never see the inside of another church again." And she smiled. "Our forensic accountants have already seized your bank accounts and they are tracing the origins of that huge deposit of money you received mysteriously."

Still shocked at what was happening, the Reverend Marsh said under his breath, "And good luck with that." He still didn't even know who sent it, and he had tried to find out. Really, the only thing he knew was the name of two of his parishioners who had found the thugs willing to carry out their attack for a fee. And so he started singing, as Kenyon had advised him to, even before they got to the station house.

"All I know is that Tony Coleman and Mike Wagner gave me the contact information for the two guys working the treatment plant last night. They weren't supposed to hurt anybody or harm the water supply," he lied. "They were just supposed to jam up the equipment… just a little trick or treating," he managed an artificial grin.

It was not very effective, and Kenyon's tick started up again. She hated it when these jerks started lying to her. It made her feel like they must think she was really stupid. But she went along with the Reverend's gag. "Yeah, I knew you wouldn't want to hurt anybody, you being a man of God, and all. But tell me, where can we get in touch with Coleman and Wagner?"

Marsh happily snitched on them, thinking it would save his skin. It wouldn't, but Kenyon wouldn't get the pleasure of telling him that, at least not tonight. They'd need to see how many verses the Reverend Marsh knew of this song, before giving him the bad news that he'd most likely be going to jail for life.

Max Leland was shocked when he heard that Tony Coleman and of all people, Mike Wagner, were involved. He hadn't heard anything about the disgraced Coleman for years. Ever since the controversy about Coleman being ousted as Commonwealth's Attorney and disbarred because of a conflict of interest in the Craswell attempted murder case. And he couldn't believe that Wagner was out of jail.

Leland drove over to Coleman's address in Virginia Beach, parked his car about a block away from Coleman's house and waited for the other members of the task force team. Since he was retired, he couldn't just go up to Coleman's house, but he certainly wanted to. That guy really turned out to be a bad apple, starting with the Wagner trial and now, trying to sabotage the water supply.

Then Leland saw a car drive into the Coleman driveway. This undoubtedly would be Mike Wagner, the lackey and jail bird who was Coleman's eyes, ears, hands and feet. It was Wagner who was listed as Coleman's Power of Attorney at the bank, according to the forensic accountants, and Wagner who drove Coleman everywhere according to the neighbors. He apparently had become Coleman's right hand man. Leland assumed that Wagner would know everything Coleman knew because it seemed as though the old man was totally dependent on him. Leland made a mental note that Wagner was just as valuable a witness as Coleman.

Next Leland spotted the black and whites coming down the street. No sirens, he was glad of that. Leland met Special Agent Kenyon and he smiled when he saw her get out of the car. Higgins was right, she was a strange bird. "Special Agent Kenyon, I'm Max Leland," he said, shaking her hand. "Just so you know," he hurried on quickly, "Mike Wagner has just arrived. So we are looking at two potentially dangerous men in the house."

"Glad to know that. Thank you, may I call you Max? Did they reissue you a service revolver?" she asked. She wanted to know how much fire power she had behind her.

"Yes, but I'm hoping we can get in without a gun fight. I was thinking Coleman may remember me. We kind of have a bit of history between us. I was thinking I could go to the door, and just ask to come in and talk to him. Want me to give it a try?"

Agent Kenyon liked a man with balls. And Max was one of those men. Too bad he was so old and married. Otherwise, she could have gone fly fishing with him, she thought wistfully.

"Let's give it a try, Max. We'll be right behind you."

Leland strode up the sidewalk to the front door, showing no signs of nervousness. He rang the door bell and waited. He heard a shuffling sound inside. Then the door opened a crack and a man in a wheel chair peered out, "Who is it? What do you want?"

"Max... Max Leland, do you remember me Mr. Coleman?"

"Yes, yes, I remember you, you bastard. You're one of the sonsabitches that made me lose my license, my career. What do you want?"

"I regret that now," Leland said. "What's happening now in the world today, it's not right. I look back on that trial and understand why you wanted to help Mike," he lied. "We men are threatened, just as you predicted. May I come in?"

"OK then, don't just stand there come inside."

Coleman backed his wheelchair away from the door and Leland entered the house, careful not to close the door shut. He was lucky Coleman didn't notice that he left the door cracked so Kenyon and her team could get in easily once he cuffed Coleman.

He followed Coleman to the living room, where he was shown a sofa. He noticed that the old man labored hard to wheel himself into the room. He also noticed that he had a blanket robe over his legs and that he used only his left hand to wheel himself into the room, making it all the more difficult to navigate his wheel chair. His right hand remained under the robe.

"Have you heard about what happened at the reservoir last night?" Leland asked.

"I'm crippled, not blind and dumb. Of course I've heard about it."

"No, you're certainly not dumb. In fact, I was wondering if you were the master mind behind the attack on the water reservoir."

Coleman tugged on his ear. Leland noticed it and immediately remembered that Coleman had that peculiar habit whenever he was nervous or angry, and that was his tip off that Coleman was about to pull a stunt; most likely, he was holding a gun under that robe on his lap. At that moment, Leland let his cop instincts take over, and pulled out his service revolver.

As always, his instincts were right on. Almost simultaneously, as Leland pulled out his service revolver, Coleman withdrew his right hand from under the blanket and aimed his gun right at Leland and fired. Leland hit the floor, shooting. His weapon found its target. And because Leland was able to hit the floor so quickly, the bullet intended for him missed.

Leland got up and went over to the wheel chair. He saw that his bullet had hit Coleman right in the heart.

He was still the crackerjack shot he once was. As he was feeling for Coleman's pulse to make sure he was dead, Leland heard a floor board creek behind him. He turned just in time to see Mike Wagner aiming his gun right at him.

"You know, Mike. I just don't think that's a great idea," Leland said to Wagner.

"Why? Don't you want to join Coleman outside the pearly gates?" Wagner asked with a sneer on his face.

Ever the asshole, thought Leland.

"Well, no! I don't want to join him where he is going since I don't think he will make it to the pearly gates. But the reason it would be an extremely bad idea to shoot me are the four guns pointing right at your head, right behind you."

Wagner turned and saw the four SWAT officers aiming their guns right in his face, much as he had done to Craswell years ago. "Shit," was all he had to say, dropping his gun. Later, in an effort to keep from spending the rest of his life in prison, he told Kenyon everything he had been told by Coleman about the international Group of Eight. Who the members were, how they were funded and what their goals were.

Wagner also told Kenyon that the Group of Eight had never met him, so she thought that Leland could easily pose as Wagner. That would be the way to make contact with the fanatics and infiltrate the organization. Once he had enough information to convict them, he could arrest them, and head off an outbreak of worldwide terrorism.

Just as soon as Kenyon finished interrogating Wagner, she passed the information onto Leland who immediately called Coleman's contact at the Group of Eight, posing as Wagner. He explained to the contact that Coleman had been rushed to hospital with symptoms of a heart attack, but that he would be Coleman's stand in at the meeting scheduled at Coleman's house in three days.

Kenyon and Leland withheld notice of Coleman's death, from the press to minimize their suspicion.

As the day approached the special task force wired the house with recording devices strategically placed in various locations throughout the house. Leland went

through the closets to dress in the same manner as Wagner.

As the men arrived, Leland was struck by their pompous attitudes. Each man was accompanied by a security guard. This worldwide gathering looked like a mini version, an evil version at that, of the UN. There was an industrialist from China, a Sheik from Dubai, a South African politician, a General from the Israeli military, two bankers, one from London and one from Buenos Aires, a deposed dictator from the Balkans, and what really surprised Leland, a two-bit Congressional Representative from Richmond, Virginia. What a motley group, Leland thought.

Leland introduced himself as Mike Wagner and offered them drinks. The smell of pizza permeated the house. "I thought you guys might be hungry, since its lunchtime. We got nothing fancy, but I've had several pizzas delivered from Little Caesars." Leland thought the piazza name was ironic, as he felt he was sitting in a room full of little Caesars.

None of the G8 members wanted pizza, just as the task force had hoped. But their body guards were starving, right on schedule for lunchtime. So the bodyguards headed to the kitchen where they would feast on Rohypnol laced pizza that knocked them out in fifteen minutes. Commonly known as the date rape drug, the FBI ironically used this banned drug for their cause so that they could rape the G8 so to speak. So much for the firepower in the group! The Special Forces cops jammed into the walk-in pantry, waited till the body guards passed out, then came out and cuffed the thugs.

Several of the G8 members lit up cigarettes, and it was a little tense when Leland had to find ashtrays. He ran into the kitchen. As he entered the swinging kitchen doors, eight revolvers were aimed right at him by the Special Forces cops. Leland immediately held up his hands, and whispered, "Easy fellows. I need ashtrays." Stepping over the handcuffed sleeping beauties, Leland grabbed some saucers and brought them back to the smokers. "Sorry fellas, when the boss gave up smoking, he dumped all the ashtrays.

"A lotta good that did him, I mean with his heart attack and all," he offered, passing the saucers around. The group seemed convinced that Leland was Wagner. Perhaps because of their arrogance, no one seemed to be concerned about a set up. After the usual small talk, the group sat down and immediately made it known that they were not pleased with the botched plan. They wanted to know if Coleman had messed up by choosing the wrong thugs to carry out this important job.

Leland, vigorously defended Coleman, trying to act the part of the loyal lackey, just as Wagner would have.

"Look, Wagner, since the old man is out of the picture, with a bad ticker, you've got to do a better job for us, this time. You think you can handle it?" the Congressman from Virginia intoned. "Yes, I'll do the job myself," Leland said, looking as earnest and convincing as possible. "Okay, we've got faith in you. This is important for the world."

Then the men started outlining their plan to attack the headquarters of AmeriBank, which was stolen from them by that woman, Tanya Jackson.

Leland innocently asked if there were others in the Group of Eight to help him. "No, we travel light; too many cooks ruin the stew, as you say here," the Balkans dictator spoke up. At that, Kenyon, who heard every word on her blue tooth headphones, signaled her men to move in. They had all the information they needed to wrap this up.

As the door flew open and several police officers came in with their service revolvers drawn and ready for action, the Israeli general was the only man packing a gun; unadvisedly, he reached for his weapon, only to find his hand blown across the room. He seemed to stare at the blood spurting out of his arm in disbelief.

"Sorry, general, but you won't be needing your shooting hand anymore," Kenyon said sarcastically. The plan had been brilliant. It was Kenyon's idea to lure the body guards into the kitchen with pizza. When Leland congratulated her, she said, "Momma always said, the way to a man's heart is through his stomach."

Leland noticed that her tick was gone. And actually, she was rather attractive when her eyes were not blinking uncontrollably. Not that he noticed, this woman was just about the age of his daughters, about the age of his wife, Mila, when he first met her. He couldn't wait to get home, get back to sanity. "Hey, you think you could teach my wife and me something about fly fishing."

"Sure," Kenyon responded. That seemed to be her lot in life, getting invitations from married men old enough to be her father. At that point, the remaining members of the swat team, some twenty men and women stationed outside the house, were swarming in, picking up the pizza laden body guards, still groggy from their afternoon snack.

THIRTY-FOUR

ALYCIA AND ALEX LELAND decided to have their baby at home. Alex had been a medical corpsman in the home guard, and he knew basic medical techniques. Even though it was her first child, Alycia was all for home birth and forgoing the hospital. They thought it would be the safest thing for their baby, especially since they didn't know the baby's sex. On the off chance it could be a boy, they wanted to do everything possible to protect the child.

The couple already felt the hostile stares of their neighbors because they had what generations ago would be considered a conventional marriage, which is a union between a man and a woman. Now, most marriages were between women. In fact, there just weren't many men left in the population. And those that were left, for the most part, weren't considered marriage material. They were thought to be infertile at best, but most likely impotent. And most children were conceived using the egg from one woman to fertilize the egg of another woman.

So when Alycia became pregnant, her neighbors made cutting remarks about Alex. They looked at her budding pregnancy almost as a perversion. It's not that they thought anyone would try to kill a baby boy born in a hospital. But they feared that if the baby was born and had any problems, he'd be the last child to be treated, the last child to get limited medical resources. He would be treated like a burden on society, and therefore not get the best treatment. Anyway, they just didn't want to take the chance.

Secretly, they both hoped the baby would be a girl, so that there wouldn't be any complications, now or as the child grew. Alex, the grandson and namesake of Police Chief Alexander Maximillian Leland, was descended from a long line of cops. In fact, his grandmother, Commander Mila Leland, was also a cop.

For some inexplicable reason, Max was one of a handful of men who had not been feminized by the estrogen in the water. Estrogen just didn't seem to affect some men as it changed other men. Some researchers hypothesized that the reason could be due to an ancestry with extremely high testosterone levels.

Nevertheless, Alex remembered paying the price for being different. It was difficult to be admitted into university; he often felt out of place; and high school was a series of confrontations with his female classmates. Alex still remembered his high school biology teacher espousing a current popular theory about the uselessness of men: "Why do we need men, anyway? One theory suggests that sexual reproduction began when some parasitic organism began injecting its genetic material into an unwitting host in order to utilize its reproductive machinery like a virus. A male may look similar to its reproductive partner, but he is still essentially a parasite." The other kids just laughed. But Alex felt less than human. He felt like a parasite.

After studying criminal justice and graduating with top honors from the university, Alex decided to follow in his grandfather and father's footsteps and join the force. It just wasn't that easy. He had to pass a series of psychological tests showing he wasn't too aggressive, that his temperament was suited to solving crimes, and that he would be a good team player. Then once on the force, getting a partner wasn't that easy.

Alycia was also in the new crop of recruits, and she offered to buddy up with Alex. When Alex met Alycia, it was like a miracle. They were drawn to each other instantly. Their love affair was scandalous, or so it seemed at the time. Her family did not approve, but one beautiful June evening in 2067 they married anyway, after they found an offbeat justice of the peace who seemed to specialize in weirdo marriage ceremonies.

As Alycia came close to delivering, she stayed in the house. She didn't like the comments she heard behind her back when she and Alex went out together. In the first few months of her pregnancy, they didn't realize how much hostility they would encounter, but then it became painfully obvious as every pair of eyes were glued to their every movement and action. Sometimes restaurant service was deliberately slow. Alycia and Alex realized that their marriage was unusual and attracted attention. But once the baby was on the way, it was as if their union was on display, and the matriarchal society of the day did not approve!

It was early in the morning in August when Alycia's labor pains began and went well into the evening. Then her water broke. One thing on Alycia's side was the fact that she was very athletic. She had also studied delivery without pain medication and had practiced birthing exercises. Every preparation she had made served her well. The baby was born in 2069 without complications, and the delivery was as painless as a delivery could be.

Cutting the umbilical cord, Alex was gentle with the baby, bathing it in lukewarm water, gently washing off the blood and fluid stuck to its body and hair. He talked softly to the baby, assuring it of their love. He kissed the baby repeatedly as he bathed it. Then he swaddled the baby in a small flannel blanket and took the baby to its mother.

As every mother does, she studied the baby's face. It was beautiful, blue eyes, jet black hair, small little button nose and cherry lips. She next examined its hands and feet. There were the requisite ten toes and ten fingers. Then she hesitated and looked at Alex. He looked away. As she opened the blanket, Alycia saw that they had given birth to a son. Tears slowly trickled down her face. These were tears not for her. She loved this baby no matter what. They were tears for the baby, for the years of hardship ahead of him. How would he fit into society? What would happen to him when they were no longer around to protect him?

Then Alex put his arm around mother and baby, kissing them both. He was such a caring man. "Your baby is hungry, Alycia," he whispered, coaxing her to bring the baby to her breast.

Once awakened to the breast, the little boy acted as if he were starving to death, as he gulped down colostrum, the rich milk which contains antibodies and good bacteria, that would be the first protection his mother offered him, hours before her actual milk would come in.

While mother and baby were feeding, Alex began making plans. He and Alycia had discussed this months ago. He'd give his notice at the police station after bragging about their beautiful baby girl. They'd be sure the baby was dressed all in pink in case fellow cops stopped by. And he'd explain that they wanted to move to be close to Alycia's family. Alycia would be able to secure a position at the local college teaching criminal justice once the baby was old enough. People in their new town would never have to know that the baby wasn't conceived by female egg to egg fertilization.

He and Alycia would bring the boy up as a girl. They had bought baby girl's clothes, not that there was any other choice in the stores. And they had picked out a name, Christine Alexia. They would call the baby Chris. In time they'd explain everything to Chris. But for now, they would surround Chris with all the love in the world. And they'd protect him from a society that was negative toward men.

"Alex, do we have to do this?" Alycia asked in days to come as she and Alex put the finishing touches on their packing.

"Alycia, we've already talked about this. We're already prepared to go. We want to make this as smooth a move as possible. There won't be any questions. And we'll tell the nosey neighbors that Chris is a little fussy and that she doesn't like to be held very much. We've already got a lease on an apartment. We've planned for this. And you will be able to get a job at the college. Let's just keep our plan going. You know it will best for our baby boy."

"Is it best for the baby, best for him to lie about who he is, his very manhood?"

"Yes," Alex said without a doubt or hesitation. His memories of high school still stung. He didn't want his child to face the same name calling, the slights, and the wounds of being shunned. No, Alex had no doubts.

And so, Alex gave notice at the station house. They showed their baby girl off, but were very protective of her, not wanting anyone to hold her. They said their goodbyes, and left for Chicago. It would be a whole new life for them, maybe even a little more accepting of Alex. And as far as the folks in Chicago would know, baby Chris was the product of egg-to-egg fertilization, and was the prettiest little girl in the world.

Alex and Alycia adjusted quickly, following the cross country move. As Chris' hair grew, it came in blond and curly. They made sure Chris was dressed in the prettiest, frilliest little dresses with matching hair bows.

They had their baby's ears pierced. If anything, they made Chris into a prissy little girl.

By the time Chris was four, the child couldn't bear to have his hands dirty. He loved his dollies. Occasionally, as they walked with Chris in the stroller, as a car or truck would go by, little Chris would go "vroom, vroom". Alex and Alycia would look at each other, smile and say something like, "Our little girl is going to grow up to be a race car driver." The neighbors in Chicago thought the little girl was darling. And if they ever had a doubt about whether she was a girl, they never let on.

As the baby got older, Alex and Alycia had to explain that they had a secret that Chris would have to keep. "Chrissie, don't show anybody your private parts. Be careful about that, okay? Even though you're a little boy, just like Daddy, we want to keep that a secret."

Chris didn't mind any of that. In fact, it was like a game to him. But once in middle school, he started noticing that he was somewhat interested in girls, that he liked the way they sashayed around. He liked the way they looked.

And he noticed that the little girls began to sprout breasts. He found it fascinating to watch the girls' bodies change.

Chris' parents got him a form fitting bra, so it seemed that Chris was developing just as the girls in his class were. Luckily, he didn't have a heavy beard and was able to keep his face perfectly clean shaven. With makeup on, no one noticed that Chris had a few facial hairs. Chris was able to modulate his voice so that it didn't sound too deep. All in all, Chris passed. His classmates called him Chrissie, and he was one of the most popular girls in school.

Chris' biggest problem was his interest in girls. He'd have to stifle his attraction to girls by day, and he'd go home and fantasize about them at night. As he touched his private parts, he enjoyed the sensation of getting an erection and quickly learned to masturbate, while imagining what his friends looked like naked.

Chris went onto nursing school, and graduated at the top of the class. Chris had everything going for him, except for an open love life. He had never had a relationship with a girl. There were plenty of girls ready to have sex with Chrissie, the beautiful young lady they thought they knew. But Chris had to keep his secret. And so, he turned down date invitations from women who thought he was a woman.

But then, everything changed when into the emergency room and into Chris' life came an accident victim, Chevon Lane.

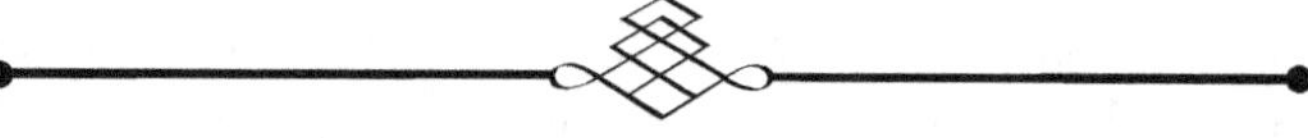

THIRTY-FIVE

JASMINE ELLIOTT SPOKE INTO a dime-size phone on her wrist. "Brigid come over and take a peek at this stormy spot on the sun's surface. I think we are in for an unprecedented eruption of radiation from this boiling inferno," she said as she flashed through stored pictures recorded by the most powerful telescope in the world.

When Brigid walked into the laboratory twenty minutes later, Jasmine was busily studying the data that was being collected in outer space and transmitted back to Earth in a constant stream of garbled algorithms. She was one of the few astronomers who had mastered the art of interpreting this complex information.

"Hi sis," she said and kissed her sister affectionately on the cheek and then settled down to view Jasmine's presentation.

Brigid and Jasmine were not only sisters but close friends their whole life and they were also research colleagues. Both had developed a fascination for astronomy, a field of science that had captured their imaginations since attending a worldwide conference with their parents and Dr. Craswell. It was in Singapore where they met Dr. Raj Pavit who was the world's leading astronomer at the time.

Dr. Pavit had been attending a global conference on male infertility. He had a theory that the viability of male sperm was being compromised not only by chemicals in the water, such as estrogen, but by global warming and solar flares. When Brigid and Jasmine met Dr. Pavit, they were captivated by his unbridled enthusiasm for astronomy, by his keen intellect and by his invitation to visit him at the Khureltogot observatory in Mongolia.

The girls, who turned thirteen during the conference, were enthralled by all the sciences. However, after meeting Dr. Pavit and visiting him in the observatory setting, they were determined to pursue astronomy. Now, forty six years later, Dr. Pavit had passed the mantle as the world's leading astronomer to these two women.

It wasn't surprising that Brigid and Jasmine had chosen the same field of endeavor, or that they did everything together. After all, they were fraternal twins, and two of the sisters from a triplet of girls born as the result of the first successful egg-to-egg fertilization by Dr. Leslie Craswell.

They were a very close-knit family and loved their other sister, Toni, born to their other mother. She was also conceived by the same egg-to-egg fertilization procedure. Toni had chosen a different field of endeavor, journalism, and she was equally successful in her own right. She loved her scientific sisters and so admired their accomplishments.

But she was a little jealous of their closeness, not jealous in the way that she envied their relationship, but jealous in the way that she wished she could experience their uncanny closeness. It was uncanny that Brigit and Jasmine looked so much the same that they were often asked if they were identical twins. They shared the same identical purpose in life and the same thought patterns. But nevertheless, Toni spent as much time with her sisters as she could and loved every minute they were together.

"Hey Brigid, look at these images, and look at this data," Jasmine said, not even needing to look around to see that her sister was in the observatory. They could sense each other's presence. The advances in solar observation had been staggering during this century. Sophisticated equipment had been designed and placed into orbit to facilitate observation of the cosmos.

Brigid was involved in the search for earthlike exoplanets revolving around other stars. This field of study had yielded many potential planets that could support life in other solar systems. But the technology to allow the human race to explore any of these extra terrestrial places was still decades away.

Jasmine used advanced apparatuses to gauge and measure the radiation emitted from the sun during solar storms. The two women watched these monstrous storms which produced staggering intensities of energy that could be compared to a hundred million atomic bombs exploding simultaneously. Jasmine had become world renown for her research into these massive explosions that occur in the solar corona and heat plasma to tens of millions of degrees.

The scientific community, if not the general public, had become intensely fascinated with these basic building blocks of all matter, electrons, protons and heavier ions spewed out into space at speeds approaching the speed of light. There was a rising concern that the late Dr. Pavit had been correct in predicting that this phenomenon could impact the ability of the human race to reproduce.

During the occurrence of a solar flare, electromagnetic radiation is produced at all wavelengths from long-wave radio to the shortest wavelength Gamma rays. Dr. Pavit had warned that, unfortunately for life on Earth, monthly averages of these massive solar storms show that the number of sunspots visible on the sun waxes and wanes with an approximate eleven year cycle. And Dr. Pavit suggested that the solar flares appeared to be increasing in intensity.

The twin sisters had been waiting for their fiftieth birthday to witness an expected escalation of activity on the surface of our life giving sun. The concern was that the life the sun gives, the sun could also take away. It was ironic that their fiftieth birthday could coincide with a peak of solar sun spot activity. Mindful of the dangerous space storm of January 2005 that left scientists bewildered and reworking their theories, they were concerned and wondering about what would happen this time around. In 2005, the solar event at two in the morning on the twentieth produced an intense burst of energetic protons that arrived frighteningly fast and surprisingly, tripped radiation monitors all over our planet.

In an interview at the time, an investigator from the California Institute of Technology on NASA's Advanced Composition Explorer spacecraft, which monitored the event said, "This flare produced the largest solar radiation signal on the ground in nearly fifty years, but we were really surprised when we saw how fast the particles reached their peak intensity and arrived at Earth."

"Since the early nineties, we've believed proton storms on Earth are caused by shock waves in the inner solar system as coronal mass ejections plow through interplanetary space," said the principal investigator for the Reuven Ramaty High Energy Solar Spectroscopic Imager satellite. "But the protons from this event may have come from the Sun itself, which is very confusing," continued the Professor at the University of California at Berkeley.

Scientists scratched their heads over the oddity of this eruption. They wanted to catch another event this powerful to study it closely, but as with anything to do with the cosmos, you have to be patient. And the Elliott sisters were patient, as well as meticulous in their research endeavors. They had studied under a professor of physics and astronomy at the University of Rochester who was inducted into the National Women's Hall of Fame for her excellence as a teacher of young women, and for the exceptional advances she had made in the field of infrared astronomy.

The Elliott sisters certainly fulfilled the prophetic assertion of Maria Mitchell, the first-ever professional female astronomer in 1848, who correctly predicted, "The eye that directs a needle in the delicate meshes of embroidery will equally well bisect a star with the spider web of the micrometer."

Both Jasmine and Brigid were snatched up by NASA directly from the University. Jasmine's initial job with NASA was to study the effects of solar storms while Brigid went into NASA's search for earth like planets in our region of the Milky Way. Just like the fairy tale, Goldilocks, Brigid was looking for a planet that is not too hot, not too cold, but just right for life.

The Elliott girls were located at the same observatory, and as their work progressed, their projects converged into meticulous tracking of the planets and the effect of solar storms on the earth. NASA stood back and watched as they saw the incredible work the two women were doing, realizing that they were most valuable when they directed their own research. And so the two were given the use the observatory as their personal laboratory and tracked and planned the research they would do.

And tonight would be the culmination of years of hard work, painstaking tracking and recording of the Hinode Solar Observatory, built at the beginning of this century to study the interaction between the Sun's magnetic field and the corona. The first mission failed to transmit the data back to Earth, so another more up-to-date satellite was designed, built and launched to continue the investigation.

"That is amazing! You are right, the sun looks as though it is about to explode from that spot, it is a cauldron." Brigid exclaimed as soon as she had a chance to view the sun's surface and review the data.

"If you look at the magnetic field lines linking those two sunspots, they have become sheared and twisted in a manner I haven't observed before. That is the prelude to a solar storm. But look at the intensity of the magnetic field, it is extraordinary. I am going to alert the International Space Station to tell the astronauts to take cover in the shielded room," Jasmine sounded near panic, which was unusual for her. She was normally a calm individual.

"I suggest you hurry and put out a general warning on the news for all electronic devices to be shut down for tonight and tomorrow maybe," Brigid urged.

Jasmine placed a call to the astronauts and warned them to take cover, and then she called her sister Toni to give her a heads up about what they suspected. She wanted to make sure her sister got the scoop. Toni was no sooner off the phone then she made plans to fly to California and be at the observatory within three hours. Next Jasmine followed protocol to release the information to the networks in general. The media was abuzz with the story and aired the announcement on all news channels.

Later that night, Jasmine could detect the increase in flow of gases from the Sun that streamed past the Earth at speeds of more than a million miles per hour. Disturbances in the solar wind shook the Earth's magnetic field and pumped energy into the radiation belts. A region on the surface of the Sun often flared and gave off ultraviolet light and x-rays that heated up the Earth's upper atmosphere. Shaking the Earth's magnetic field can also cause current surges in power lines that destroy equipment and knock out power over large areas.

In the hours following the solar flare, Jasmine went to the observatory to watch the series of loops above the surface of the Sun. These loops were best seen when viewed in the light emitted by hydrogen in the red region of the solar spectrum.

The radiation levels were high and Jasmine was alarmed as she monitored an increasing level of gamma rays and X-rays penetrating the atmosphere. The Earth's magnetic field would normally protect us from the solar weather by deflecting the harmful radiation around the atmosphere keeping it in outer space. This coronal mass ejection was the largest in recorded history and Jasmine realized that there would be consequences to human life on Earth.

Over the next few days the emergency rooms and all the hospitals around the world were busy as men complained about excruciating pain in their groin. After the Center for Disease Control noted an increasing trend of this malady they started investigating possible causes. Panic ensued among men, but since they only made up thirty percent of the world's population, the problem was not considered to be a high priority.

Dr. Teresa Theron was examining yet another biopsy from another male patient, "This one shows the same radiation levels again, just like the last couple of thousand we have examined." She looked up from her electron microscope and sighed.

Her nurse was preparing more slides for the doctor to examine, "Thank goodness there does not seem to be any reports about women experiencing pain."

Dr. Theron was a leading reproductive medical researcher. "I fear that that what is left of our male population has been rendered infertile by the solar flare."

The nurse sniggered, "Have you tried to have sex with a man recently? They can't even get an erection anymore. I know because I have tried."

"Well now even if they are able to get an erection, they are probably infertile," the doctor replied. "This natural disaster seems to have performed the equivalent of a vasectomy on most of the world's male population."

"What a shame, I thought it would be nice to experience sex with a man and now I will not get that opportunity," another nurse observed.

At this, Dr. Theron looked very concerned. "You realize that this could have been the end of the human race. We need to thank Dr. Leslie Craswell for her innovative approach to reproduction. Ironically there were many that tried to stop her and if they had succeeded then our species would now be in danger of extinction."

"Really, you mean this isn't a temporary issue?" the nurse replied. This time all the joviality was gone from her voice.

"That is right," the doctor confirmed, "A man's testicles are located in a sac outside the body to keep them several degrees cooler than the rest of the body for sperm production. That is why they seem to have been damaged by the high levels of gamma rays from the solar flare. Now the human race is solely dependent on women being able to be fertilized by other women using the procedure perfected by Dr. Craswell half a century earlier."

THIRTY-SIX

CHEVON LANG WAS PRETTY badly injured when she was admitted to the intensive care unit and placed in Chris Leland's care. She was brought into the emergency room all battered and broken after a less experienced skier had collided into her. The other woman skier was not badly hurt. But Chevon had a broken leg, broken pelvis, and was in a coma.

The emergency room doctors worked on her for several hours, and then sent her to the intensive care unit with instructions to put her in the care of an exceptional nurse. That would be Chrissie Leland. Chrissie had a way with patients. The worst cases seemed to respond to her.

When Chris first glimpsed Chevon, he was struck by her good looks. She looked like a snow princess. Coal black hair, contrasted against a very fair skin with burgundy lips. He was in awe of this beautiful woman entrusted to him to nurse back to health. He reminded himself that his first task was to get her situated into bed.

"Ready ladies," Chris said to the orderlies when they wheeled Chevon into the room. "Let's get this snow princess into bed as gently as possible." They lined the gurney up parallel to the bed, and with Chris on one side of the bed and the two orderlies on the other side of the gurney, they lifted the blanket to transfer Chevon onto the hospital bed. "Gently now, on my count, one, two, three."

Then, Chris talked softly to Chevon. He always did this with coma patients. There still wasn't any solid scientific evidence that coma patients could hear you. But Chris thought they could. And he'd had a lot of success doing this.

"Chevon, my name is Chrissie, and I'm going to be taking care of you. I was told you took a bad spill on the slopes. I know it wasn't your fault and it's not fair that you are the one that is all banged up. So, what I would like to do is to help you get back on the slopes as soon as possible." Actually, he didn't know if she'd ever be able to ski again, but there was no reason to tell her that. If she was athletic enough and if she worked hard in rehabilitation and if she didn't get an infection, and if she was lucky, maybe she'd get back. There were always so many ifs in this job, which was the part of his job that Chris didn't like. Chris always did everything he could to beat the ifs.

He played a very old recording of the Boston Symphony doing the Beatles, a singing group from the twentieth century. He'd found the old recording among his great grandfather's possessions, and burned it onto a memory chip. It was part of Chris' collection that he played for patients. As they got better, he'd put on more lively music. But for starters, this symphonic version of Beatles tunes was perfect. It was soothing and seemed to relax patients.

Then Chris started bathing Chevon. As modern as medicine had gotten, there were still some things that required the human touch. And a gentle warm sponge bath was one. When Chris opened up Chevon's hospital gown, she took his breath away. Chevon was the most beautiful woman he'd ever seen. It wasn't just her figure, which was fabulous. But her skin looked and felt like silk. Her breasts weren't large, but they were perfectly proportioned and perky. Chris was mesmerized.

Chris stopped and reminded himself to be professional and detached. Besides, he could feel an embarrassing erection taking over his libido, and after years of practicing self control, so that he would appear as one of the girls, he wasn't going to expose himself or his penis. So Chris stood for a moment, looked out the window and took a deep breath. He tried to imagine all the pain this young girl was going through and all the difficulties she'd have while recovering. Then, he turned back to his patient, and began to bathe her gently.

"Well, let me tell you a little bit about me." He told her about his grandmother and grandfather, and about how they fell in love at the diner the night some thugs came in to rob the patrons. Sometimes, his coma patients would later ask him about his grandparents. They didn't quite remember the story, but they remembered to ask, and so he'd always tell them his story again proudly.

"So now, snow princess, tell me all about yourself. Not yet ready to talk, huh? But when you get to know me, you will find out that I am patient. I can wait until you feel like talking."

Day after day, it was the same routine. Chris talked to Chevon in his soft lilting tenor voice trying to coax her out of her coma. When his shift ended and another nurse took over, Chris had to tear himself away from Chevon to go home and get a good night's sleep.

Chris was glad that his patient load was light, because it gave him more time to spend with his patient that he was starting to love. On the fourth day, Chris was in the middle of another story when he realized that his snow princess had ice blue eyes, ice blue eyes that were for the first time looking back at him. He smiled his infectious smile that was the best medicine of all.

"Oh, so you decided to join the party after all! Chevon, it's good to see you. I'm Chris, your nurse. You know you had a bad spill on the slopes."

"Chris," was all she said. Then she began looking around the room, looking down at her leg in a cast. Her face winced as she sensed the pain of her injuries.

"I know you're in a lot of pain right now. But, Chevon, you're going to be fine. We'll work together on getting you up soon. You'd like that. Right?" he said, taking her hand and smiling. He was surprised at how tightly she gripped his hand. She was strong. And that was going to be a good thing for her.

"What happened? Please tell me again. I feel like I've been dreaming about a diner where you can get free hamburgers. Can I have a hamburger?" Oh, she was hungry! That was a great sign, Chris thought. And he realized she was remembering the story he'd told about his grandparents at the diner, and after the robberies, how the owner had told his grandfather, 'come back anytime, the hamburgers will be free for you'.

"One hamburger, coming right up."

Chris paid one of the aides to get two burgers, fries and a coke. That was their first meal together. By the second bite of her hamburger, Chevon was already laughing at Chris' jokes. This hamburger meal became a ritual with them. They'd have one every day for the month that Chevon was in the hospital. While eating a hamburger every day wasn't endorsed by the hospital, the doctors realized it was great medicine. And the hospital snack bar made great, greasy hamburger and fries.

Chris watched the physical therapists as they worked with Chevon in her hospital room. They showed Chris how to help Chevon with the exercises to strengthen her muscles. Chevon improved daily. During her monthlong stay, the two became close friends. When it was time for Chevon to leave, Chris hugged her good bye.

Chevon kissed him first on the cheek, and then on the mouth. The kiss was more passionate than she had intended and it surprised Chevon. She had never really felt any passion for her girlfriends in the past. She'd had sex with other girls, but Chevon always felt like she was just going through the motions. She had decided that she just didn't care too much for sex. But this kiss with Chris, this was different.

Chevon thought that maybe because Chrissie had taken such good care of her, she was emotionally charged. But as they continued to kiss, Chris couldn't hide it any longer. His manhood took over, and Chevon realized the girl she was kissing was no girl. She was kissing a real man, a man with an erection. She had never done that before, and she was turned on to feelings she had never experienced.

A few months after Chevon went home from the hospital, the couple announced their engagement. Most of the hospital staff knew that these two had fallen in love anyway. And everyone was so happy that Chrissie had at last found someone. And they all thought the two women would make a very happy couple. Neither Chris nor Chevon were about to explain that Chris was not a real woman. The reduced numbers of men left in the society were oddities. Most, like Chris, were keeping their identities secret.

Chris and Chevon started their family, and they realized that if they had a boy, they'd have to continue the charade. Chris hoped that their babies would all be girls and then they would not need to live the secret life that he was subjected to. He remembered that his life was complicated because of his secret. Chevon, on the other hand, wanted a boy. But all three pregnancies produced three beautiful baby girls who looked just like their mother, snow princesses in Chris' eyes.

They adored their parents, believing that both were women, just like the mothers of all their friends. As the girls got older and into their teens,

Chevon and Chris felt that it was time to explain to their daughters that Chris was really a man.

It was unusual at this day in time for a couple to include a male and female partner, even though it was only a few generations earlier that marriage had been defined as a union between one man and one woman, as husband and wife.

"When your father and I kissed for the first time in the hospital, I realized I was kissing a man," Chevon explained.

"How did you realize that, mom?" Eve, the most inquisitive of the girls asked innocently.

Chevon laughed nervously and smiled. They had always been open with their girls about sex and she wasn't going to stop now. "Your father had an erection, honey."

The girls looked at their mother blankly.

"Your father, of course, like all men, has a penis. As I left the hospital we kissed and I felt his penis press up against my thigh."

The girls, Eve, Zoe and Mila looked at each other, and in chorus, echoed, "Eww! That's just gross." And as the story unfolded, about their hospital romance and their first kiss, the girls began to realize that their parents had engaged in traditional sex to conceive their children. All were blushing at that moment, including Chris. But being the loving family that they were, the five burst into laughter, hugged and that was it, nothing more was said.

There was no argument from the teens when Chevon asked their girls to keep the family secret. No problem there. While they adored their father, it was certainly an unexpected revelation that one of their parents was a male and they were not proud of that. Like all teenagers, they didn't want to stand out or be considered weird. And this definitely classified as weird.

However as the girls got older, their feelings towards their father changed. They loved him so much, that they begin to get angry that he had to hide his true identity. The girls began to actively lobby their dad and suggest that he reveal his masculinity. They were proud of their father and the fact that he was a male didn't affect their love.

If anything, it made their love for him stronger because they realized how much he had sacrificed for them, to make their lives as normal as a child's life could be. And they realized how much he had suffered because he had to keep his true identity secret. They just couldn't understand how he could be so accepting of the world's intolerance. And these Leland girls were strong willed just like their grandmother. They had apparently inherited some of her genes and like a chip off the old block; they wanted to reverse society's discrimination. After all, this was their dad, not their mother, and they had become so proud of him.

Eventually the girls got married to wonderful young women, who were enlightened about Chris' real identity. Like their wives, they also accepted Chris totally. His kindness and generosity won them over and they loved him too. Anyway, by this time, men were so few that they were nearing extinction.

Eve, who had become a magazine writer, asked her dad if she could write a feature article about him. She urged him to tell his story. To her, his story was precious; his struggle, which he had managed with such grace and ease, was legendary.

Chris was in his sixties, and he too was getting tired of always pretending, having to make sure there was never a whisker on his face, having to always pretend to be something he wasn't. Chevon encouraged him too. And so, Eve Leland wrote a prize winning story for Chicago Today about her other mother, her father, the man in her life. It caused a sensation.

Eve would eventually write a book about her dad. And it became a best seller. Eve dedicated the book to her dad, whom she described as "the most immortal mortal I've ever known."

In a way, the book made Chris' life easier. Not having to pretend to be something he wasn't was a relief. It gave him a freedom he'd never experienced before in his life. His daughter had given him the greatest gift of all; she had a restored his dignity as a human being, with the right to live as he was without having to pretend.

He even gained some celebrity status and began receiving invitations for speaking engagements to describe his life as a secret man. He and Chevon loved the speaking circuit. Not only was it fun, but lucrative as well. Adding to their happiness, their life together was crowned by the birth of many adoring granddaughters.

But as in all lives, the cruelest blows eventually come in the end. Chevon died unexpectedly, with no warning from an aneurism, when she was seventy three. Even though his daughters and grandchildren rallied around him, Chris was lost without his true love, Chevon.

Then Eve came to his rescue once again. They launched a search for other men. It was a fascinating project, and the handful of men worldwide who revealed themselves seemed so relieved to reveal their identities, just as Chris had been. There were eight men in all. And Chris stayed in touch with each one, and grieved as each man passed away.

At ninety seven, Chris, with his children and grandchildren around him, passed away. His girls were devastated. He was the kindest and gentlest person they'd ever known. To others, he was a museum piece, an oddity, a short obituary in the paper. But to them, he was Dad.

The Most

Immortal Mortal

Has Fallen

"Christopher M. Leland, the last known living man, succumbed to pneumonia at his home in Chicago today. Mr. Leland was 97. He was surrounded by his loving family, three daughters and seven granddaughters. Chris' wife, Chevon Leland, preceded him in death.

Mr. Leland kept his true identity a secret until 35 years ago, when his daughter, noted author, Eve Leland, persuaded him to tell his story. Following the publication of her bestselling book, "My Dad's Secret Life", Mr. Leland was popular on the speaking circuit throughout the United States.

Mr. Leland was a nurse for 35 years which is how he met his wife, Chevon, who was his patient in the hospital. Theirs was the old style traditional love story which endured through the ages.

Mr. Leland enjoyed skiing with his wife and daughters and he was an avid scrap-booker, keeping track of his family history.

To the end, he seemed to live up to his daughter's description of him as "the most immortal mortal." A private service will be held for the family and close friends.

EPILOGUE

LUCINDA ELLIOTT CLOSED THE file as a tear trickled down her cheek. She was touched by the biography of the last man on Earth, written by his daughter. And she had also located Chris Leland's scrapbook. As she leafed through its pages, she saw his life, and how he had been forced to live a lie for much of it. She could see in the faded photos how much he loved his girls. She could see the kindness on his face. She could see his pain.

Lucinda walked to the wine keeper and opened a bottle. She needed to think about this and try to get away from the emotional aspects of what had happened to Chris Leland. After all, he had been dead for over two hundred years now. As she poured herself a glass of chardonnay, she realized that her sadness wasn't for Chris Leland only; it was for all of humankind.

To most scientists, Lucinda included, the extinction of any species represented society's greatest failures. But to think that society let men go extinct, the enormity of it struck her. As in all of nature, when something goes extinct, it throws the natural order of things out of balance. And when men went extinct, it eventually resulted in an imbalance of power held by women. Ironically, Lucinda reflected on the fact that women had become as powerful and arbitrary as men were reported to have been. It was ironic and sad that women had become as treacherous and self centered as the male of the species. The checks and balances were missing.

She leaned back in her chair, wine in hand and reflected on the papers she had read. Dr. Craswell was the researcher that saved the human race from total extinction with her reproductive technique that enabled women to fertilize the eggs of other women. Ancestors of hers had unwittingly begun the change to the matriarchal society when they became pregnant with the first babies produced by egg-to-egg fertilization. While their intent was not to change society or replace men, that became the result.

She also realized that governments had not taken seriously the threats that increases in estrogen in the water would lead to the impotence of males. Everything that had happened could be chalked up to chance. Or the blame could squarely be put on a modern society that was too busy to cope with life threatening issues, too preoccupied with self interest to project consequences, and too influenced by power to stop the powerful.

At first, she wondered why this bothered her so much. It was a done deal; society was changed forever. Or was it? Her scientific mind was racing ahead, considering how to undo the curse of extinction. Not only would such an attempt pose incredible scientific and intellectual challenges, it would also produce societal issues and maybe even power struggles. But the scientist can't be dissuaded from honest scientific pursuit. Plus, Lucinda believed she had a personal stake in this. She felt she owed the world payback for what her ancestors had unwittingly done.

She picked up her notation computer and reviewed her research. There were places, cryobanks where they froze the sperm of men to help women get pregnant before the egg-to-egg fertilization was available. Maybe she could find one and search for any remains that might be useful. Before she even realized it, Lucinda was starting to formulate a secret plan that would enable her to resurrect the male population. What if frozen sperm could last for a long time? How could the sperm stay frozen all this time and still be viable? No, that would be impossible. Or was it?

First and foremost, Lucinda was a scientist and she decided that it was worth the research time to try and find some ancient evidence. The first thing they would do is locate any possible cryobank sites that might have stored sperm. She would keep her plan secret, sharing it only with her sister, Shakti, the only person in the world she trusted with her life. And that would be an issue. The two of them would have to be extremely careful. Their efforts to turn the clock back would be fought by the powers that be. After all, they did live in a society where Big Sister was watching.

"Hi Sis, this is Lucinda," she spoke clearly into the answering machine. She made sure her voice was cheerful, in case anyone was listening. "Come on over tonight and have a glass of wine with me. There are some things we need to discuss."

And so it begins anew....